Heart Magic

Heart Magic

Metaphysical Stories About
Finding Love and Answers

Dick Sutphen

Also By Dick Sutphen
(From Pocket Books)
You Were Born Again To Be Together
Past Lives, Future Loves
Unseen Influences
Predestined Love
Finding Your Answers Within
Earthly Purpose
The Oracle Within

(From Valley of the Sun)
Master of Life Manual
Enlightenment Transcripts
Lighting The Light Within
Past Life Therapy In Action
Sedona: Psychic Energy Vortexes

Some of the stories first appeared in *Master of Life WINNERS* magazine, or as part of audio books on cassette.

First Edition: June 1992

Valley of the Sun Publishing, Box 38, Malibu CA 90265

ISBN Number 0-87554-500-9
Library of Congress Card Number 91-068565

To All The
Metaphysical Seekers
Who Have Been Reading
My Nonfiction Books
For 16 Years

And Are Now About To
Take A Chance
On My Stories

Thank You

Contents

THOSE WHO SHARE OUR ENERGY

Chapter One

Sedona, Arizona: On a red-rock ledge a hundred feet above the floor of Boynton Canyon, Darci Farrell sat alone—naked, eyes closed, and cross-legged in deep meditation. The image of an Indian flickered before her inner eyes. Eagle feathers dangled from the leather strands that bound his braided white hair. His floating image appeared to glow against the sheer red walls on the far side of the canyon.

"Welcome home, my child." His silent greeting filled her mind.

She responded with a thought. "I don't understand."

"You understand it is time to dry your tears."

"Easier said than done," Darci smiled.

The Indian raised his hands in the air as if to embrace the sky. "Easier than you think." He was beginning to fade as he pulled an eagle feather from his hair and thrust it toward her. "Full moon," he said and disappeared.

"Come back. Please come back." Darci's words were no longer silent and the sound of her own voice pulled her out of the altered state of consciousness. She opened her eyes to see the same scene she had observed in meditation, minus the Indian. Chaparral grew from the cracks in the rocky ledge. Her sweaty clothes were spread over their branches, drying in the sunshine. Four feet in front of her the ledge dropped off, the sheer rock wall plunging down to the green canyon floor. Dry red washes spider-webbed the terrain. The rock wall at her back ascended hundreds of feet into the sky, and was streaked many shades of red by a million years of wind and rain spiraling through the canyon. At the end of the canyon a giant monolith rose out of the chaparral and manzanita as if in tribute to God.

Darci stood up slowly and twisted her well-toned torso from side to side, then backwards until her long raven hair brushed the ground. When she bent forward she saw the black-tipped eagle feather between her feet. She picked it up, and brushed it with her fingers, parting the webs and stroking them back into place. She kissed the feather and blew gently on the fluffy down at the base, then held her spiritual gift to the sky. She twirled it slowly against the April sun. Orange streaks flared behind the flowing translucent patterns within the vane. She was fascinated, inhaling deeply and dancing delicately with her bare feet to unheard music.

Both arms in the air, one holding the feather, she turned and turned, her eyes closed, her naked body kissed by the sun as she expressed the exhilaration that filled her soul. It was the sort of joyous emotional display that her ex-husband deplored—an uninhibited expression of her metaphysical beliefs that he found intolerable. As she thought of Jack her foot came to rest on the loose rock at the edge of the ledge. It crumbled and gave way.

Darci's eyes snapped open. She lunged away from the edge, falling flat on her stomach, grasping for a hold in the rock surface. She felt her fingernails painfully bending and breaking as she balanced momentarily, her lower body hanging over the edge. She held her breath, her sapphire eyes wide with fear. The only sound was the wind strafing through a channel in the canyon wall, spawning a ghostly moan that ascended into a wail and then rolled away down the canyon.

When Darci finally inhaled she slipped, maybe an inch, her fingertips leaving tiny trails of blood. The chaparral trunk was a foot to her left. If she reached for it she'd surely fall.

If I don't, I'll fall anyway, she thought in horror.

Simultaneously attempting to claw a fingerhold into the rock with her right hand, she lunged for the tree trunk with her left, grasped it, and felt her body slip free of the ledge to dangle over the edge by one hand. She clawed desperately at the tree with her right hand, her clutching fingers only grasping leaves that shredded from the branches. As her left hand began to lose its grip, she clutched heavier branches with her wildly flailing right hand.

"HELP! Oh God, please, someone, help," she screamed. Her mind raced. Her hands felt torn from her body.

Do you want to die here, like this? The thought jack-knifed through her mind. *Jack would deem it appropriate.*

The thought gave her the strength to wrench herself up enough to lock one arm around the trunk of the small tree. She was momentarily more secure, but her lack of strength and the angle of the cliff negated any chance of pulling herself back up over the edge.

"HELP! HELP!" The words reverberated through the canyon like a multitude of pleading voices echoing the word until it became a ghostly whisper indistinguishable from the wind.

There were hikers. I saw them, she thought. *So what? It would take somebody too long to climb up here. I can't hang on.*

Trembling, whimpering, she imagined herself falling through space, screaming until she hit the rocks with a sickening thud.

The pain was streaking down her right arm as if her blood were beginning to boil. The arm crooked around the trunk was turning white and going numb. Her mind reeled.

What do I have to live for? A divorced thirty-year-old woman with no special talents. Let go. Let go. No, don't let go.

A wave of dizziness jumbled her thoughts. Breathing deeply to push it away, she clutched the trunk tighter.

Bad karma, Darci . . . haven't earned enough good-girl credits. Her eyes flooded with tears that rolled lazily down her cheeks then tumbled off into space to splash on crystal-encrusted rocks ten stories below.

"Don't let go." The faraway voice was male.

Did I really hear it? No. Yes. I think.

"It will take me time to get to you," said the voice. "Hold on."

"Hurry, please hurry!" Darci screamed.

"Hurrypleasehurry, hurrypleasehurry." The echo sounded like her own voice mocking her for being such a cosmic fool. *I was dancing, naked with my eyes closed on the edge of a cliff and fell off the edge.*

You need help, Darci. New Age ideas are for retards. Jack's voice prodded her. *You should be locked up and deprogrammed like a cult convert. Why don't you let go? You're too stupid to live.*

"Leave me alone, Jack." Darci realized she was yelling out loud.

The dizziness was coming in waves now. She fought to focus upon holding the chaparral trunk.

"Are you still coming?" she screamed.

There was no answer. As she strained to hear, she noticed the eagle feather lying on the ground a few feet from the edge of the cliff. It stirred lazily in response to the wind.

Her bloody hand twisted on the trunk. *Oh, God, don't let me die. Let me live long enough to fulfill my purpose, what-*

ever it is.

"You'll be okay. I'm going to loop my belt through your hands to strap you to the trunk before I try to pull you up."

Darci looked up into the reassuring blue eyes of her smiling blond rescuer. He was lacing a leather belt around her wrists and to the tree. Once it was secured he laid flat on his stomach and reached over the edge.

"You're going to have to swing your body back and forth until I can grab your leg," he said. He locked his feet around the trunk of the tree and leaned further over the edge. Darci attempted to swing her body from side to side, the motion shooting pain through her arms and hands in nauseating waves and scraping her chest against the ledge. He pushed her hip for momentum and on the third swing he grabbed her, one hand clamping her buttocks, the other clasping her upper leg.

"Now," he yelled, pulling her up, twisting his own body into a roll that flipped Darci safely back on the ledge, her savior lying on top of her.

For a frozen moment they looked deeply into each other's eyes, before he kissed her tenderly on the lips. He then reached over her head to unlash the belt binding her hands, and helped her up into a sitting position.

"Are you all right?" His voice was deep and rich. He pulled a canteen from his hip, twisted off the cap and started to hand it to her, when he noticed her bloody trembling hands. Instead, he raised the canteen to her lips and tilted it carefully. She swallowed twice and pulled away.

"Thank you," she said. "Thank you."

"I dropped my backpack down the trail. It has a first aid kit," he said, gesturing and standing up. "I'll be right back."

When he returned Darci was feebly trying to put on her tee shirt.

"I have a solar blanket," he said, zipping open the backpack, and extracting a foil-backed sheet that he shook open and placed around her shoulders. "Let me help you with these." He picked her white lace bikini panties and a pair of denim shorts off the bush and helped her put them on.

"A rather intimate way to meet a woman," he said, and blushed.

He's beautiful, she thought, watching him search through the first aid kit. He was classically good-looking, with a square, sun-bronzed face, and a thick crop of straw-colored hair. Late thirties she guessed. She could sense the power coiled within him.

"I'm Darci Farrell."

"Calum O'Keefe," he said laying out gauze, tape and first aid cream. "Can you move your arm?"

She raised her shoulder and winced at the pain.

"Let me see it," he said, holding her arm with one hand while lightly stroking it with his other. After a couple of minutes, he massaged a little deeper and stopped to apply pressure at one point.

"What are you doing?" she asked.

"Acupressure point. The energy needs to be released."

"You know about things like that?"

He looked into her eyes again. "I was climbing and saw you meditating."

"Yes."

He nodded and returned his attention to her arm.

"Aren't you going to ask me how I fell over the edge?"

"I would imagine it's embarrassing," he said, his warm smile reflected in his laughing eyes.

"Yeah."

"I wouldn't want to embarrass a beautiful woman."

He was now bending her arm at the elbow, up against her body and down, drawing the blood back into the muscles. Each time he closed her arm, his hand brushed the side of her breast. She tried to repress the resulting shivers.

"I can take you to a hospital in Cottonwood, but I don't

think anything is broken."

She shook her head.

"Your chest needs to be cleaned and treated, and I don't think you can do it." He smiled, embarrassed.

Darci looked at the bloody, ragged scrapes across her breasts. Her nipples were raw. She looked at Calum. "Please," she said.

He ripped open a package containing a clean gauze pad, folded and dampened it with water from the canteen. Then gently, without meeting Darci's eyes, he began to clean her ample breasts. The gauze was soon soiled with oozing blood and the red-colored earth. He repeated the process with new gauze pads, wiping the contours of her body, carefully lifting each breast to clean beneath it, and lightly dabbing the raw nipples. It hurt but she was too distracted to respond.

"Your body is beautiful," he said as he removed the cap on the first aid cream. "I wish this were under different circumstances."

Darci smiled but he didn't see it. He applied the cream to her chest with his fingers, then cleaned and treated her hands in the same way.

"Let it soak in for a few minutes before I help you put your shirt on," he said, tucking the solar blanket tighter around her shoulders.

"You saved my life. Thank you."

"Who is Darci Farrell?" Calum asked, sitting cross-legged in front of her.

"Her ex-husband would tell you she's a cosmic foo-foo. Maybe he's right."

Calum smiled.

"But I think maybe she is just a silly woman looking for answers that may not exist."

"What kind of answers?"

Darci looked away, across the canyon. "Oh, answers to

questions like who is Darci Farrell, really? Why am I here? What's my purpose? Simple questions like that."

"God sent me to tell you," Calum said. "She did. She said, 'Go save Darci and tell her why she's here, and what she's supposed to do.' "

Darci looked directly into Calum's eyes, her own eyes wide and serious.

"Just kidding," he said, breaking into a laugh. After a moment, Darci laughed with him.

"See, I believed you. I am a foo-foo."

"I *can* tell you why you're here, Darci. Everyone on earth has reincarnated to try to get it right. We want to rise above our karma by learning to let go of fear."

"Fear?" Darci replied.

"Fear-based emotions—prejudice, guilt, greed, jealousy, envy, malice, blame, repression, stuff like that."

"Oh my God, you're a foo-foo too," Darci said. She smiled warmly.

"Maybe. I'm also one of three partners in a Phoenix restaurant. And divorced with a twelve-year-old son that I see on alternate weekends. Your turn."

"I'm a bookkeeper for a Denver real estate agency. No kids. I live with a roommate named Sally, and I came to Sedona on a mini vacation after reading a book on the energy vortexes."

Calum took an apple from his backpack, sliced off a piece and placed it in Darci's mouth. They talked for an hour about their respective lives and metaphysical beliefs.

The sun was casting long shadows and bathing the canyon in a golden glow when Calum leaned over and removed the foil blanket from Darci's shoulders. "Put your arms out and I'll help you put on your tee shirt."

When she was dressed, Darci picked up the eagle feather and wove it into her hair. "A gift," she said in response to Calum's questioning look.

"Are you all right?"

"Fine. I'm sore, but that's all."

"There's a creek a couple miles from here where we could swim. And I can fix dinner." He patted his backpack.

"I accept," she said, wrinkling her nose as she smiled.

They made their way off the ledge and slowly, through smooth rock washes, down to the canyon floor. It was dusk when they reached the swiftly running creek. They followed the water a few hundred yards into pine trees to a natural pool that was formed by the rocks. Calum removed his pack, and unzipped it. He took out a sleeping bag, spread it on the ground and gestured for Darci to sit down.

"I'll gather some wood for a fire," he said, then quickly disappeared into the trees.

I don't think I've ever wanted to make love to anyone so much in my entire life, Darci thought, lying back on the sleeping bag and looking up through the sycamore boughs at the first stars twinkling in the darkening sky. *No. It's a psychological reaction to nearly dying. No, face it, Darci, it's lust. Just lust.*

Returning, Calum quickly dug a hole, built a fire and placed a pot of water on a portable grill to heat. He then stirred dehydrated fruit into another bowl of water. "Hungry?" he asked as he removed his hiking boots.

"What's on the menu?"

"Dehydrated chicken and rice in cheese sauce, fruit salad and a granola bar if you're still hungry. Not exactly what I'd serve you at the Indian Nation, but it will do."

"The Indian Nation? Is that the name of your restaurant?"

Calum stood up and stretched, then removed his tee shirt. "Native American and Mexican food. Really different." He unzipped his faded Levi's and stepped out of them, then slipped off his underwear. He turned toward Darci who was lying on the sleeping bag looking up at him. "Do you want me to help you undress? To swim," he added.

Oh my God. Be cool, Darci, be cool. "I think I can do it," she replied. She was untying her shoes when Calum ran the few steps to the edge of the pool and dived into the dark water. Surfacing, he swam to the far side.

"It's cold, Darci." There was a shiver in his voice.

"It's deep enough to dive?" she questioned from the bank, her nude body silhouetted against the orange flames.

"In the middle," Calum replied from the darkness.

The icy water sucked the breath out of her body as she surfaced in the middle of the pool. Treading water, she turned, shivering as she surveyed her surroundings. The fire cast flickering reflections on the wet rocks as she swam into the shadows and Calum's waiting arms. He kissed her gently, then guided her to submerged rocks where they could stand waist deep. He held her with one arm, and traced her lips with the index finger of his other hand, before covering her mouth with his own, his tongue entwining with hers in sensuous exploration. Darci whimpered when he pulled her body tightly to his.

"Oh, yes, Calum, yes."

He slid his hand down her back and gripped her buttocks, then ran his fingers between her flesh and lifted her. Her body opened, aching with the promise of fulfillment as he entered, each deepening thrust generating a trembling response. She felt as if he had penetrated her soul as she matched his thrusts in the churning water—tensing and releasing in single purpose—joined together as one soul pursuing an unquenchable desire.

When she opened her eyes the fire was several fires and Indian women were cooking an evening meal. She closed her eyes and drowned in the dizzying, uncontrollable joy.

When he emptied himself into her the warm rush seemed to flood her body and mind, and she said, "Welcome home, Shellaka."

"I hope I didn't hurt you," he said, still holding her tightly.

"Didn't notice if you did," she giggled, cupping his face in her hands. "It was wonderful."

He nodded and smiled, the biggest smile she'd ever seen. Then he kissed her again and still holding her tightly, asked, "Who is Shellaka?"

"Shellaka?"

"You said, 'Welcome home, Shellaka,' right after I came."

"No, I didn't. You must have tripped out." She looked into his eyes dancing with reflected firelight. "I'll race you back to the dinner table."

They spoke primarily with their eyes as they ate the meal, sitting crossed-legged on the sleeping bag, facing each other. Following dinner they made love again and then lay in each other's arms looking up at the nearly full moon and listening to the night sounds of the high desert; coyotes, owls, crickets, and the creek cascading over rocks into the pool and out again. The dwindling fire hissed and crackled, sending occasional sparks into the air.

"When is the full moon?" Calum asked.

"I don't know. Why?"

"In meditation I was told to return to Boynton Canyon on the night of the full moon," he said.

Chapter Two

Alone in her room at the Los Abrigados resort, Darci tried unsuccessfully to go to sleep. *I'm acting like a lovesick schoolgirl,* she thought. *All I can think about is Calum O'Keefe. He even overshadows the fact I nearly died this afternoon.*

She snapped on the bedside lamp. The clock read 3:10

A.M. *I've got to get some sleep or I won't look good for him tomor* . . . she caught herself in mid thought. *Jeeze. Listen to yourself, girl.* She blinked her eyes, adjusting to the light and looked around the room which was filled with Sante Fe style Southwestern furniture and fabrics of pink, orange, red, and brown.

She stretched her naked body and felt pain in her arm and chest. She took a Diet Pepsi from the refrigerator bar and walked out onto the second-story balcony. Beyond the tennis courts was Tlaquepaque, a colonial Mexican village reproduced as exclusive gift shops. Beyond Tlaquepaque the erosion-carved red-rock buttes rose majestically into the moonlit sky, surrounding the area like a fortress.

Located above the Mogollon Rim, Sedona's mile-high elevation was the same as Denver, so Darci had experienced no shortness of breath while mountain climbing. It was a tourist-supported town of shops that ranged from Western art by Cowboy Hall of Fame artists to Pink Jeep Tours through the back country. On any given day twenty tour buses would be lined up in the main street waiting for their passengers to return with exposed rolls of film and bags full of overpriced souveniers.

Darci's thoughts drifted back to the events of the day. *How could you make love to a man four hours after you met him, Darci? Granny would call it whorish behavior. Maybe she'd be right. But it was the first time since Jack and it has been a long* . . . She jumped at the sound of the ringing phone.

"I sensed you were awake. I hope I didn't . . ."

"I was awake. Where are you?"

"In the lobby."

She laughed. "You can come up but I don't have any clothes on."

"So what else is new?" he said. The phone clicked off.

"The door's open," she called out upon hearing his approaching footsteps.

Calum entered the room carrying an armful of wild flowers. Darci was sitting up in bed beneath the quilt.

"Do you have something I can put these in?" He held up the flowers.

She pointed at the ice bucket by the bar. "Thank you, Calum. Don't tell me you've been gathering those in the moonlight?"

"Couldn't sleep."

"Maybe we can sleep together. You've got twenty seconds to get out of those clothes and into bed."

"We won't sleep," he said as he undressed.

"Probably not," she said as he climbed into bed.

At sunrise Darci Farrell, wearing tan shorts and a bulky white sweater, and Calum O'Keefe in jeans and a racing jacket, sat with their arms around each other on a large boulder overlooking the Airport Mesa energy vortex. It was located midway between the main highway through Sedona and the top of a mesa that served as the town's airport.

"For such a famous healing place it looks just like the rest of the pine tree and red-rock terrain," Darci said.

"Why were we both told to be in Boynton Canyon during the full moon, Darci?"

"The full moon is two days away. Saturday. I checked. And I wish I knew why."

"You saw an Indian. I just heard the words in my mind. But there must be a connection." He picked up a small flake of rock and tossed it through overhanging pine boughs into the vortex. "I feel like I've always known you," he said, looking toward the horizon.

She hugged him tighter. "Me too."

"But I know so little about you, except that you're incredible in bed," he said.

"What do you want to know?"

"What do you read?"

"Metaphysics. And believe it or not, anything and everything that's ever been written about antique dolls."

"Antique dolls?"

"My mother died when I was five and I was raised by my grandmother, who collected dolls. I guess I caught it from her. When Granny died, I inherited her collection."

"Your turn, Calum. What do you read?"

"About American Indians. If there's anything you want to know about Southwestern tribes, just ask. And I study the psychic sciences because they help me deal with people."

"Give me an example," she said.

"Okay. According to personology, the slant of your eyes says you're not critical of others, and the arch of your eyebrows tells me you're informal and easy with people. Your visible eyelids and that stubborn chin say you're a direct actionist. You often act before you think, which sometimes creates problems, but it makes things happen. And the space between . . ."

Darci interrupted. "You can really tell all that about me just by looking at my face?" He nodded. "Well, I know about me—tell me what your face says about you."

Calum gave a lopsided grin. "That I'm analytical, somewhat introverted and that I want to make love to you again."

"Maybe it's just a physical attraction," she teased.

"It wouldn't scare me if it were."

"Do I scare you?"

"It's been years since I cared about anyone but my son and building the Indian Nation into the best restaurant in Phoenix."

"A workaholic?" she asked.

"I like to spend time, not waste it," he replied. "And I

have had trouble trusting women. My wife left me for someone else."

"My husband left me because he never wanted to hear about the New Age again, or so he said."

Calum smiled at that and shook his head, not understanding. "Meditation helped me get through it," Calum said. "But that was a long time ago."

"But you still come to Sedona to meditate?" she said.

"And take part in the psychic activities." Calum's eyes followed a morning dove flying out of the fiery sky. "Look," he said, pointing. "I'll bet you a kiss her nest is in that tall strand of prickly pear."

Darci watched the bird circle twice and then flutter gently into a nest in the cactus. She turned to Calum, closed her eyes and puckered her lips. The kiss quickly turned passionate as she parted her lips and let him possess her mouth.

"Shellaka, my killer," she said in his ear, her voice as raw as sandpaper.

Calum pulled free of the embrace, and stared at Darci's glassy eyes.

"Why did you say that?" he demanded.

"What? Say what?" Her eyes focused.

"You said, 'Shellaka, my killer.'"

"Calum, what's wrong with you? I didn't say anything." She looked at him as if he were crazy. Seeing his fear and confusion, she whispered, "I swear, I didn't say anything."

"Yes, you did, Darci."

She looked down for a few moments, then slid off the boulder, and started walking away. "I think we need some coffee."

Without talking they followed the rocky path through scrub desert growth down the hillside to the road where Calum had parked his Jeep Cherokee. Five minutes later they entered the Ranch Kitchen at the highway intersection. It smelled of fruit cobbler and coffee and the cigarette smoke drifting lazily over the dozen tables. The sun through the window blinds striped the patrons with slivers of horizontal light. A waitress in a checkered uniform seated them at a table next to two cowboys. Darci watched in fascination as one of the men rolled a cigarette.

"The Old West lives on," she said.

"The guy rolling the cigarette owns one of the gift shops across the street and sells rubber tomahawks," Calum replied. They both laughed. Neither mentioned the incident at Airport Mesa. "Has anyone ever done your astrology chart?" he asked.

She shook her head.

He continued. "There's a lady here in Sedona who keeps me informed of my fate. I'd planned to see her this morning. How about coming with me?"

Three miles from the restaurant they turned right off Highway 89A and followed the road into the shadows of a red mountain shaped like a coffee pot.

"I love Sedona," Darci said as they pulled into the driveway of a modest tract home.

"So does everybody else," Calum replied. "But unless you want to be a clerk or a waitress, you have to bring your job with you. I've often thought about opening a Sedona branch of the Indian Nation. Maybe someday."

The middle-aged woman who answered the door wore a white blouse with a paisley vest, jeans and running shoes. Amanda Bateman was plump, red-haired and freckled. She greeted Calum with a bear hug.

Calum turned to Darci, "Amanda, this is . . ."

Amanda finished his sentence. "The woman I've been telling you about for the last several months."

Darci smiled and extended her hand. "Darci Farrell. And I want to hear more about your prediction."

Amanda led them through the living room, down the

hall and into a bedroom that was set up as a reading room. She sat down behind the desk and gestured for Darci and Calum to take the chairs facing her. A computer, several books and a statue of Buddha sat on the desk. The walls were decorated with astrological symbols and visionary art. Amanda snapped on the computer and it hummed to life.

"Your birthday?" Amanda asked, looking at Darci.

"But this is Calum's appointment," Darci responded.

"Yes," Amanda said. "Your birthday?"

Darci looked at Calum who nodded his approval and then at Amanda. "December 10th, 1961. 2:50 P.M., Denver, Colorado."

Without responding, Amanda's fingers danced over the keys. She sat back, read the screen and punched Enter. "This thing does in a few minutes what used to take me hours," she said, returning her attention to the couple sitting across the desk. "You met yesterday, didn't you?"

Darci and Calum looked at each other. "Right here in Sedona," Darci said.

"Come on, Amanda. Astrology can't be that accurate," Calum said.

"Only in the hands of a gifted professional," she teased, returning her attention to the computer screen. Her fingers flashed over the keys momentarily, then she sat back and smiled. The printer on the credenza behind her desk began to chatter.

"That's your chart, my Sagittarius," Amanda said to Darci, "and now I want to combine it with Calum's Aries chart for a compatibility reading."

"Amanda, I . . ."

"Hush, Calum. Destiny brought you to Sedona this weekend, and destiny brought you to me today. Don't fiddle with destiny."

"Do you really think we were destined to meet here?"

Darci asked as Amanda was tearing off the second print-out.

"Tell you in a minute," Amanda replied.

While Darci and Calum watched silently, Amanda examined the charts, her eyes darting from one page to another. "Of course," she muttered, then traced a line, flipping back and forth through the dozen or so pages. "Ah, yes. Sure. Mars, Venus. Venus, Mars. Interesting. Hmmm." She scowled a moment then went on.

"Yes," she said to Darci. "You and Calum are soulmates with several double whammies in your chart to seal it. He probably won't accept it, but he doesn't have any choice in the matter."

Darci laughed.

"Neither do you, young lady," Amanda said to Darci. "Well, what else do you want to know?" Amanda tilted back in her desk chair, placed both hands behind the back of her head, and smiled knowingly.

"Well, well . . ." Darci stammered. "What does that mean, really?"

"It means that you were born to be together. Everything that has ever happened to you has been leading up to your meeting yesterday."

Calum smiled at Darci, who mirrored his expression.

"Let me see your left hand, Darci," Amanda said.

Darci extended her hand, and the woman across the desk took it gently in her own, turning it sideways and stretching and pulling the skin.

"Okay, now let me see yours, Calum." After a similar examination, Amanda laughed loudly.

"What?" Calum asked.

"I told you that you were going to have more children, Calum. You've got three on your hand and Darci has two. Isn't that interesting?" She laughed some more. "Two girls," she said to Darci.

Amanda explained their charts for over an hour. As they walked out the front door to leave, she said, "You two should attend the past-life regression sessions at the Eagle's Eye bookstore tonight."

"Group regressions?" Calum asked.

Amanda nodded. "Hold hands as you go into the altered state. Place a crystal between your hands and . . ." She stopped in mid-sentence. "Just a minute." She ran back into the house and returned moments later with a translucent purple stone that looked like two pyramids attached at the base. "Hold this between your hands."

Chapter Three

They slept through the afternoon in Calum's room at the Poco Diablo resort. Darci awakened filled with a terrible sadness and a sense of impending doom, her body drenched in sweat. She looked at Calum lying next to her, sleeping soundly. She attempted to recall her dream but it was rapidly dissolving into fragments; a mist, a waterfall, anger, fear. But the important images remained just beyond the realm of perception. *Death,* she thought. *Death was part of it.*

She pushed the thoughts out of her mind and recalled the conversation with Amanda. *You don't have any choice, young lady. No choice. No choice.* That wasn't quite true of course. She was perfectly free to get up, get dressed, get in her car, drive home and never see Calum O'Keefe again. *Of course I have a choice. So does he.* But at this moment she didn't want any choice. She wanted Calum to be her soulmate and live happily ever after.

She had showered, washed her hair and ordered room service before Calum awakened. When he opened his eyes, she said, "All those orgasms must have drained your energy, sleepy head."

"Oh yeah, come here and we'll find out." He held out his arms.

She shook her head. "Room service is due in five minutes."

"So? We've got five minutes."

She laughed. "Calum, after being celibate for nearly a year, my poor body is . . ."

She was interrupted by a loud knock on the door. Moments later a young man carried the dinner tray into the room, and Darci directed him to set it on the patio table overlooking the golf course. Calum opened the bottle of Sauvignon Blanc, tasted it, then poured it and offered a toast. "To us." As their glasses clicked, a barrage of lightning pulsed through the darkening sky beyond the red-rock buttes. It was followed by an ominous peal of thunder that sent shivers up Darci's arms as she sipped her wine.

A few minutes into their meal a wild mallard duck meandered out of the golf course pond to join the couple and beg for scraps. His aggressive honking alerted others and soon a dozen ducks padded back and forth demanding a hand-out.

"I think they ate more of your meal than you did," Calum said.

"I'm a sucker for kids and animals," Darci replied. Then looking at Calum, she added, "And blond-haired Irishmen who save my life."

"Half Irish. My mother was Dutch."

"My distant ancestors were blond-haired Swedes, but Granny claimed great-grandma messed around with a Cherokee Indian." Darci combed her hand through her long ebony hair.

"I thought you looked natural wearing that eagle feather," Calum replied, putting the dinner dishes back on the service tray.

At seven o'clock they were in the small classroom at the back of the Eagle's Eye bookstore. Twenty folding chairs were set up but only fifteen were filled. White candles flickered on both sides of the stage and New Age music played softly in the background. The scent of incense drifted into the room from the bookstore.

Darci whispered to Calum, "Have you ever noticed that there are always three women to every man at metaphysical gatherings?"

"Maybe women are more open to new ideas?" he said.

"Less fearful of new ideas would be another way to look at it," she countered, then added, "You don't see many young people either."

"Probably because you have to experience life's ups and downs before you start looking for answers," he replied.

A doe-eyed, florid-faced man in his fifties walked up onto the stage and stood behind the podium. He had shoulder-length salt and pepper hair, and high cheekbones; he was dressed in a flowing white shirt and pants. "Good evening. I'm Lawrence, your past-life guide for tonight's explorations. Thank you for joining me. I'm going to conduct a past-life hypnotic regression to the lifetime that is affecting you more than any other. Before we begin our time travels, I want to talk to you about karma.

"You have to decide for yourself if karma is reality for you. I contend that there can be no halfway karma. In other words this is either a random universe or there is some kind of plan. By random universe, I mean that over millions of years we evolved through the animal kingdom to become who we are today. If this is the case, there is no meaning to life—we will all live and die and that will be the end of it."

Darci snuggled closer to Calum and squeezed his hand. Lawrence continued. "But if this isn't a random universe there must be some kind of plan. And if there is a plan, doesn't it follow that there would be an intelligence behind the plan? Now we could call the intelligence George, or Ginger, or God. The name doesn't matter. But if an intelligence set up the plan, doesn't it also follow that justice would be part of the plan?"

Lawrence looked around the small audience, making eye contact with each person. "But look at your own life. Watch the television news. Where is there justification for the misery and inequality in the world? How can you justify mass starvation, abuse, and murder? How can someone rob others and live the good life as a result? Only karma can explain it all. There is no other philosophy or religion that can. None."

A middle-aged woman raised her hand, waving it to get Lawrence's attention. He stopped and nodded at her. "The Christian Bible explains it all," she said. She was scowling.

"Not so," said Lawrence. "As an example, let's look at two lives. Two little girls were born on the same day in different parts of the city. One was born healthy to loving, nurturing parents. The other was born with a club foot to parents that didn't want her and showed her no love. When grown, the first girl married well, had children, and a happy life. She died peacefully at an older age. The second woman lived life as a cripple, and had children out of wedlock she couldn't support. She suffered and died painfully in her early forties."

Lawrence took a deep breath and continued, "Now, according to the Bible we reap our rewards in heaven. If this is the case does the woman who lived the good life receive a lesser reward? How do you justify the miserable life? Does she receive a bigger reward? It just doesn't work. It isn't fair. I think George, or Ginger, or God would be fair."

Darci noticed that the woman didn't challenge the speaker again. Lawrence stopped to take a drink of water. Calum was about to raise his hand to ask a question when

Lawrence said, "Karma rewards and punishes. It's a multi-life debit and credit system that offers total justice. It even explains a seemingly senseless murder, as Kahlil Gibran said, and I quote, 'The murdered is as guilty as the murderer.' "

Lawrence recognized Calum who had his hand in the air. "So, you're saying absolutely everything is karmic?"

"Yes. And I'm saying you need to decide if you're going to accept karma as your philosophical basis of reality. There is no halfway karma. It either is or it isn't. And if it is, then everything in your life is a karmic effect and everything you think, say and do creates more karma."

Calum spoke without waiting to be recognized a second time. "Then if karma is, there is no one to blame for anything? All our experiences are to balance past deeds, and to test our awareness?"

"Right," said Lawrence. "And the rewards are to be enjoyed."

"Then when my wife left me, it was my karma? I can't blame her for that?" Calum asked.

"You may have left her in a past life. If you blame her in this one you'll probably have to experience a future lifetime with her. But if you can let go of your resentment, you'll have learned your lesson."

Darci spoke without raising her hand. "I thought wisdom erased karma?"

"It does," Lawrence replied. "The purpose of karma is to teach. If the young man beside you is wise enough to release his resentments, he won't have any further karma in that area, or with that soul."

Someone else asked, "Then before we are born we make decisions about who we'll have relationships with while on earth?"

"Yes, but it may be a little more complicated than that. My research indicates the oversoul theory is accurate. Maybe I'll talk about that after the regression. But now, let's explore the past life that is most affecting your current life."

Lawrence explained how the regression was to be conducted. He told the participants they could experience the hypnotic session sitting in a chair or lying on the carpet-covered floor. Darci and Calum chose to lie down, holding Amanda's crystal in the palms of their entwined hands.

Lawrence paced his voice to the amplified clicking of a metronome. "Deeper, deeper, deeper, down, down, down." He directed a body relaxation and induced the altered state with patterned speech at forty beats per minute. "And you are now in a deep altered state of consciousness," he said. "And in the memory banks of your subconscious mind there is a memory of everything that has ever happened to you in this life you are now living and in any of your past lives. Every thought, every word, every deed is recorded in the memory banks of your subconscious mind, and you are now going to go back in time to the lifetime that is affecting your current life more than any other."

Lawrence continued to direct the process and guided the participants through a tunnel into the past. "Number one, you are now there and vivid impressions are beginning to form."

Darci felt a terrible sense of foreboding as she began to emerge from a haze, running, running, running. She was gasping for breath. She? No. *He* was gasping for breath. Chest pounding, heart about to explode, he fought to keep his footing on the wet grass. Dodging between pine trees, he climbed higher and higher through the tendrils of fog. "Lakato." The voice was calling him, pulling him up the mountain into the clammy mist.

The full moon broke from behind the clouds, casting an eerie glow through the mist as he made his way across the river, and up to the top of the waterfall. He leaned against a tree and felt the rough bark on his back, as he fought to get his breath. Frowning into the mist he whispered, "I'll find you, Shellaka."

For a moment the ticking of the metronome drew Darci away from the Indian, but the mist seemed to reach out and draw her back to the thundering roar of the waterfall dropping onto the rocks below. The mist parted and the full moon illuminated two Indians standing facing each other— glaring at each other with looks of seething hatred. Both were young, wearing only loincloths, their long black hair braided in the same style.

"You stole my life," shrieked Shellaka.

"Not yours," Lakato roared.

They each drew obsidian knives and dropped into a crouch, circling in the wet grass, looking for an opening. The knives flashed in the moonlight as each thrust at the other, nearly missing flesh. They snarled and trembled in rage. Circling. Growling. Slashing. Lakato's blade sliced across Shellaka's chest, and as he twisted he felt a devastating pain in his side. The blade ripped loose and plunged into him again. He lashed out and felt his own knife connect—felt the wet ooze of blood, or was it the damp grass, or the water as they fell?

Darci's eyes snapped open. She saw the white ceiling of the room and felt Calum's hand clutching her own. The metronome ticked monotonously. She took a deep breath. She wanted to whimper but she didn't. Tears ran out of the corners of her eyes and down into her ears. She wiped them with her free hand and noticed that Lawrence was watching her. She closed her eyes again and counted herself awake.

Sitting up, she gently removed her hand from Calum's. The rest of the room was still in a deep altered state of consciousness. She took a pen and small notebook from her purse and wrote, *Shellaka. Lakato. Indians. Terrible anger.* She attempted to remember the name Calum had accused her of whispering in his ear.

Lawrence awakened the participants with instructions to remember everything. "I'd suggest you make some notes about what you just experienced," he said. "Subjective impressions are much like quickly forgotten dreams."

Calum sat up, stretched, and noticed Darci's red eyes. "Was it a bad experience?"

Smiling, she handed him her pen and notebook. He made a few quick notes, tore out the page and handed the notebook back to her. Lawrence announced a ten-minute break and everyone moved from the classroom to the bathrooms or into the bookstore.

Standing by themselves in the Eastern philosophy section of the store, Calum asked, "What did you experience, Darci?"

She handed him her notes. He read them, looked at her with an expression of disbelief, shook his head, and drew his own notebook sheet from his shirt pocket. She unfolded the paper and read, *Chasing or being chased. Mountains. Indians. Water. I feel hatred. I call after him, "Lakato." I know I will kill him. My name is Shellaka.*

"Did you catch him?" Darci asked, her eyes wet with unspilled tears.

"No," Calum said. "I didn't. When Lawrence awakened us I was coming to a waterfall."

"Maybe I just made it all up because you told me I called you 'Shellaka,' " Darci said, shivering as she turned away from Calum to scan the bookshelves. She decided not to tell him about the knife fight at the top of the waterfall.

Back in the classroom, after several participants had shared their regression experiences, someone asked Lawrence to explain his oversoul theory.

"Yes," he said. "Let's go back to the beginning of life on

earth . . . and initially, please be aware that I am speaking symbolically. There was a time when there were no intelligent humans on the planet, but a great energy gestalt existed in the nonphysical realms. We'll call this gestalt 'God.'

"Now, science tells us that energy cannot die, it can only transform. And it cannot stand still. It must, by its very nature, expand or contract. So, as an expansion of the energy gestalt called God, the cells within the great body of God constantly divide and subdivide, creating new energy, just as the cells within your physical body divide and subdivide. This is a good analogy, for human beings are in fact made up of units of energy.

"When life on earth evolved to the point of sustaining intelligence, oversouls began implanting their soul atoms into these beings as another way to expand the energy gestalt. In other words, at some point your oversoul cell divided and you are one of the new ones that were created. You are one more in a long lineage of cells in the body of God—the part and the whole at the same time.

"After you experience physical death, you will cross over and find that you now have oversoul status. The way you will resolve your karma and engender additional energy is to continue the oversoul's process of division. In other words, you will implant your soul atom into a new baby with a karmic configuration that supports your learning needs. Maybe you'll decide the best way to resolve your karma is to explore simultaneous lives as a businessman in England and a poor woman in Mexico. So, with the assistance of higher understanding, you implant your soul atom into two lives in those settings. And these new human beings become extensions of you. But once anything is created, it is freed, so they will be free individuals. They are on your 'frequency' and you will feel and experience through them. You will have to totally experience all their joys and misery, their successes and failures, their learning, which is your learning. So you will continue to evolve through these additional lifetimes, raising your level of awareness.

"Both the Englishman and Mexican woman will share the same past-life lineage. In other words, if they were both hypnotically regressed in the year 2075, they would experience a past life as you, or any of those in your direct lineage. You would all exist on the same frequency.

"The karma of your two creations will be to master the lessons you didn't learn while you were on earth. When they die, they will become oversouls and shape new explorations of their potential. Thus the energy continues to multiply and expand."

Lawrence stopped to take a drink of water. The participants began to ask questions. A woman in the front row asked, "Then the past life I just experienced was that of my oversoul or someone in my lineage?"

"Yes," Lawrence answered. "And you are here on earth to master the lessons your oversoul didn't learn."

Darci whispered, "I don't think I can absorb any more."

"Me either," Calum replied. They got up quietly and slipped out of the room unnoticed. A young woman wearing a crystal headband and a Levi's jacket was sitting behind the cash register near the bookstore front door.

"Spring storm came in," she said, gesturing toward the window and the dark film of rain that rippled down the glass, blurring the lights and images outside.

"Thank you, we enjoyed the seminar," Darci said, taking one of Lawrence's cards from a display unit by the door. It said, "Lawrence," offering no last name or address. Beneath it was a local phone number.

They stepped out into cold rain blowing under the overhang of the roof. The unseen moon illuminated the edges of the dark thunderclouds from behind, casting an anemic light over the rain-swept parking lot. A single sodium-vapor lamp at the street entrance reflected in the rain-splattered pools of water.

"Let's run for it," Darci yelled, taking Calum's hand. They sprinted across the gravel, jumping the puddles, but by the time they reached the Jeep the rain had plastered their hair to their heads and was dripping down their necks.

Once inside the vehicle they shook themselves like wet dogs, the water splattering over the interior. Calum started the engine and snapped the heater to high. When he turned to Darci and noticed the mascara streaks on her face, he laughed.

"I'll get you for that," she said, snickering.

He took a handkerchief from his pocket, and dabbed her face dry then put his arms around her, kissing her gently. Lightning slashed the sky behind the mountains, followed by a peal of thunder that to Darci seemed more like a growl of frustration and pain. She shivered and snuggled into Calum. She felt as if somehow the Indian in her regression had followed her up out of the altered state, and was now manifesting itself as a malevolent presence that lurked just out of sight, watching her from the shadows.

Die, Lakato. Die, Lakato. Soon. Soon. Soon. The thought reverberated through her mind like a shock wave. She pushed it aside and shivered uncontrollably.

"Are you all right?" Calum asked.

The heater was beginning to warm the interior and clear the fogged windshield. Calum switched on the windshield wipers which flicked back and forth like the beat of Lawrence's metronome. "Deeper, deeper, deeper, down, down, down."

Darci shook her head trying to toss off the oppressive feeling and clear her thoughts. "Let's go get some coffee," she said.

Phil and Eddie's, a "fifties-style" diner, was just down the street. As they walked in the front door, Hank Williams was wailing 'Lovesick Blues' on a vintage jukebox. A tired-looking waitress gestured for them to sit where they wanted. A dozen customers, mostly rainsoaked high-school students, filled the booths. Old 45 RPM records were mounted on the walls, along with baseball hats and school banners.

"You're a sight," Darci said, looking across the booth at her lover, whose blond hair was hanging in his eyes.

He smiled. Taking handfuls of napkins from the table dispenser, he tried to blot the wetness from his hair. Darci did the same. The waitress brought two mugs of steaming coffee.

"I'm still trying to understand the oversoul bit," Darci said. "According to Lawrence, we've never been anyone else in a past life and we'll never be anyone else in a future life, is that right?"

Calum was stirring cream into his coffee. "That's the way I understood it. We're the living result of past lives, and the lives we experienced tonight were those of someone in our oversoul lineage. But the lives are affecting us just as if we had actually lived them, which in a way, I guess we did."

Darci shook her head. "But then my karma isn't my karma, it's my oversoul's karma."

"I don't know," Calum replied. He sipped from the steaming mug. "Maybe when the oversoul cell divides, it creates a clone of itself. You began your life as an exact duplicate of your oversoul. So you were born with a background, a history, and with karma to experience. Your oversoul's desire was your desire, but with experience you started to make free choices."

Darci seemed deep in thought, then said, "But in the future, as an oversoul myself, if I pass on my soul atom to others, it will be the others who experience the future life. I'm really off the hook."

"What's the difference if you feel and experience through them?" Calum asked. "Maybe you should view it as a larger, multidimensional you."

Outside, stroboscopic slashes of lightening ripped the sky, followed by rumbling thunder that sounded as if it were trying to force its way into the diner. Pellets of rain pounded the windows with frenzied intensity.

Darci, elbows propped on the table, cradled the mug and blew on the steaming coffee. "If those I create will continue to work on my unfinished karma, you and I may be working out the unfinished karma of Shellaka and Lakato," she said, a concerned look on her face.

Deep in thought, Calum didn't respond. He was running his index finger slowly back and forth on the sharp edge of the dinner knife. His expression was blank and his eyes unseeing.

Chapter Four

"Are you sure you don't want company?" Calum asked as he pulled the jeep into a parking slot in front of Darci's room at Los Abrigados.

"Everything is happening so fast, Calum. I just need a few hours to breathe deeply and think about it."

"I can understand that," he said. "And I'll miss you. How about breakfast?"

"Make it lunch," she said, leaning over to give him a kiss.

She was halfway up the rain-slick steps to the second floor when Calum yelled, "Sweet dreams, Lakato."

Midnight. Darci was still wide awake. She telephoned Sally, her Denver roommate, to explain that she'd be in Sedona two days longer than planned. She wanted to tell her about Calum, but Sally was too sleepy to carry on a conversation.

Darci ran a tub of hot water and poured in the bottle of bubblebath from the bathroom gift basket. As she soaked in the bathtub, she sipped a glass of wine from the refrigerator bar. Her chest was no longer sore but the hot water stung her nipples. As she lay blissfully relaxed in the soothing water, her thoughts revolved around Calum. Finally, when the water had cooled, she reluctantly stood up, stretched, then slowly toweled herself dry.

She climbed into bed with *Sedona Life* magazine, but couldn't keep her mind on the tourist-oriented articles. Images of herself hanging over the cliff's edge kept filling her mind and again she relived the fear of letting go, tumbling, twisting, turning, screaming through space to land in the water. *Water?* There had been no water.

Deliberately, she turned her mind to memories of Calum, on top of her, kissing her with her hands still bound to the tree; Calum on top of her, making love; Calum on top of her as they rolled through the blood-wet grass and plunged — *NO!* She sat up in bed and shook her head.

Outside, bursts of blue-white lightning ripped the sky in pulsing staccato stabs, and thunder growled angrily out of the red rocks. Wind-driven rain blew against the patio door. The water rippled down the glass, turning the sodium-vapor street lamps a ghostly-bluish blur.

The sound of the rain on adobe was different. She noticed that and remembered the village built under the overhang of a sheer rock wall. Standing on the adobe steps, looking at the green fields and swiftly running river, Lakato watched the rain and thought of Seanna. Shellaka wanted her. He wanted her. She would not choose and Shellaka grew angrier by the day.

"Don't let her come between us," he said to Shellaka. "Let the customs of our people determine the outcome." But Shellaka would not listen. His love was more important than customs. Once Lakato's closest friend, Shellaka now shunned him. They fought once but they were well matched and there had been no winner and no loser. Shellaka shunned the council and would disappear for days at a time, always returning with gifts for Seanna. But Seanna wouldn't choose. Seanna wouldn't choose. Seanna wouldn't . . .

A thunderclap of lightning sounded like it was shattering the walls of Darci's room. She bolted into a sitting position and rubbed her eyes as lightning barrages illuminated the sky, silhouetting the blurry figure of a man on her patio. Panic surged through her. *He's trying to open the door,* she thought, fighting to breathe and find her voice. "I'VE CALLED HOTEL SECURITY," she screamed. She sat in frozen anticipation, her fingernails digging into the comforter. When the lightning flashed again the patio was empty.

Trembling, she rolled out of bed and padded to the patio to check the door. *Locked.* Outside she could see only the blurred images of the rain-slashed parking lot. She crawled back in bed and thought about calling security. She would have called if beautiful Seanna hadn't waved from across the meadow, beckoning to be followed. He was running through the tall grass and wild flowers. Running down the green hillside, through the trees to the sycamore grove where she waited for him, lying on a bed of leaves. "Love," she said, stroking his face. "Love, love, love."

Seanna faded away as Darci waded into the bloody water to help the Indian who was floating face down below the waterfall. He coughed, and trembled as she raised his head out of the water. His black eyes looked directly into hers and he whispered, "Love, love, love."

"Ah-h-h-h-h-h-h," she screamed.

Moments later there was a sharp pounding on the door. Darci stirred, sat up and looked at the clock. 4:24 A.M. The knocking continued. "Who is it?" she yelled.

"Hotel security."

She quickly got out of bed. Pulling on a robe, she padded to the door and looked out the peep hole. A clean-cut looking man in a suit and raincoat was holding up his identification card. Darci opened the door.

"I'm really sorry to disturb you, Ms. Farrell," he said. "But your neighbors heard you scream. And we had a prowler report from this complex about an hour ago."

Quickly, she explained about the nightmare. "But I think there was someone on my balcony awhile ago," she said. "I could have just dreamed it, but I don't think so."

"Keep your door locked, and call if you need us. We can be here in two minutes."

Darci closed the door, switched the bolt and inserted the chain lock before checking the door to the balcony again. *Locked.*

Sitting on the edge of the bed, she let the details of the dream fill her mind then entered them into her notebook. "What if there's still karma between my oversoul and Calum's oversoul?" she wondered aloud. "What if we want to resolve it, but our oversouls don't? What if Shellaka created Calum with soulmate astrology only to bring us together to extract revenge?" She shuddered uncontrollably.

By 9 A.M. Darci had finished breakfast in the hotel restaurant and was back in her room. Searching for Lawrence's calling card in her purse, she punched the numbers on her phone.

"Mr. Lawrence, my name is Darci Farrell. I attended your session last night at the Eagle's Eye bookstore. It says on your card that you take private appointments. I'm not interested in a past-life regression, but it's very important that I talk to you as an expert on reincarnation." She paused. "No, I won't be here next week. I need to see you today. This morning if possible." She heard him flipping through a notebook. "Ten o'clock will be fine, thank you very much. Can you tell me how to get there?"

Wearing black jeans, a black turtleneck sweater, and a lightweight ski jacket, she was preparing to leave the room when the telephone rang. She hesitated, looked at the phone, then walked out the door without answering. The storm had passed and the sun had broken through the overcast sky. It was already too warm for a jacket.

At 9:55 A.M. she pulled her Ford Probe GT to the curb in front of a small home in an area called "uptown Sedona."

Lawrence greeted her at the door. "Oh yes, I do remember you from last night," he said, holding open the door.

Up close, she could see the lines spiderwebbing his face. He was older than she had thought. Shorter too. His long hair, more white than black, was drawn back in a pony tail. He wore white pants and an open-neck white shirt with billowing sleeves. Around his neck hung a small silver pentacle.

"Let's sit on the patio," he said, gesturing to the open sliding door across the room. The living room was furnished with nondescript pastel-colored furniture, and the walls were decorated with montages of certificates with official-looking seals. There was no visible sign of his metaphysical interest.

Outside, Darci sat down in a metal lawn chair beside a glass-topped table. The patio looked out over Lawrence's well-kept backyard and the backyard of another house on the next block. Beyond the houses, in stark contrast to civilization, the magnificent red rocks appeared as brilliant temples filling the horizon.

Beside the table an iron kettle steamed on a hibachi filled with glowing coals. "Cha-no-yu," Lawrence said, bowing.

"Excuse me," Darci replied.

"Tea ceremony. Would you like some?"

43

"Please."

She silently watched him fastidiously prepare the elements. He poured the boiling water into two drinking bowls. Next, some finely powdered green tea was spooned into each bowl, and well stirred into the water with a tea whisk. A sugar bowl and spoon were set before her.

"First, we'll drink tea, then we'll talk," he said, handing Darci a bowl.

"Okay," she smiled. Five minutes passed. Lawrence relished his tea and obviously wasn't bothered by the silence, but it made Darci nervous. Or maybe it was his hooded eyes that looked sleepy until one noticed their intensity and the strange way they locked on their target.

"The tea is good," she said.

He nodded.

"It's beautiful here," she said, trying to start a conversation. "Do you live alone, Lawrence?"

"All my life," he said, placing his bowl upon the table.

"Can I tell you why I'm here?"

He bowed again. It took Darci twenty minutes to relate all she had experienced since falling off the ledge. She explained the astrological configurations, the regression experiences, the dreams and her oppressive feelings. She ended by sharing her fear that Shellaka had created a soulmate to extract revenge.

"That's quite a story," Lawrence said, leaning back in his chair. "But I think you may have missed the most obvious consideration. You're younger than Calum, aren't you?"

Darci nodded and leaned forward in her chair. "Eight years younger."

"It's more likely that your oversoul created you with soulmate astrology that would assure a bond with Calum. You could be a love offering."

"A love offering?" Darci said, shaking her head.

"Maybe Lakato wants to rise above his karma with

Shellaka and this is the only way to do it. In a soulmate bonding the love works both ways, so Calum can't help but love you."

"Love conquers all, huh?" she asked.

"Maybe. But realistically, Shellaka's hate may be too strong for Calum to resist. The oversoul may be able to channel his anger through his creation."

"How do you mean, 'channel'?" Darci asked.

Lawrence raised his hands indecisively. "The oversoul theory is just that, a theory. Maybe the Indian in your vision meant for you to fall off the ledge."

"You mean Shellaka might have manifested the vision? But that doesn't make any sense—Calum was the one who saved me."

"A creation always has free will. Calum was acting on his own at that moment, but at another time he might have been influenced by Shellaka. Or your fall could have been a setup for Calum to get close to you. Maybe Shellaka has other plans. I just don't know how to figure it, Darci. I've never encountered a case like this." He wiped his brow with a handkerchief.

"Have you been in this work long?" Darci asked, distracted.

"I was a hypnotist in New York for twenty years. Five years ago my health forced me to move to a drier climate. I'm supposed to be retired, but it hasn't worked out that way."

Darci asked to use the bathroom.

"Second door on the right, down the hall," he pointed.

On the way back to the patio Darci noticed a bedroom door slightly ajar. She hesitated, then stopped and peeked in. The neat bedroom was as nondescript as the living room, but the two framed posters on the wall facing the bed were of handsome young muscle men. She smiled.

Lawrence started talking before she sat down. "Darci,

the way I see it, you have two choices. You can leave and never see Calum again. That's probably the safest choice, but you may be passing up the love of a lifetime. Or you can attempt to resolve the situation by exploring it in more depth, or by going to Boynton Canyon tomorrow night during the full moon."

"How would I explore the relationship in more depth?" she asked.

"I'm remembering a hypnotic technique called ultra-depth," he said, stroking his chin. "I've only used it a half a dozen times. It takes over an hour of intense induction to put good hypnotic subjects into an ultra-trance. Obviously, you and Calum are good subjects. Initially, the technique was being explored at a California university but they were forced to stop the experiments."

"Why?"

"The subjects, usually a man and a woman, were driven so deeply into hypnosis that they reached a point where they rejected the commands of the hypnotist and entered their own subjective world. Upon awakening, the hypnotist would find that his subjects had explored some kind of joint alternate reality."

"But why did they stop the experiments?" Darci insisted.

"Because the men and women who volunteered to be part of the experiments developed such intense bonds they divorced their mates to be together with their hypnosis partners."

"I'd welcome a more intense bond with Calum, but I don't see how it could serve us. What could we find in an alternate world that would help us in this one?"

"No, I'd do it differently," Lawrence said. "It would be an ultra-depth, past-life regression to your lives as Lakato and Shellaka. I've never conducted one. I don't think anyone has."

Darci looked Lawrence directly in the eyes, frowning.

"You said the subjects rejected the hypnotist. In other words, you'd lose control of us once we were under."

Lawrence nodded. "Yes. But if I sensed trauma I could wake you up. I have no idea to what degree you might enter the past life."

Darci nodded.

"There's one other thing," Lawrence said. "One of my subjects found ultra-depth so disturbing he lost all memories of the experience and the whole week prior to the session."

Chapter Five

The message light was blinking when Darci returned to her room at the resort. She dialed the operator. "The message is from a Calum O'Keefe, who asked that you meet him at Bell Rock at 1 P.M. He'll bring the bread and wine."

It was 12:10 P.M. She'd passed Bell Rock on her way into town, so she knew the location. *Plenty of time.* She lay down on the bed. Closing her eyes, she placed her hands at her sides, connecting her index fingers and thumbs in the mudra position, and began yoga breathing. She held each breath for as long as she could before letting it out slowly through slightly parted lips. When the breath was all the way out, she contracted her stomach muscles pushing it further out, then repeated the process. When she was mentally calm she directed a body relaxation and countdown. Floating in a peaceful void she sent out the thoughts:

I call out to the positive powers of the universe, to my guides and Masters, and those who share my energy. Protect me during this meditation, and throughout this day and the days that follow. Protect me from all things seen and unseen, all forces and all elements. As above, so below. I ask it, I beseech it, I mark it, and so it is.

She floated without thoughts or concern, awaiting any visualizations or subjective impressions. There was nothing but the blackness and peace until the sound began. Far away at first. Rattling. A baby's rattle. No. It was closer now. More intense. Darci focused on the sound. Goosebumps shot up and down her arms as the vision of a coiled rattlesnake appeared before her inner eyes. Its head darted up and down as its tongue flicked in and out, its body twitching and its serpent eyes watching her. Evil eyes waiting for an opening; lusting to sink its fangs into her flesh and fill her body with deadly poison.

Love, love, love, Darci said the words in her mind. She imagined herself projecting white light at the quivering reptile. *Love, love, love. Love, love, love.* The snake tightened its coil as if preparing to strike. *Love, love, love.* There was another sound. *Swish.* A hawk shot into the vision, grabbed the snake by the head and disappeared into the black void.

When she was calm again, she called out to Granny Farrell. *If you're not too busy over there, I'd sure like to see you, Granny Farrell. Please. I love you.* Blackness faded into deep purple that melted into a cloudless blue sky. Granny Farrell sat on the edge of a gleaming white fountain in a temple garden. She radiated a shimmering light. Darci bounded across the lawn to embrace her grandmother, then sat on the grass at her feet and dropped her head into her grandmother's lap.

I miss you, Granny, Darci said. Her grandmother stroked her hair.

I miss you, my child. You're doing well, your time is near.
What time?

Whatever time you want it to be. Remember to love, love, love.

Darci raised her head and looked at the woman who was no longer Granny but a smiling Seanna, as young and vibrant as she'd appeared in the sycamore grove. Darci shivered and stumbled to her feet, looking around in confusion. *Granny?*

Love, love, love.

Darci counted herself up out of the meditation and lay on the bed, staring at the ceiling. *Am I going over the edge or what?* She sat up and made a half page of notes in her notebook.

Chapter Six

As she drove to Bell Rock, Darci thought about the book she'd read on the Sedona vortexes—the reason she was here. According to a scientist quoted in the book, the earth's magnetic field was riddled with deviations and irregularities, but three vortex areas were noted to be most powerful: the Bermuda Triangle near the Bahama Islands; Sussex, England; and Sedona, Arizona.

She remembered that American Indian legend claims there are four power places in the world; two positive and two negative, the positive being Sedona and Kauai, Hawaii; both red-rock country. The Indians say that the towering crimson peaks stimulate sensitivity and that here a man realizes his true dreams and ambitions. The mountains are like a great magnet and people are drawn to them to come face to face with themselves and the potentials of their nature.

Darci slowed down as a tour bus pulled out onto the highway ahead of her.

The energy vortexes were supposed to intensify all energy, positive and negative; psychic energy, relationship energy, sexual energy and physical energy. Darci accepted this. She'd never experienced such vivid meditative visions. There was no question about the relationship and sexual energy. As far as the physical energy was concerned she'd hardly slept since arriving in Sedona.

Five minutes out of town the road curved out of the pines and Bell Rock filled the horizon. The mountain was considered to be a beacon vortex, emitting energy from the base through the top and extending miles into the air, supposedly explaining numerous UFO sightings. Psychics suggested it was a place for stimulating consciousness and communicating with higher forms of life. *Hopefully not lower forms of life,* Darci thought as she pulled off the road to park her car beside Calum's Jeep.

He sat near the base of the mountain, a picnic basket in his lap.

"You make my heart smile," she called ahead, happy to see him.

"I missed you," he yelled in response.

They embraced, playful at first, the kisses quickly turning passionate. When they paused to look in each other's eyes, she rumpled his blond hair and drew a finger gently across his forehead, then down his nose to his lips. "What's in the basket?"

"A loaf of bread, a jug of wine, and four packages of Gummi Bears."

She laughed. "I'm the woman, but you keep preparing the meals."

"I don't want any feminists claiming I'm sexist," he said, taking her arm for the climb up the mountain.

They passed people sitting in meditation. Chaparral and clumps of cactus appeared to grow out of solid rock along the ascending path. A hawk swooped out of the darkening sky and Darci remembered the rattlesnake vision. She shivered and pushed it out of her mind.

Shielding her eyes, Darci looked up at the peak of the bell. "Want to climb all the way to the top?" she asked.

"Are you kidding?" he replied.

She smiled gleefully. "I'll bet we could make it."

Calum shrugged his shoulders. "Okay, but not with a picnic basket. Let's eat first, then climb."

A red-and-white checkered cloth served as a table on the ground. He laid a fresh loaf of French bread in the center, a small butter crock beside it, two apples, a block of cheese, and two crystal wine glasses. Darci sat on the edge of the cloth, holding her knees to her chest, watching the man she wanted to love. He presented a bottle of wine like a waiter, holding it out for her inspection. French Chardonnay. She snobbishly turned up her nose, gestured acceptance with her fingers, and broke into laughter.

"You are a very special man, Calum O'Keefe."

"And you are a very special lady, Darci Farrell." He handed her a glass of wine.

"To soulmates," she said.

"To soulmates," he repeated.

Lightning flashed in the black sky beyond the mountains to the northwest, but the warm spring sun continued to bathe the lovers. Calum broke the bread and drew a black-bladed knife from his pocket to spread the butter.

"What an unusual knife," Darci said. "What's it made of?"

"Obsidian. Before metal, it was all that was available. Today some surgeons use them because they're sharper than a razor." He held it out to her.

Darci shook her head. Calum dipped the knife into the butter and spread it on a large hunk of bread, then deftly shaved several slices of cheese, which he placed on the bread. With a flourish he presented the sandwich to her.

"Tell me something about Mr. Calum O'Keefe that nobody else knows," she said, sipping the wine as she balanced the sandwich on her knee.

"Oh boy, now you're getting personal," he said.

"Wouldn't want to do that," she replied, licking her lips.

He laughed, raised his eyebrows and nodded his head slowly. "Something nobody else knows, huh?" He took a bite of bread and chewed slowly. "Well, nobody knows that sometimes when I'm all alone in my apartment I eat Gummi Bear sandwiches."

Darci shook her head. "Not good enough. Something else."

Calum looked off at the horizon, mustering his thoughts. Finally he said, "Nobody knows that on Sunday nights, after I take my son back to his mother's house, I often cry."

"Oh, Calum, I'm sorry." Darci put down her wine glass and sandwich and leaned over to hug him. She kissed his ear and whispered, "I didn't mean to bring up anything painful."

He smiled, kissed her playfully on the lips and said, "Finish eating so we can go climb a mountain."

They were halfway up the nearly vertical portion of the climb when the sun disappeared behind dark clouds. Calum was leading. "Maybe we'd better forget it," he said, looking back at Darci. "It may rain."

"Hey, I'm the direct actionist, remember? I always finish what I start."

"Okay," he said, continuing to climb.

They were nearing a fissure in the upper arch of the bell when the first fat droplets of rain began to splatter the earth. "Oh, that feels good," Darci said, putting out her arms to embrace the rain. "I don't think I've ever felt so energized in my life."

"Maybe we'll be beamed up by a UFO," Calum laughed, taking her by the hand to walk into a wide crevice at the crest. They stood with their arms around each other, looking down at the dwarfed world. Darci's Probe GT, parked beside the road, looked like a toy. People meditating on the flange of the bell looked like ants. In every direction the eroded buttes ascended out of the blood-red desert into the cloud-shrouded sky. They inhaled the scent of ozone like an exquisite perfume. The charge of negative ions in the air exhilarated their bodies and minds. Tilting their heads back, they let the pellets of rain splatter their faces, and they laughed until they nearly cried.

"CAN YOU BELIEVE THE ENERGY?" Darci yelled, her eyes dilated and wild.

She slipped away from Calum and pirouetted on one toe, gaily dancing for her lover, a ballerina on a heavenly stage. She whipped her long black hair from side to side as she danced, turning, twisting, expressing the energy with wanton joy; whirling and spinning on the crest of the mountain, catching Calum's eye as she twirled, watching him clap to the beat of unheard music.

A barrage of lightning slashed blue-white out of the black clouds, striking Cathedral Rock several miles away. The growling thunder rumbled angrily across the desert floor like a demonic beast seeking a kill.

Darci seemed not to notice as she whirled and spun in uninhibited excitement, removing her black turtleneck with one graceful flowing movement; a free soul, cupping her bare breasts up into the rain as she twirled around the torch-lighted circle, to the beat of the primitive drums, and the smiling faces of the tribe. She pirouetted into a savage flat-footed stomp of animalistic intensity as the Indians parted to make way for Seanna, her hair braided with flowers. Darci smelled the fire, heard the clapping, and tasted the joy of victory. And she felt the pleasure in her genitals; the orgasm bubbling up from lifetimes past to erupt like a volcano spewing death over those she loved.

The torches flickered and died as Darci ended the dance on a thunderclap, unsnapping her jeans as she slid to her knees. She laughed at the increasing velocity of the storm that now lashed the mountain with wind-driven sheets of rain—howling phantoms plunging headlong into the abyss.

"WHAT'S HAPPENING?" she shrieked, gasping for breath. She was trembling violently as she crawled on her hands and knees toward her lover.

Calum lifted her into the air. Her frenzied eyes met his as they both collapsed on the rocky earth, rolling over, Darci on top. She dropped forward, throwing her breasts into his face and grinding her hips into him. His tongue flicked madly over her nipple with crazed intensity. Her guttural cry was a mixture of pleasure and pain.

Thunder exploded nearby, the marrow-piercing crackle jolting Darci into a sitting position. She tilted her head back into the driving rain and screamed, "I LOVE YOU!" She rose up on her knees and peeled her jeans off her hips. He grasped her thighs but she slipped away, slithering backward off of him, down, until she was tearing at his Levi's with her teeth while her hand ripped at his zipper. With her free hand she skinned one leg out of her jeans. "Oh, my gawd, Darci," he moaned, arching his hips into the air and shaking the rain out of his eyes.

She rose up on her knees, looked down at him whimpering beneath her and dropped upon him, violently fusing the two of them into one screaming, thrusting, orgasmic mass. They rolled over and over, off the crest, dangerously close to the edge of the mountain top.

As their frenzy raged, murderous barrages of stroboscopic lightning sliced the sky; bolt after bolt striking the nearby mountains; deafening claps of thunder exploding like mortars around them, shaking the mountain, parting the veil, transcending desire in a savage effort to absorb the other's soul.

Chapter Seven

Her face in a shallow pool of water, Darci opened her

eyes to find herself topless with her jeans half off, chilled and trembling. The rain had stopped; an unholy light shrouded the mountain. She sat up and rubbed her eyes then slipped her bare leg back into the wet jeans. A few feet away her turtleneck sweater lay inside out, in a pool of water. *What happened?* She tasted blood in her mouth. She stood up shakily, and turned around. "CALUM," she called in each direction, and listened intently for a response that didn't come.

Wringing the water out of the sweater she put it on, trembling. The wet material strafed her nipples and she remembered. *Sex. Wild sex.* She shook her head. *What else?*

"DAMN IT, CALUM, WHERE ARE YOU? IT'LL BE DARK SOON." She recognized the fear in her voice, and felt it sink to the pit of her stomach when she looked off the mountain to see her car parked by the road. Calum's Jeep was gone.

Tears streaming down her cheeks, Darci took one last look at the mountain top before making her way to the trail down. Slowly, carefully, she inched her way off the top of the mountain, traversing the cuts and crevices, her feet sometimes slipping out of the wet toe holds in the rocks. Once she dangled by her hands over a ten-foot fissure, but managed to hang on until she found a footing. By the time she was sixty feet below the crest it was nearly dark.

"DAMN YOU, CALUM," she yelled, crouched in a crevice, searching for the best path of descent. To the left she thought she recognized the route they'd taken to the top. But a path to the right looked like it might offer an easier way down. She looked up at the almost-full moon, appearing and disappearing from behind scattered clouds. Thanks to the exertion of the climb, she wasn't cold, but would be if she stopped for long. Frost could settle over a wet April night at 5,000 feet.

Mountain karma, she thought as she worked her way along a narrow path. With the exception of the shadows, the terrain was momentarily illuminated by moonlight. *I used to live a rational, stable life. No soulmate, no sex orgies on mountaintops. But no near-death experiences either.*

No matter how hard she tried to concentrate upon the climb, other thoughts tumbled in. She was lost in Aunt Emmie's cornfield, racing through the plowed rows, clutching her doll, and crying as the corn leaves slapped her face and sliced her arms. Exhausted, she stopped to catch her breath, the blood on her arms dripping onto Rebecca's plastic face. She screamed. Throwing the doll down she stumbled backward, grasping cornstalks, and fell into the dirt, her hands filled with green corn worms.

"DADDY! GRANNY!" she screamed, crawling on her hands and knees down a corn row that only led to another row and another as the sun faded from pink to purple to black.

"Darci, wake up, honey, wake up." She opened her eyes in her father's arms as he carried her out of the cornfield.

"Daddy," Darci said out loud, resting for a moment on a rock ledge. "Why did you die? Why am I always left alone?"

When she saw auto headlights coming out of the high desert, she realized she was climbing down the back face of Bell Rock. *Bad move, Darci. You've seen enough of this mountain to know that people climb from the other side. Better go back.*

"Better go back, Darci," Sally said, when she'd finished telling her about the separation. "Jack's not that bad. Believe me, good men are hard to find."

"He asked for the separation, Sally."

"Well, talk him out of it."

"Sally, you know I've seen a marriage counselor. Jack

wouldn't go. He wants me to be interested in what he wants me to be interested in. And he wants me to give up all interest in the New Age."

"Darc, you live in a beautiful home in Cherry Creek, you drive a brand-new car, and you don't have to work if you don't want to."

"That's three mercenary reasons to remain in an intolerable situation."

They were lunching in a trendy downtown Denver restaurant. Sally motioned for the waiter to bring another round of drinks.

"I don't need another drink, Sally."

"Sure you do. This is a major crisis."

"You love crises. It's why you only fall in love with married men."

"Darci, I haven't averaged more than three or four crises a year since high school." Sally raised her wine glass to make a toast. "And you've helped me through every one."

Darci laughed and shook her head. Sally was a vivacious blonde with close-cropped hair who lived for the day she'd find the ideal relationship, while doing everything in her power to make sure it never happened.

"We could rent a place together," Sally suggested.

"That's why I asked you to lunch," Darci replied.

A small plane flashed across the night sky on approach to land at Airport Mesa. Darci visually tracked the landing lights, wishing she were in the comfortable cockpit. She was getting tired. Her clothes were almost dry, but the temperature had dropped. When she stopped moving, the shivers set in. *I'm probably a third of the way down.* She was following a narrow path into the blackness of a shadowed crevice. The ground crumbled beneath her feet. Grasping futilely at the rocks, she tumbled into a groove, and slid several feet on her back before plummeting off into empty space.

Chapter Eight

Calum was sitting on a gurney in the Cottonwood Hospital Emergency Room when he saw the nurse point at him as a deputy sheriff stepped into view. *Oh, no.* He stiffened and held the ice pack a little tighter to his forehead.

The deputy was a tall, stone-faced man in his forties with crew-cut hair. Hands on his hips, the fingers of his right hand drummed on his holster with a distracting, rolling rhythm. "Sergeant Tompkins," he said, nodding at Calum. With predatory eyes, he examined Calum's wounded face from the front and side. "Do you mind?" he said, gesturing for Calum to remove the ice pack.

Tompkins shook his head. "Hope she was worth it. I need a report." He took a pen from his pocket and flipped open a clipboard. "Course you know, we get any rape reports tonight, you'll be the first guy I'll come looking for."

Calum looked beyond the officer to the mirror along the wall. Four deep fingernail scratches raked down both sides of his face. His temple and shoulder were both bandaged. His shirt and pants were saturated with blood.

"The nurse said she bit off half your eyebrow."

Calum nodded.

"Also took a bite size chunk out of your shoulder."

"Yes."

"Either she's the devil's daughter or else she didn't want you doin' it to her. Which was it?"

"We were having sex and she just went crazy."

"You give her drugs or somethin'?"

"No. We shared a glass of wine a couple hours earlier."

"I need her name."

"Why?"

"I ask the questions. You answer 'em."

"Darci Farrell."

"Address?"

"I don't know. She's from Denver, visiting Sedona."

"Where did this happen?"

"On top of Bell Rock."

"The very top?" The officer scowled at Calum who nodded. "Where is she now?"

"I left her there."

"On top of Bell Rock, at night?"

"It was afternoon when I left. I was losing a lot of blood and she just sat there laughing and calling me strange names."

"What names?"

"I don't know. Past-life names, I think."

"Aw-w-w, for gawd's sake. New Age looney toons, right?" He shook his head and made some quick notes. "You do mushrooms or LSD, looney toon?"

"Neither, I told you."

Officer Tompkins took the radio off his belt. "Donna, this is Tompkins, I'm over at M.J. Lawrence Hospital, get Summerfield at Ranger Headquarters. Tell him we may have a stoned looney toon sitting on top of Bell Rock."

"She's staying at Los Abrigados. Room 2511," Calum said, getting off the gurney.

"Where do you think you're goin'?" Tompkins said, looking Calum straight in the eye.

"I've got to find her."

"You ain't goin' anywhere, buster, til we have a talk with your girlfriend."

Chapter Nine

The moon was much higher in the sky when Darci opened her eyes. Her ears rattled. Her head aching, she pulled herself slowly into a sitting position. She was on a ledge. Behind her was the sheer crevice she had fallen down, in

59

front a three-story drop to another ledge. There was no way off.

No-o-o-o-o-o, her mind raced. As she tried to stand, excruciating pain ripped through her ankle and she fell back against the rock wall, and slid down into a sitting position. Rattling again. *Rattling?* The sound was coming from the shadows on the far side of the ledge, ten or twelve feet away. She carefully massaged her ankle and tried to move it. *Not broken. Probably sprained. I don't believe it.* She rubbed the goose egg on the back of her head, bit her lip to keep from crying, and then almost laughed. *What you resist, you draw to you. Resist being abandoned, guess what?*

Several deep breaths did little to quell her increasing fear or the feeling that a malevolent presence was nearby, maybe watching her, maybe finding pleasure in her pain. She held her hands to her face, felt the cold sweat, and whimpered like a frightened child.

She shifted her position. *RATTLING!* "Oh, dear God, give me a break," she said, her voice wheezing with repressed fear. She strained to see into the shadows. Long moments passed. When she started to think she had imagined the sound, a large diamondback rattlesnake slithered into view. Darci stared, her eyes glistening with terror, her hand over her mouth to stifle a scream. The snake inched toward her. It stopped, slowly raising and lowering its head, sensing with the flicking forked tongue.

"Shoo," Darci screamed, waving her arms. The snake coiled itself sinuously and the rattling started again. "I'm too big to eat. Go away," she shrieked, shaking her good leg at the pit viper. She desperately tried to think of a weapon. Nothing. Her purse was in the car. There was no growth on the ledge, not even a rock to throw.

The snake vision flashed through her mind. "Love, love, love," she said aloud, mockingly. The rattling had stopped.

The rattler remained tightly coiled, watching her, twitching, its tongue flashing in the moonlight.

Panicked, she considered taking off her jeans and using them to swat at the snake. She envisioned the snake sinking its fangs into the denim and then tossing snake and jeans over the edge. *Great. That way I could be naked again, if I'm ever rescued. But no snake would be stupid enough to get its fangs stuck. I'd probably just end up losing my pants.*

She sat motionless, silent, in pain, watching the snake as the moon slowly crossed the sky, inch by inch, illuminating more and more of the far side of the ledge. When a second rattlesnake came into view she let out an audible gasp. *RAT-TLE!* As the moonlight crept up the wall it illuminated a small hole from which a third snake crawled.

A den of snakes! She recalled a newspaper story about Colorado snake hunters—how they would find dozens of snakes sleeping in balls in dens and caves. "Can this possibly get any worse?" she wondered aloud. *RATTLE! RATTLE!* The second snake joined the first. *Yes, it can.* Darci looked up to see the moon disappear into a blackness that enveloped her world. *I can't see the snakes. Oh my, God, I can't see the snakes.*

Metaphysical teachings about fear replayed in her mind. "There is only one fear—the fear of being unable to cope. Fear is always about what is going to happen, not what you are experiencing. It's about the future. You wander into the desert and you fear encountering a rattlesnake in the future. Then you meet the snake and you fear it will bite you in the future. Then the snake bites you and you fear you are going to die in the future. Rise above fear by concerning yourself with NOW. The future will take care of itself."

Yeah. Sure. Right on. Just handle now? Peering into the darkness she could see only an occasional car on the highway far below. She held her arms tightly to her chest in an attempt to suppress the trembling and waves of nausea. She swallowed hard and bit back the tears, but they trembled on her eyelids and slipped down her cheeks . . . down her cheeks . . . down her cheeks . . . onto the bed as she said goodbye to Jack and hung up the phone. Sally was sitting on unpacked moving boxes in the new apartment, her hair in rollers, green goo all over her face.

"I hope you take that jerk for eighty percent of all he's got and ten years of alimony."

Darci shook her head. "I want to let go with love."

Sally made a disgusted face. "Yeah, after the settlement."

"No, Sally. I don't want any future karma with Jack."

"Karma, sharma. You talk about living in the *now*, right?" Darci nodded. "Then why worry about your next life before you get there?"

"Why worry about facial wrinkles before they appear?" Darci pointed at Sally's reflection in the dresser mirror.

Her roommate laughed. "An investment in the future."

"Touché," Darci quipped.

Darci thought she heard the snakes slithering closer. *Did it brush my leg?* She gasped in horror. *RATTLE!* It was closer.

Closing her eyes, she began to mentally draw upon metaphysical protection. *I call out to the positive powers of the universe, to my guides and Masters, and those who share my energy. Protect me through this night from all things seen and unseen, all forces and all elements, and all snakes.*

Darci imagined a bright white light coming down from above, entering her crown chakra and filling her body and mind to overflowing. She concentrated the light around her heart area, then imagined it emerging from her heart area to surround her body in a protective aura. *The universal light of life energy, the God light,* she thought, as she felt the rattlesnake slither up on her lap, coil into a ball between her legs and stop moving.

Chapter Ten

"I'm sorry sir, Ms. Farrell still doesn't answer," said the Los Abrigados operator.

"Thank you," Calum said, hanging up the phone. His eyes met those of the young deputy sheriff assigned to stay with him in the hospital waiting room. "I should never have left her up there," he said to the Deputy.

"Chicken-hearted, if you ask me," the Deputy drawled, and returned to reading the sports section of the newspaper.

Chicken-hearted. Chicken-hearted. Chicken-hearted. The words exploded in Calum's mind as he slumped into a chair. "Don't be chicken-hearted," his father said, handing him the shotgun. "It's time you learned to hunt like your brothers."

"I don't want to kill anything," he whimpered, setting the gun on the ground. "You said you wouldn't make me shoot anything if I came with you. You promised, daddy."

The blow caught Calum on the side of the head, knocking his feet out from under him. "Don't talk back to me, and don't you ever set a gun on the ground."

Tears blinding his vision, Calum struggled to get up. Gil and Johnny were laughing at him. "I'm not killing anything," he screamed defiantly.

"Then you'll clean our kills," his father said, jerking the eight-year-old boy to his feet.

The piercing wail of an ambulance siren pulled Calum out of his shameful past as tires screeched to a halt outside the emergency room. The doors flew open as two grim-faced, blood-splattered attendants wheeled a man through the waiting room, the unrecognizable mass of flesh that had been a face now a bloody ruin.

Calum gagged. For a brief moment, he thought he was going to vomit. Like before. Just like before. "Like this.

Watch closely, lad, because you're going to clean the rest."
His father grabbed one of the pheasants lying on the table,
and slit open the bird. Reaching in, he ripped out the
bloody guts, and held them dripping before Calum's face.
The boy recoiled and gagged, then the hot pressure in his
stomach forced its way up through his throat and he vom-
ited. He began to scream as he fell backwards. Still screaming, he scrambled to his feet, and ran, and ran, and ran.

Chapter Eleven

The worst had happened and she'd handled it without
falling apart. *No, not the worst,* Darci thought as she felt a
second snake crawl over her leg to curl up next to the first
one. *To be bitten is the worst.*

"You drew them to you, Darci." The silent words whispered as the image of the Boynton Canyon Indian appeared before her inner eyes. "They're cold-blooded and they
seek your warmth."

"How did I draw them?"

"The white light and high vibrations."

Darci quickly changed the subject, momentarily forgetting about the snakes. "Are you Lakato, my oversoul?"

"No."

"Are you Shellaka?"

"No."

"Who, then?"

The Indian image faded away to be replaced in rapid
succession by images of Granny Farrell, then Seanna, and
finally a wise-looking Chinese elder.

"Who do you want me to be?"

"Anyone who can make the snakes go away."

"You are protected as you requested, my child." The
image began to fade.

"Protected?" Darci said aloud. The snakes moved and she held her breath, trying not to tremble. She returned to thought language. *Great protection. I'm half frozen, my ankle is sprained, I have two rattlesnakes in my lap, and no way off this ledge. Why don't I feel protected?*

"Protected," the voice echoed in her head, but there was no visual image and she wondered if she had imagined it. Maybe she had imagined the whole conversation.

The temperature was dropping, and she was struggling to remain in an altered state of consciousness.

The moon emerged from the cloud cover and the light that fell on her face drew her up out of the void into the terrifying reality.

She opened her eyes and lowered her gaze without moving her head. The two large diamondbacks lay entwined in her lap, their scaly skin glistening in the moonlight. She thought briefly about snatching them from her lap and heaving them over the edge but decided she was sure to be bitten in the process.

As if responding to her thoughts, the snake on top raised its head, forked tongue flickering, and looked at Darci. Darci's eyes locked with the reptilian slits. Death was now bobbing its head up and down a foot from her face, but, strangely, she was no longer afraid. *What? The last-minute acceptance of the inevitable?*

Darci recalled a friend's claim that a firewalk over a bed of red-hot coals had given her the courage to do anything. *Two rattlesnakes in the lap should equal a bed of hot coals,* she thought, as the awakened snake uncurled and began to slither up her stomach toward her face.

"Lower your temperature, my child." The voice exploded within her mind.

Like yogis? According to mystical writings, they could raise and lower their temperature at will. She closed her eyes as the snake slithered up to her breasts. She imagined herself jumping from a mountaintop, tumbling through space, twisting and turning as she fell. Deeper, deeper, deeper. Down, down, down. Falling, falling, falling. She allowed her feet, ankles, lower legs, and upper legs to relax into numbness as she fell into the void. Her upper body relaxed. Colder and colder. Relaxed and numb. She continued dropping into an imaginary world of ice, sleet and snow, and winds that howled at her ears—deeper and deeper until she landed in the snow on a steep slope, sinking into the freezing whiteness of the snowbank. She lay still, numbed and frozen, her thoughts crystalline and still as ice.

An ear-shattering sound awakened Darci with a start. She tried to remember where she was and why her foot hurt so badly. *The snakes. Oh, my* . . . The snakes were gone. The sound intensified as a helicopter swept into sight like a giant, raging bird, its 30-million candle power spotlight a primeval eye sweeping crazily over the mountain terrain. The light flashed across her, up the mountain and down before settling upon her as the chopper hovered noisily in the air not twenty yards away.

Chapter Twelve

"This the guy that left you up there to die?"

Calum looked up to see Darci in a wheelchair beside Deputy Sergeant Tompkins. Their eyes met, but neither moved.

"Darci! What?" Calum stood up, warily.

"He didn't leave me to die," Darci said, her eyes fixed upon Calum as she answered Tompkins.

"Mr. O'Keefe claims you scratched him up and took a few bites. That true? And what'd he do to you?"

Darci looked disbelievingly at the law enforcement officer, then at Calum's scratched face and bandaged eye. "Calum?" she said, shrugging helplessly, her hands raised in confusion.

"Are you all right?" he asked, kneeling beside the wheelchair.

"I think I sprained my ankle." She watched the tears suddenly well up in Calum's unbandaged eye. "But, tell me, Calum. Tell me. Did I really do that to you?"

He took her hand, looked at it, stalling. "You acted possessed," he said in a hushed voice.

Darci shuddered. "Oh, my God." She slumped in boneless exhaustion. "What's going on, Calum?"

"If you'll excuse me just a moment," Tompkins interrupted. "Does anyone here want to file charges?" Hands on hips, he drummed his fingers noisily on his holster.

Darci and Calum looked at each other. They both shook their heads without acknowledging the deputy.

"Crazy damn New Age looney toons," he grumbled. As he swaggered out the doors of the waiting room he called for the young deputy to get a report from Darci.

It took a half-hour for the Sheriff's report and another hour for the emergency room physician to examine Darci's head and tape her ankle. "It's not a bad sprain, but you shouldn't put any weight on it for a few days. If you have to walk, use crutches," said the young doctor.

"It's my left foot, at least I can still drive." It was more a question than a statement.

"Let someone else drive you for a few days," were the doctor's parting words.

Darci purchased a pair of crutches from the hospital, and they left the emergency room. It was midnight. A chilling wind had replaced the rain, and moonlight reflected in the shimmering pools of rainwater dotting the blacktop parking lot.

"Are you sure you trust me to ride with you?" Darci

asked, as Calum helped her into the passenger side of the blood-splattered Jeep.

He smiled but Darci noticed that it didn't reach his eyes.

"We can pick up your car at Bell Rock, or I can take you back to Los Abrigados," he said.

"Los Abrigados," she said. "And on the way I want you to tell me everything that happened on that mountaintop."

"You really don't remember?"

"I remember dancing in the rain. I have vague memories of wild sex. But I can't remember anything else until I woke up naked in a puddle of water, freezing cold, and alone."

Rainwater splashed over the windshield of the Jeep as Calum wheeled out of the hospital parking lot. "Coffee?" he asked, pointing to a Taco Bell down the street.

"Please."

"Anything else? We haven't eaten since lunch."

She shook her head. "I loved your picnic lunch."

A young Indian woman handed two large cups of coffee through the drive-in window, then excused herself to find some cream. Calum flicked on the heater control and punched a tape into the cassette player. The soulful, bluesy voice of Marianne Faithfull filled the vehicle with "Boulevard of Broken Dreams."

"I need to know what happened, Calum."

He glanced at her as he stirred the cream into his coffee. Balancing the cup carefully, he pulled slowly back onto the main street out of Cottonwood.

"We were having sex in the rain—fantastic sex. I've never experienced anything like it in my life, Darci. You were wild, and getting wilder." He glanced at her quickly, then back to the dark highway. "At the height of your frenzy, you started scratching and screaming. You bit my face and I kicked you away. You became a demon, growling on your hands and knees, calling me weird names. I was trying to get away when you leaped on me and took the hunk out of my shoulder. You were screaming, 'Time to die, Shellaka. Time to die, Shellaka.' "

Darci stared at the yellow line flickering down the center of the empty highway. Slow, hot tears began to trickle down her cheeks. "I'm so sorry, Calum. I don't remember any of it."

"And you didn't remember calling me Shellaka the first time we made love, or at Airport Mesa?"

She shook her head. "I thought Shellaka set up the soul-mate astrology and our meeting in Boynton Canyon. But it looks like my oversoul, Lakato, is the one who wants revenge."

"Why?" Calum asked without looking at Darci.

"Hello Stranger" was playing on the stereo. Marianne Faithfull was asking about the person in the mirror. The song caught Darci's attention.

"Is the person *I* used to be just a fading memory?" Darci whispered in response to the lyrics.

"Why revenge?" Calum asked.

"For something that happened in the Indian lifetime. I don't know. But Lakato seems to be able to control me whenever he wants."

They drove the midnight highway, sipping their coffee silently. In the distance the buttes of Sedona came into view, illuminated by moonlight. After each passing car, Calum switched on the windshield wipers for a few cleaning sweeps. The tape snapped off. The tires hissed on the wet pavement.

As they entered West Sedona, Calum slowed to forty-five. The lights of a bar advertising "Live Country Music Saturday Nights" still flashed. The parking lot was full.

"Calum, I talked to Lawrence about a hypnotic technique called ultra-depth. I think he'd be willing to direct a joint regression back to our past lives as Shellaka and Lakato. Maybe if we explored the past together . . ."

Calum interrupted. "I don't think so, Darci."

"But, if we could do it tomorrow night in Boynton Canyon, we might be able to find out once and for all . . ."

"No."

Darci looked at him sadly.

He continued. "I think I love you, Darci. But obviously we don't seem to be too good for each other."

"Calum, if we have soulmate potential, wouldn't it be worth it to take a chance?"

The jeep pulled up in front of the stairs to Darci's room at Los Abrigados. "I can't, Darci. I'm sorry, but I can't." He shut off the motor. "Can I help you up the stairs?" he asked, turning to take her crutches from the back seat.

"I can make it," she said opening the door and sliding out of the vehicle, balancing on her right foot. He passed the crutches across the passenger seat to her. "Tomorrow night at eight, Calum, I'll be in Boynton Canyon on the expanse that leads to the ledge where you met me."

He nodded.

She was on the second step when the Jeep reversed, turned and fled into the blackness toward the highway.

Chapter Thirteen

The hotel's bell captain sent someone to pick up Darci's car at Bell Rock while she ate breakfast in her room—Huevos Rancheros with specially requested fresh cilantro on the side. Her ankle was badly swollen, the pain a dull, distracting ache. When the phone at her side rang, she answered on the first ring. It was Amanda Bateman.

"Hi, Amanda. How'd you find me?"

"While I did your astrology chart, you mentioned you were staying at Los Abrigados and Calum was at Poco Diablo. I called Poco to talk to him, but they said he had checked out last night. I thought he might be with you."

Darci felt as if her breath had been sucked out of her body. Her head swam. Finally she said, "He's not here, Amanda."

"Not a lover's quarrel?"

"Worse than that." Darci explained what had happened as she understood it. When she had finished, Amanda was silent for a while.

"Dear God, it explains the one disturbing aspect in your combined chart. Your charts are so unique, I studied them some more last night. I was calling Calum to tell him that today is a day of destiny for both of you."

"What does that mean?" Darci asked warily.

"You'll have to interpret it yourself. But what you do today will affect the rest of your life. To see the same aspect in two soulmate charts on the same day is beyond coincidence. Somehow you have to solve your problem."

"Any suggestions?" Darci asked.

"It's not my area of expertise," Amanda said. "But hate is fear. And if fear is the problem, love is the answer."

Darci promised to keep Amanda updated. As she hung up the phone, someone began knocking at the door. She struggled to her feet with the crutches, decided they were too much trouble, and hopped across the room on her right foot. A bright-eyed teenage bell boy held out her car keys.

"Your car is parked right down there, ma'am."

"Thank you. Please come in for a moment while I get my purse." She hopped across the room, rummaged through her purse and found a ten dollar bill, which she handed to the young man.

"Bad foot, huh?" He folded the bill and slid it into his pocket. "Thanks. Your car's great. Wish I could afford one," he said as he went out the door.

Darci's next call was to Lawrence. "Lawrence, I need you to conduct the ultra-depth regression with me, tonight, in Boynton Canyon. The situation is out of control and I have to handle it."

"I don't know about doing it in Boynton Canyon," he said.

"It has to be there. I'll pay you whatever you ask. Please."

"Will it be a joint regression?"

"Just me. I'd like to be there at dusk."

"It will be cold out there after dark. It might rain," he said.

"It's very important, Lawrence."

There was a long pause. "Is a hundred and fifty dollars acceptable?" he asked.

"Yes. I'll pick you up at six-thirty."

Hanging up the phone, she spent the next thirty minutes getting familiar with the crutches by walking around the room, then, as gracefully as possible, easing herself from a standing position into a chair. Confident at last in her new-found ability, she ventured outside, traversed the stairs and walkway to the empty tennis courts. Storm debris still covered the green surface. Below the courts were picnic tables beneath giant oaks and sycamores that lined Oak Creek. The swiftly flowing water looked so inviting she rolled up her jeans, unwrapped her ankle and sat down on the bank. She put both feet in the icy water, and the cold quickly numbed her aching ankle. She smiled appreciatively.

Sunlight flickered through the tree leaves, turning her watery reflection into surrealistic swirls and sparkles. A squirrel chattered in the tree above her and the world seemed fresh and new, until thoughts of Calum began to seep into her mind. All night long she'd dreamed of snakes and of falling. Upon awakening the pain in her ankle had distracted her. When she did think of him she told herself, *I'll see him in a little while and we'll work it out.* That thought allowed her to eat breakfast. But now, knowing that he was gone, a gnawing sadness crept in—a penetrating sadness that conjured memories of her lost family, of death and funerals and final partings that became desperate nightmares that never went away. *I miss you, Calum. I love you. But my creator wants to kill you.*

Anger began to replace the sadness. *LAKATO. I can't believe you created me for revenge—you're a god now. Why? What happened?* She felt a flash of awareness. *Maybe when your anger erupts, I go over the edge.*

Staring at the fast-flowing water, she remembered her regression: Shellaka and Lakato, struggling in the creek, the knives flashing, the blood, and both men falling down the waterfall. *Dead. I know they both died together.* Then, for the hundredth time since awakening on Bell Rock, she tried to remember what had happened during the storm. Nothing.

On the other side of the creek, a man and his young son strolled along the bank, stopping occasionally to skip stones across the water's surface. They waved at her. She waved back.

I want to have your children, Calum. Darci felt the thought echo out across the universe. She closed her eyes and visualized herself standing on a mountain top, saying it over and over. *I want to have your children, Calum.*

Back in her room, she called directory assistance in Phoenix and asked for the number of the Indian Nation restaurant. It was almost noon.

"Yes, Mr. O'Keefe is in, but he isn't taking any calls today," said the woman who answered the phone. "Can someone else help you?"

Chapter Fourteen

Although it was still daylight the full moon appeared

through the windshield of her car as Darci pulled the Probe GT into Lawrence's driveway. She honked twice. Lawrence opened the front door and stuck his head out.

"Sorry for honking, Lawrence. I sprained my ankle."

He nodded, looking confused, then disappeared inside. He returned with a black bag over his shoulder, carrying a folding lawn chair. A cheap see-through plastic raincoat covered a topcoat, which was open to reveal a white shirt; his white pants were tucked into shiny black cowboy boots. He loaded the bag and chair into the back and climbed into the passenger seat.

"Pretty snazzy," Darci said, nodding at the boots.

"Snakes, you know. They crawl at night."

"That's what I hear," she replied, backing out of the driveway.

"How did you sprain your ankle, Darci?"

She told him the Bell Rock story as they drove down Dry Creek Road. They passed the last houses on the edge of town and were soon in the high desert. Giant buttes bordered the road to Boynton Canyon.

"I'm glad Calum isn't coming with us," Lawrence said.

"Why?"

"He evidently sets you off. Without him we can have a nice quiet regression."

"Unless, of course, we don't," Darci said, and laughed. Her hair was braided into a long tail. She had pulled a blue ski jacket over her T-shirt and jeans. The jacket was too warm, but she knew from experience how cold it was going to get.

The interest in the energy vortexes had forced the U.S. Forest Service to develop a small parking area near the canyon entrance. No other cars were there.

"It's at least a mile back into the canyon. How are you going to manage that on crutches?" Lawrence asked as they pulled to a stop.

"After the rattlesnakes, I can do anything," she said, opening the car door. The tips of the crutches sank into the damp ground. It was dusk. The moon rode higher in the sky. A cool, damp breeze rustled through the trees. She heard something else—a strange unearthly sound, so faint and far away, she wasn't sure if it came from the canyon or deep within herself.

"Do you come here often, Lawrence?" she asked, as they started down the trail.

"I'm not too fond of nature," he said, his eyes darting from side to side.

Leaves blew across the trail into the shadows as they made their way through the trees to a fire-break road. A large Indian medicine wheel marked the turn leading into the canyon area.

"Ever take part in any shaman rituals, Lawrence?"

He shook his head.

Darci continued. "I understand that the wheel depicts the universe and the sacred way that balances all creation." She turned from the medicine wheel and looked down the rock-strewn fire-break road. "I don't feel too balanced right now," she said.

"How are we going to get out of here when we're done?" Lawrence asked, as they walked and hobbled along the rough path.

"I have a flashlight in my pocket," Darci said.

"Well, yes. I have one too. But you're having a terrible time and it's still light enough to see the path. This is not a good idea, Darci."

"It's the only idea I've got, Lawrence, and we're going to see it through." The statement strengthened her determination, and she plodded faster.

An owl hooted from somewhere in front of them. The moon was nearly overhead. For several minutes the breeze was blocked by a rock wall, but upon entering the mouth of the canyon a damp wind spiraled out of the shadows with a thin high-pitched wail.

Like a banshee, Darci thought.

As darkness enveloped the canyon, the shadows cast by the moonlight became especially treacherous for a woman on crutches. Lawrence snapped on his flashlight to illuminate the path, and cautioned Darci to be careful.

"What's in the black bag?" Darci asked when they were half way into the canyon.

"A battery-powered speaker and microphone, so I can surround you with the sound of my voice."

A crutch snagged in a hole and Darci fell. She landed on her sprained ankle and cried out pitifully. Lawrence helped her to her feet. "I wish I could carry you," he said, "but I'm huffing and puffing as it is."

"It's not much farther," she said, settling her crutches under her arms and hobbling grimly down the path.

Leaving the fire-break road, it became more difficult to maneuver the scrub desert growth that covered the canyon floor. After she fell several more times, Lawrence insisted on holding her arm for additional support.

At 7:45 they finally reached the open area she had intended for the regression. Lawrence set up the chair and she fell into it, exhausted.

"I'll do the regression lying down," she said.

"Yes. I brought the chair for me," he replied, as he carefully removed the electronic equipment from the black bag.

When he was set up, Darci eased out of the chair and made herself as comfortable as possible on the flat rock surface. The portable speaker was situated a few feet from her head. Lawrence placed the chair at her side and sat down heavily.

The full moon was directly overhead as he started his patterned speech, beseeching Darci to breathe deeply and relax completely. He slowly directed the body relaxation and initial countdown, his words clicking away like a metronome at forty beats a minute.

The wind was increasing. The outline of a bat darted across the face of the moon. Far away, thunder rumbled as if in warning. For a moment Lawrence thought he saw a light on the fire-break road, but when he looked again it was gone. A coyote howled at the far end of the canyon, its disturbing cry reverberating slowly toward him. The hypnotist shuddered and buttoned the collar button of his topcoat.

"You're going deeper, deeper, deeper, down, down, down." He held the microphone to his chin; although his mind was spinning fearfully, he didn't miss a beat. His subject went deeper and deeper into hypnotic sleep. He leaned over and looked closely at Darci. She was deep in hypnosis, but for ultra-depth, she still had a long way to go.

Out of the corner of his eye, Lawrence thought he saw the light again. He searched the oily shadows, straining his eyes. There was a light, and it was coming toward him. Fear gripped his throat. For a moment his voice faltered on the hypnotic words, as he watched the light closing the distance between them. When it was a hundred yards away, he heard a man's voice say, "Darci, Lawrence, it's me, Calum."

Lawrence snapped on his flashlight, cupping the beam with his free hand. When Calum broke through the scrub growth into the rocky expanse, Lawrence flashed the light upon Darci to show him that she was in trance. Continuing his hypnotic patter, the hypnotist gestured for Calum to lie down beside her and take her hand.

Calum said a silent "Thank you," as he took Darci's hand in his own, holding Amanda's crystal between their clasped palms. He closed his eyes as he made himself comfortable beside his soulmate.

At 8:30 Lawrence was still inducing the trance, driving the couple deeper and deeper into their shared past. "You are going back to your lifetimes as Lakato and Shellaka, back to the situation that is still affecting your lives today. Deeper, deeper, deeper. Down, down, down."

Beyond the canyon dark clouds were approaching, and lightning zigzagged above the buttes. The thunder boomed closer now. Much closer. The air smelled of ozone, and something else—something decayed, something dank that the hypnotist could not place. Although his anxiety was increasing by the minute, his voice remained calm. "Ever deeper. Ever deeper. Ever deeper. You're together now traveling back to other lives. Further and further back in time. Letting go of the present and returning to the past."

At 9:15 a bat swooped out of the night sky and brushed Lawrence's face. "Gag-g-g-g-g," he screeched, dropping the microphone from his chin. His eyes wildly scanned the darkness as the screeching bat circled, once, twice, then dropped on his head and sank its fangs into his skull. Another flew directly into his face. He swatted wildly, losing his balance and tumbling over backwards. As he stumbled to his feet he glimpsed an animal dart out of the shadows, and felt a searing pain in his leg as powerful jaws ripped into flesh.

Lightning sizzled out of the storm clouded sky, striking the monolith at the end of the canyon and exploding into a crescendo of thunder that ripped along the walls in earth-shaking waves.

"What was that?" Lakato asked, turning to Seanna who was walking beside him across the meadow.

"Storm coming," Seanna replied.

"Maybe it's Shellaka coming," he said.

"Not funny, Lakato."

Before the entire tribe at the full moon council, Seanna had announced her acceptance of Lakato's proposal.

Shellaka arose, drew his knife and plunged it into the palm of his own left hand, shrieking, "Never! Never! Never!" He threw his blood upon Seanna and Lakato, then turned and ran from the torch-lit gathering. No one had seen him since.

According to the customs of their people, the ceremony would take place on the night of the following full moon— the moon of flower blossoms. Tonight, the lovers would be mated for life. Both had purified their bodies by fasting for three days, eating only the sacred herbs. The cleansing rituals of dry heat and spiritual visions had purified their minds.

Standing side by side at the rim of the canyon, looking down on the river and their village built into the cliffs, Lakato spoke. "I long for Shellaka's blessing."

"If he has made peace with himself, he will come," Seanna said. "If not, it is better that he never comes again."

The moon was almost overhead when the torches and the fire in the center of the circle were lighted. The drumming and flute playing began. Lakato, wearing a headdress of white feathers and a cloak of yellow, was one of thirteen men who danced the sacred dance. With every seventh revolution of the wheel of dancers, one man spun away to disappear into the shadows, until Lakato alone danced the savage ritualistic mating steps. As the drumming and clapping intensified, the tribe parted to make way for Seanna. Her hair was braided with flowers, and her lips dyed red. A red mating stripe was painted across her bare breasts, and bleached skins dangled from her waist. Her dance mirrored Lakato's dance.

The fire leaped and crackled into the night sky, whipped by the howling wind that swirled along the canyon walls. Lightning ripped open the sky beyond the mountains and thunder pealed mournfully like the moans of a dying man. The drumbeats raged violently as Lakato and Seanna danced closer and closer to each other. Their eyes locked, their steps the same, they advanced to the rhythm, meeting at the top of the circle. He lifted her into the air, turned three times to the left, three times to the right, and returned her to the ground beside him.

Silence.

Hand in hand, heads bowed, the couple awaited the blessing of the elder. Standing before them, the old man was raising the cup of sacred water when an arrow hissed out of the darkness and struck Seanna in the stomach. The second arrow, the one meant for Lakato, hit the elder in the back.

A horrified wailing rose from the tribe. Lakato could still hear the lament when he reached the rim of the canyon. The sounds of grief carried on the wind, echoing across the high desert all the way to the mountains.

Driven by blind rage, Lakato pursued Shellaka into the foothills. Gasping, heart pounding, his chest feeling as if it would explode, he fought to keep his footing on the wet grass. Dodging between pine trees, he climbed higher. Tendrils of fog snaked eerily through the trees like ghoulish apparitions echoing Shellaka's demented laughter.

"La-a-a-ka-a-a-t-o-o-o." The voice was above him, calling him, pulling him up the mountain into the clammy mist. He dove into the icy river water and swam to the other side. The moon broke from behind the clouds as he climbed out of the river. Above, the cascading roar of the waterfall nearly drowned out the mocking laughter.

Shellaka was at the top of the waterfall. He knew that. They had come here as childhood friends and later as young men on hunting expeditions. They had lain side by side at this place, sharing their dreams and confessing their fears, before being lulled to sleep by the water's roar.

Lakato made no sound as he crept between the trees,

over the rocks, climbing slowly to the top, where the mists parted. The full moon illuminated the two men, glaring in seething hatred at each other. Both wore only loincloths, and their long black hair was braided in the same style.

"You stole my life," shrieked Shellaka.

"Not yours to steal," Lakato roared.

"You were my friend," Shellaka screamed.

"You killed Seanna," Lakato cried.

They each drew their knives and dropped into a crouch, circling in the wet grass, looking for an opening. The knives flashed in the moonlight as each thrust at the other, nearly missing flesh. They snarled and trembled in rage, circling, growling, slashing.

Lightning exploded out of the sky with the savagery of a hundred storms, one sizzling bolt after another striking the ground around the men.

Lakato watched his enemy circling him. But an image of Calum was bleeding through that of Shellaka. His blond hair glowed with unearthly light, and his blue eyes flashed like the lightning.

"NO-O-O-O-O-O-O-O," Lakato screamed, unheard over the thunderous celestial onslaught. "NO-O-O-O-O-O-O-O," Lakato dropped his knife and sank to his knees.

The lightning stopped.

"LOOK AT ME, SHELLAKA. LOOK AT ME, CALUM."

Calum looked momentarily confused, then shook his head and leaped forward, grabbing his enemy's long black hair. He raised the knife over his head, his face a fiendish mask of hate, his laugh demented.

Their eyes met. "Agh-h-h-h-h," Calum uttered the sound in bewilderment. He was looking down into the face of a beautiful young woman.

"WE CAN END IT, CALUM. WE CAN END IT RIGHT HERE, RIGHT NOW. ONCE AND FOR ALL." Darci's words were an agonizing plea. "I LOVE YOU. I LOVE YOU,

SHELLAKA. I LOVE YOU, CALUM."

The lightning struck again, exploding in a blinding flash of heat and searing pain that diminished into numbness and the blackness of the abyss.

Chapter Fifteen

Darci opened her eyes to see her roommate sitting beside her reading a magazine.

"Hi, Sally," she whispered. "What's happening?"

Dropping her magazine the slender woman vaulted into a standing position. "Gawd, Darci." Sally leaned over and carefully hugged her friend as if she might break. "I've been so-o-o-o worried. I'd better get the nurse."

"What? Wait a minute. What's going on?"

"You're in the hospital, you ninny. Don't you remember?"

Darci shook her head and tried to sit up. When she moved, sharp pain shot through her left foot.

A middle-aged nurse walked into the room. "Welcome back to the world," she said to Darci. "You'll have to leave for a few minutes," she said to Sally.

"No, please," Darci pleaded. "I need to talk to Sally. I don't know what's happening."

The nurse began pulling the privacy curtain along the rail around the bed and gestured Sally out of the room.

"I'll be right outside, Darci. It won't be long."

"Where am I?" Darci demanded of the nurse who was about to stick a thermometer in her mouth.

"Flagstaff Medical Center. Now open, please."

Darci accepted the thermometer. While she waited for the nurse to remove it, she decided the woman looked like a stern grandmother. Darci took the thermometer out of her mouth long enough to ask, "Why am I here?" and quickly replaced it.

"You were admitted thirty-two hours ago in shock, with a badly sprained ankle and a number of bruises. That's all I know. What can you tell me?"

Desperation began to well up within Darci at her inability to remember any circumstances that could have put her in the hospital.

When the nurse walked out, Sally returned. "Okay, Sally. My mind is really fuzzy. Start at the top, and tell me what you know about what happened and why I'm here."

Sitting in the chair beside the bed, Sally looked anxiously at her roommate. She took Darci's hand. "The hospital called the apartment yesterday morning at seven-thirty. They wanted to know about your family, nearest relatives and things like that. It scared the hell out of me. When I told them you didn't have any family and explained who I was, they told me the police had admitted you into the hospital."

"The police?" Darci's hand clutched her throat.

"I flew in from Denver twenty-four hours ago. The police told me you were driving up Oak Creek Canyon, from Sedona to Flagstaff and went off the road about 3 A.M. You weren't hurt, you just ran off into some deep brush, but you were in shock. Another motorist used his car phone to call the highway patrol."

Darci shook her head and her eyes glazed with wetness. "Sally, I don't remember any of this."

"What do you remember?"

Darci looked past the white walls of the room, out the window at the San Francisco Peaks, still covered with snow. "I remember arriving in Sedona, checking into Los Abrigados, and exploring the town. I loved it there. That was Tuesday. I went out to Cathedral Rock and did a sunset meditation that evening. Then Wednesday I decided to explore Boynton Canyon. It was quite a hike back in. I remember climbing up to a ledge that looked down on the whole canyon. It was beautiful there. Then . . ."

Sally waited. "That was Wednesday. Then what?"

"Then I went into meditation, I think. Yes, I'm sure I did." Darci looked into Sally's eyes. "I don't remember anything more."

"Don't you remember calling me, to tell me you'd be staying a couple more days?"

"No. What else did I say?"

"Not much more. You woke me up. I don't remember."

"What day is it today?" Darci asked, a touch of desperation in her voice.

"Monday. Almost noon."

"Monday? What the hell happened during those five missing days?"

A doctor walked into the room, accompanied by a man in a dark suit. "Darci, I'm Doctor Grant Weisman. This is Detective Sergeant David Mallory." The balding doctor looked his part—middle-aged, stout, serious, with great bushy eyebrows. The policeman was about Darci's age. He had good features and sharp green eyes. When he turned into the light, she noticed a long scar running down the side of his face.

Weisman and Mallory repeated the facts as Sally had reported. The detective then said, "The sleeve of your ski jacket was torn, your arm was badly gouged and you had a lot of bruises, some a few days old. None of the injuries related to the accident in Oak Creek Canyon. Can you remember anything about how you got them?"

Darci shook her head sadly.

"I think somebody beat you up." Mallory looked at Weisman and the doctor nodded in agreement. "You weren't wearing a shoe on your left foot. Your jacket was covered with red dirt, so whoever did this to you probably did it in Sedona."

"I've lost five days of my life," Darci said, dropping her head into her hands.

"That's not unusual in cases of trauma and shock," the doctor said. "You may remember in time. You may not. We thought you might have been raped, but that wasn't the case."

"You checked while I was unconscious?" Darci asked, surprised.

The doctor nodded.

The detective continued. "You were carrying a Los Abrigados room key. I checked the resort. You're still registered. Neither the desk clerk, room service, the bell boys or hotel security ever saw anyone else there with you. And, as they pointed out, they all noticed you." He smiled.

"What about my car?"

"It's fine. Maybe a few scratches," Mallory said. "But in all twenty-five miles of Oak Creek Canyon, there's only a few places where you could have run off the road without hitting a tree or dropping off into the creek. You must have had a guardian angel riding with you."

"When can I leave?" Darci asked.

Chapter Sixteen

November sleet slashed the windows of the apartment, rattling the glass. It was Sally's turn to fix Sunday dinner and the smell of frying chicken wafted into the living room where Darci lay curled up on the couch, an unnoticed book held loosely in her lap. She was comfortably dressed in grey sweats, her face bare of makeup and her hair pulled back in a pony tail. Soothing flute music played on the stereo. A fire hissed and snapped in the fireplace.

"Are you going to fondle that book until it falls apart?" Sally asked, walking into the room, a glass of wine in each hand.

Darci smiled and accepted the wine. "Thanks."

"Boring weekend, huh?" Sally was wearing an apron over tight jeans and a sweater. A rhinestone headband encircled her short blonde hair.

"You aren't capable of looking domestic, Sally," Darci chided, raising her glass in a toast.

"And you aren't capable of forgetting about Sedona," Sally said, nodding at the book in her lap.

"My problem is I did forget about Sedona. Maybe if I could remember, I could let it go."

"That was seven months ago, Darc. If I added up all my hangovers they'd amount to a lot more than five lost days."

"There's more to it than the lost days. Sedona seems to be calling me back. I don't know. It's weird."

Sally scowled at her.

Darci continued. "During the day, in the middle of my work, I remember the red rocks and feel a warm pull in my guts. At night I dream about the place."

"Not a very sexy subject to dream about," Sally laughed.

"Not so. A blond man is always there. I can't see his face, but we're always in the red rocks, laughing and making love."

"Making love?" Sally asked, raising her eyebrows.

"Yes. Intense sex."

"That, my dear roommate, is the natural result of deprivation. Why not resolve it by accepting a few of the dates you're offered? I would."

"You date two or three times a week, Sally."

"But not the kind of hunks that pursue you."

Darci laughed and downed the last swallow of wine. "Maybe someday. I just haven't been interested."

Sally shook her head in mock disbelief.

"My office is closed between Christmas and New Year's. I'm thinking of going back to Sedona for a few days. Maybe

I can get it out of my system."

"Do I make the instant mashed potatoes with milk or water?" Sally asked, returning to the kitchen.

Chapter Seventeen

The Los Abrigados desk clerk welcomed Darci with a huge smile. "Good to have you back, Ms. Farrell. Did you have any trouble on the highway?"

She shook her head. "I can't believe how beautiful the buttes look covered with snow."

He handed her the registration form and a pen and accepted her American Express card. "The restaurant is offering Santa Fe holiday dishes this week, and the bar is featuring a new jazz trio." Along with the room key he gave her a copy of the *Red Rock News.*

She snapped on the TV in her room. While unpacking her suitcase, she listened to the Flagstaff station report on local skiing conditions. "More snow is expected above the four thousand feet elevations," the announcer said.

It was 4:30 in the afternoon and light snow blew lazily against the windshield as Darci drove down Highway 89A. She checked the movie playing at the local theater; she'd seen it in Denver. The vegetarian restaurant looked inviting but she wasn't hungry yet. The lights of the Eagle's Eye bookstore caught her attention and she turned into the parking lot. The young man behind the cash register looked up from a book he was reading and said, "Hi. Let me know if I can help you."

Darci smiled and nodded. The store smelled of incense, vaguely familiar somehow. She browsed the aisles, stopping at the section on reincarnation where she found two books she wanted. At the back of the store was another room. She peeked in to see a small stage, a podium and five rows of chairs. At the New Age music display she found a new classical guitar tape by a favorite artist. After picking out several red-rock postcards to send to Denver friends, and a visionary note card to send to Sally, she carried her purchases to the cash register.

"Good books," the young man commented. He was in his twenties with curly brown hair and rosy cheeks, and wore a plaid lumberjack shirt with Batman suspenders.

"What kind of classes do you offer?" Darci asked, as she opened her checkbook.

"Oh, all kinds. Psychics and teachers use the room on a percentage basis. Last night was a palmistry class. Every Thursday is astrology, and Friday is psychic development."

"What about past-life regression?"

"We used to offer it. Lawrence was really good, but he moved back to New York City last spring."

"How could anyone choose New York over Sedona?" Darci wondered aloud.

"He claimed he'd seen enough of mother nature," the young man said.

Darci chuckled.

Dinner was a quiet, satisfying culinary adventure at a restaurant called "Food Among The Flowers." Darci dined on eggplant casserole and read a few pages of one of her new books.

The snow had begun falling heavily by the time she left the restaurant, and she drew the hood of her black ski jacket over her head. The Probe GT sideslipped as she pulled onto 89A. No other cars were on the road. Back at Los Abrigados, she ordered a hot buttered rum in the bar, listening to the jazz trio play old Ramsey Lewis and Mose Allison material. A dozen couples sat listening to the music in the semi-darkness. Darci felt sadly alone.

In her room she shook the snow off her ski jacket and hung it over a chair to dry. After a leisurely hot bath, she snapped the guitar tape into her portable player and curled up in bed with the books and local newspaper. The paper was filled with ads for after-Christmas sales and local activities, from pot luck suppers to a community dance. The full page ad on page seven caught her eye. *OPENING JANUARY 1ST—THE INDIAN NATION. Phoenix's Finest Restaurant Comes To Sedona, Offering Exquisite Native American And Mexican Food.* There was a picture of the restaurant and a location map. The type down the side of the page said, *NOW HIRING: We need two more dinner waitresses and a bookkeeper who will also serve as lunch manager. Applicants apply in person weekdays, 10 A.M. to 3 P.M.*

"Bookkeeper?" Darci said aloud. The possibility of living and working in Sedona electrified her. She pondered the idea until she fell asleep with the reincarnation book in her hands, unopened.

Darci stepped out of her room to see a Jeep with a snowplow roll past, cutting a path through the six inches of newly fallen snow. Beyond the resort the bluffs were nearly white, only their sheer walls shimmering red in the morning sun. Lazy twirls of smoke spiraled out of chimneys in the resort and beyond at Tlaquepaque. Smiling happily, she took a deep breath of the clear air and exhaled, her breath pluming around her head. She was wearing a navy blue topcoat over a blue hand-woven wool dress, black leggings and beaded, knee-high Indian boots.

Breakfast was a black bean Spanish omelet in the resort restaurant. Afterward, Darci walked across the parking lot to Tlaquepaque and spent an hour looking in the windows of the exclusive shops, noting those she would return to during business hours.

At 10 A.M. she pulled into the parking lot of the Indian Nation Restaurant. Workmen were busy installing a hand-carved sign at the entrance. The architectural style of the building was contemporary, but it was constructed of logs.

Stained-glass windows were set into the double-entrance doors. Inside, workmen were busy painting and applying finishing touches.

"Can I help you?" asked an older man wearing paint-splattered coveralls.

"I came about a job. Bookkeeper," Darci said, not believing she said it.

"Upstairs." The man pointed. "Knock on the door. The owner's name is Calum O'Keefe."

Darci nodded a thank you and ascended the stairs. She raised her hand to knock, but hesitated. *This is ridiculous,* she thought and was about to turn and go back down the stairs when the door opened.

The man at the door stared at her in seeming recognition, then, shook his head. "Hi," he said. "Can I help you?" He smiled. He was beautiful.

She open her mouth, but nothing came out. "J-j-job," she finally sputtered. "I'm a bookkeeper."

"Oh, yeah. Great. Come on in." He opened the door and stepped out of the way, gesturing for her to enter.

"Let me take your coat," he said. "Coffee?" he asked, smiling directly into her eyes.

"Please," she said. "Black."

"I'm Calum O'Keefe." He handed her a steaming mug of coffee and sat down behind his desk.

"Darci Farrell."

"I feel like I know you"—he sipped his coffee — "that's not a line."

"I feel the same way, but I'm sure I'd remember."

"Where do you work now?" he asked

"A Denver real estate agency."

"And you want to move to Sedona?"

"I love it here," she said.

"So do I," he said.

Darci fought to keep her mind clear, wondering at the

wave of dizziness that swept through her in response to his smile.

They discussed her bookkeeping expertise. "More than adequate," he said.

They discussed her duties at the Indian Nation. "Sounds like an exciting challenge," she said, feeling euphoric.

They discussed her salary requirements. "Fine," he said.

"I can start on the first," she said.

"You're hired," he said. "Are you visiting Sedona?"

"For a week," she said.

"Alone?" he asked.

"Yes," she said.

"I hate to be forward, Darci"—a shy look flashed across his face — "but I'm so attracted to you, I have to ask you if you'll have dinner with me tonight?"

"Me too," she said, with a dreamy smile. "I mean yes, I'd love to have dinner with you, Calum."

THE OTHER LINDY

The psychic opened her eyes as she finished shuffling the cards and set the tarot deck on the table. "Concentrate on your question, then cut the cards."

Lindy looked at the old woman, nodded and thought about her relationship with Daniel. *Will we eventually be together? Will he leave his wife? Will there ever be any end to the pain?*

She cut the cards.

Expressionless, Madam LeFarr picked up the deck, flicked up the first card and snapped it down on the table.

The atmosphere regarding the question, Lindy thought. Five of wands. *The games people play will lead to misery.*

The second card was laid across the first.

My personality. The Queen of Wands. *Yes, my card.* Now she knew the reading would be accurate. The third card, her conscious reactions, was also accurate. The fourth card represented her unconscious motivations. *Yes, that makes sense.*

Madam LeFarr flicked up the fifth card, which would represent influences present in Lindy's life that would be passing away soon. The psychic caught the eye of her client and quickly laid the King of Swords in its proper place in the spread.

Daniel's card! Lindy's stomach tightened.

Card six, the immediate future, was Justice. Cards seven, eight and nine were observed through a blur of tears. The tenth card representing the final outcome was the Hierophant. *The ability of man to humble himself before God and, in so doing, to gain inner peace and strength.*

"I read it as the possibility of a marriage or alliance." Madam LeFarr tapped the card.

"How could that be?" Lindy's voice broke. "The other cards show that Daniel is going out of my life."

"You fell in love with him before you knew he was married, didn't you?"

Lindy nodded, looking deeply into the psychic's all-seeing eyes. Madam LeFarr could be a Gypsy, Lindy had decided before the reading began. She was dark-skinned, her long, once-black hair was nearly grey, and she seemed stockily built though she hid her body beneath a loose-fitting black dress and flowering lace shawl. A silver pentagram hung around her neck.

"I'll get some tea." The psychic slowly rose from her chair and left the room.

Lindy looked again at the tarot spread. Although she was very familiar with tarot cards, this was her first experience with a psychic reader. She shook her head in denial. *Just because this woman is accurate with Lorraine doesn't mean she can read me.*

The small dimly lit alcove off the living room seemed appropriate for a reading room. Incense sweetened the air. The circular reading table was set in the center of the room and covered with a black tablecloth. A brass floor lamp lit the alcove. The reading chairs were straight-back mahogany with padded tapestry seats. Behind lace curtains, drawn venetian blinds filtered thin horizontal bars of patterned sunlight on the carpet by the wall.

"You are an attractive woman," Madam LeFarr said returning with a tea tray. "You're thirty-five, aren't you?"

Lindy nodded and nervously fingered her long brunette hair. She wondered if the remark came from psychic knowledge, a good guess, or if Lorraine had told her.

"There will be another man."

"I don't want any other man. I want Daniel."

"The outcome is positive." The psychic pointed to the outcome card with one hand while pouring tea with the other. "But you can read the cards yourself, can't you?"

"Yes."

"I use tarot to make a mental connection with my subject, then I rely upon psychic input." She took a long sip of tea before leaning back in the chair and closing her eyes.

Lindy watched closely. After a lengthy silence the woman's eyes began to flicker beneath her closed eyelids, as if she were dreaming.

"Your Daniel is tall, thin with dark hair and a Roman nose." There was a long pause as if the psychic were waiting for confirmation. Lindy remained silent. "You've been together in many lifetimes which explains why you were so attracted to each other upon first meeting. In the life before this one, American during the time of Civil War, you were married. You lived in Maryland." She paused again. "When your husband went off to war you took a lover."

Lindy shivered.

"You were found out, and when your husband returned he was told of your indiscretion. He was terribly hurt and said he would never trust you again. Eventually, you left him. Your current pain is karmic retribution for your past actions."

Tears formed in the corner of Lindy's eyes.

"Are there any questions you'd like to ask?"

"Is there any chance we can be together in this life?"

"Not in this reality."

Lindy looked ruefully at the psychic, who still slumped in the chair with her eyes closed.

"What other reality is there?"

"There are many realities—many frequencies of time and space parallel to the one we are experiencing within."

"Other frequencies?"

"In which your counterparts are living other explorations of your potential."

"You mean Daniel and I are both someone else in some other place?"

Madam LeFarr opened her eyes and slowly sat up in the chair.

"Please tell me about this," Lindy said.

"It might be easier to show you, if you're interested in seeing for yourself?"

"Please."

"It's called a frequency switch, and is conducted in an altered state of consciousness." Madam LeFarr led the way into the adjoining living room and directed Lindy to sit on the sofa. The psychic sat in a side chair.

The room reminded Lindy of her grandmother's house, with its worn, overstuffed furniture from another era.

"You'll judge the results of the frequency switch from your own experience." Madam LeFarr adjusted her body in the chair. "So go ahead and lie down, stretch out and make yourself comfortable. That's it. Now close your eyes and begin to breathe very, very deeply. Very, very deeply."

The psychic's voice was as soothing as the steady ticking of a clock. "So relaxed and so at ease. So relaxed and so at ease." Soon the old woman was directing her "down, down, down, deeper and deeper down."

At first Lindy was fully aware of lying on the sofa, of the incense wafting out of the reading room, and of an occasional car passing on the street outside. But the longer the psychic talked, the more Lindy began to drift. *Swinging . . . in a hammock. No, just swinging in space . . . floating and swinging back and forth, back and forth.*

"In your higher mind you are fully aware of your totality," Madam LeFarr's voice was louder now, and she was no longer pacing her words. "Your soul exists on many levels of manifestation, and you have the power and ability to mentally transfer your awareness to any of these frequencies at will. And in just a moment you will relocate to the most similar reality in which you share a relationship with Daniel. On the count of three, you will be there. One, two, three."

As the psychic's voice faded, Lindy sensed movement, although there was nothing she could relate it to in the blackness. As fear started to creep up her spine, the blackness faded away into a kitchen. *I'm standing in a kitchen . . . I think it's a kitchen.* The stove wasn't right—instead of gas burners or electrical coils there were two units, small metallic fingers formed circles to cook on. Beside the stove was what looked like a sink, but instead of a faucet and knobs there was an opening above the basin.

"I've got to go, Mama," yelled a child as she burst into the kitchen. That wasn't what the words sounded like, but that's what Lindy heard.

The little girl was probably seven or eight, with long dark hair. Obviously she couldn't see Lindy, who stood right beside her. Lindy watched as the girl took a mug from a cupboard, placed it below the opening above the sink and slid a latch. Water poured into the cup.

"Here's your lunch, honey." An attractive woman followed the girl into the kitchen.

Lindy gasped. It was herself, Lindy. The woman didn't look like her, but something about her was so familiar that she knew.

"I have saloball practice after school, Mama."

The other Lindy nodded and kissed her daughter. "Do well." The girl sprinted out the kitchen door carrying her lunch bag.

Lindy watched the woman turn to what looked like a calendar hanging on the wall. Above the squares indicating days were letters that didn't look like any letters Lindy had ever seen. Within the squares were handwritten notes.

Hair appointment at twenty-seven long. Take the dog to zinseera. Buy quadlicken supplies.

One moment Lindy was reading the woman's thoughts, standing watching her go over the calendar, and the next she was observing through the other woman's eyes. *Oh, my God. I'm inside her. Does she know I'm in here?*

"Shilbrima, I'm going to pick up some lensill on the way home tonight," a man said, walking into the kitchen with a newspaper under his arm. He looked at the woman, quizzically. "Are you all right, sweetheart? You look strange."

"I think so. I just felt lightheaded for a moment. It was weird."

Daniel. It's Daniel in a different body, Lindy thought. *And her name is Shilbrima.*

He kissed the woman tenderly and Lindy felt a flood of warmth spreading through her body and mind. *But I don't have a body. I have her body and she doesn't even know it.*

"I love you," Daniel said.

"I love you," Shilbrima said.

Daniel walked out of the kitchen. A moment later the woman glanced out the window to watch her husband drive away in a three-wheeled car.

Shilbrima poured steaming black liquid into a mug, then sat down at a kitchen table with the hot brew. Lindy recoiled at the heat and the taste. *Like hot mud spiced with curry. Yuck!* The woman took a little file from the pocket of her robe and began to work on her nails. When her nails were done and the drink gone, she stood up, stretched and padded down a long hallway to the bedroom. When Shilbrima dropped her robe, Lindy noticed her body in the mirror. *Better than mine, even though she's had a child. But she's probably younger too.*

Shilbrima sat naked at a dressing table and began to apply makeup to her face. Around the mirror were photographs of her and Daniel and the child—at an amusement park, in front of their strange-looking car, with an older couple. As Lindy watched Shilbrima outline her eyes, the word "return," echoed through her mind.

"Return. Return. Return."

She doesn't hear it.

"On the count of three you will be back in your physical body, remembering everything you just experienced. Number one, number two . . ."

Lindy felt as if she was being ripped out of the other woman's body.

" . . . three."

She opened her eyes to find herself in Madam LeFarr's living room. Her body trembled and tears ran down her cheeks.

"You successfully made the transfer, I see." The psychic leaned forward in the overstuffed chair.

"How can it be?" Lindy blotted the tears with the sleeve of her blouse, not looking at Madam LeFarr.

"Why should your soul be limited to only one exploration of potential at a time?"

Lindy sat up and crossed her arms in an attempt to quell the trembling. "How many realities are there?"

The psychic pointed across the room at a radio sitting on a small table. "How many stations could you find turning that dial? On one frequency you're working out some negative karma, on another maybe you're experiencing a karmic reward. One experience appears better than another, but from a higher perspective, you are the totality . . . an ever-evolving soul attemping to attain perfect harmony."

"But it was like here, but not like here . . . people like us, but as if they evolved a little differently."

"I directed you to the reality closest to this one in which you are interacting with the soul you know as Daniel. Otherwise you might have experienced little green people, or light forms, or . . ."

"Can I return there?"

Madam LeFarr took a long look at Lindy. "Yes, anytime."

"On my own?"

The psychic nodded.

"Teach me, please."

Nighttime. Lying in her own bed, in her apartment overlooking the city, Lindy stared at the lights below. She smiled as she closed her eyes and began to relax her body, one part at a time, just as Madam LeFarr had taught her to do.

As she counted down, deepening the altered state, she focused upon Shilbrima and the man who was also Daniel . . . the Daniel she loved and could not have. The Daniel who told her it was over. The Daniel who said he would never see her again. The swinging and swaying started and continued for a few minutes before her body filled with an incredible warmth. *Oh-h-h-h, my God . . . my God.* Erupting in spasms of orgasm she opened her eyes to see Daniel above her, Daniel looking into her eyes and smiling, Daniel making love to her with an intensity she'd never experienced before. The other Daniel who would be hers forever.

THE WALK-IN

Kevin Forester left his body on February 1st and didn't return. On February 2nd the new inhabitant started getting Kevin's act together for the first time in his life.

The transition had started two weeks earlier while Kevin was asleep, out of body on the astral plane. "We need to communicate." The man was dressed in white.

"Why?" Kevin tried to push past him.

"I can offer you a way out of the life you seem intent upon destroying."

When freed by sleep, Kevin often visited a lake in the Ozark Mountains. The environment was a tranquil contrast to his waking life, and he very badly wanted to go there now. "I don't know what you're talking about."

"Are you happy?" asked the man.

"Who is? I gotta go."

"I can help you stay at the lake as long as you want."

"You know about the lake?"

"You lived a simple, happy life near there in the late 1800s."

"I always have to leave the lake before awakening." The man in white had Kevin's full attention.

"Kevin, you're a drug addict, you love no one, and you're irresponsible to your family, friends and employer."

"I'm also two months behind in my rent and they're about to repossess my car. Tell me something I don't know."

"I'm offering you a painless way out of the physical, without incurring any negative karma. You would then be free to remain here on the astral plane until you're ready to move on."

Kevin looked closely at the man and perceived the intensity of his vibration. "You're a Master?"

The man smiled.

"I don't remember what happens over here when I wake up."

"It doesn't matter."

As the two entities talked, others drifted past; sleeping incarnates exploring out of body, new discarnates still adjusting to the astral plane, upper level souls, guides, and Masters. They flowed past and through each other like fish beneath a sea of ever-changing colors.

Although this was a nonphysical realm of existence, each soul appeared to the others in attire of mental manifestation. Those who were projecting in their astral bodies while asleep on earth, appeared as they did in life, clothed as they preferred. The discarnates existed within their etheric bodies, usually projecting an earthly appearance from a previous life. These etheric bodies were electromagnetic fields of a particular vibration—the intensity indicating their soul level. The soul atom containing the chakras, all memories and a pattern of character traits, talents, and attitudes were contained within the electronic field as a blueprint for a future incarnation.

"I'd leave my body without dying?" Kevin asked the man in white.

"You'd go to sleep, and your etheric body would slip away as another soul replaced you, retaining your memories. His etheric body would replace yours, and he would agree to set your life in order or incur the karma you've created."

"Why would he do that?"

"For the opportunities offered by incarnation. Maybe to accomplish a task or fulfill a goal. Walk-ins always have a purpose."

"Does someone out there want my body?"

"No one in particular, but there are always souls wanting to walk-in if an opportunity arises."

"So this new guy would have two minds, mine and his own?"

"For a few weeks. But by the time he established new directions, his own conscious memories would fade, leaving him remembering your past, with an intuitive awareness of his totality."

"His totality?"

"He'd maintain subconscious recognition of ties with other souls. This isn't conscious recognition; it's the intense attraction or repulsion you sometimes experience upon meeting a person for the first time."

Kevin inhaled smoke, opened his eyes and coughed. A naked blonde with smeared mascara was sitting up on the other side of the bed, taking a long hit on a roach. "Mornin', sweetie." She spoke without exhaling, offering him a hit.

He shook his head. *Pain!*

The woman—*Pam*—blew smoke and stared at the empty apartment wall.

Kevin swung his feet out of bed, sat up and lowered his head into his hands. It was the first time he'd experienced physical pain in 12 years.

"We closed down the Hideaway," Pam said.

He couldn't remember.

Naked, standing unsteadily, he took a deep breath and

shuffled to the bathroom.

"You couldn't get it up last night."

He closed the bathroom door. The alien reflection in the mirror had red eyes with dark circles beneath them. *What a way to start a life*, he thought, searching through the medicine cabinet for aspirin and a toothbrush.

The hot shower helped. He stood before the mirror looking at his foggy image in the condensation. *Kevin Forester, 34 years old, six-foot-one, thinning brown hair, blue eyes, attractive enough, with a flabby but well-proportioned body. Circumcised.* He smiled.

"Kevin." Pam knocked and immediately opened the bathroom door. Leaning against the door frame, she stared at him with unfocused eyes. "I thought we'd shower together." There was disappointment in her voice.

"Next time." He forced a smile. "I have some things I have to do."

"Go to hell, Kevin." She punched the door, slamming it into the bathroom wall.

"What?" Kevin said, surprised.

"I always look good to you when you're stoned, but not in the cold light of day." She stretched eye wrinkles with an index finger and patted her pouchy stomach.

"You look good right now, Pam. You have no idea how long it's been since I've made love to a beautiful woman."

She sighed, looked at the ceiling, then met his eyes. "Last Saturday, with me in that bed, or didn't that count?"

"No, you don't understand how . . ."

"I'll make the coffee," she said, walking away.

They left the second-floor apartment together. Kevin walked Pam to her car, parked at the curb a half block away. They kissed quickly. "See you at the Hideaway," she said, gunning the motor and pulling away.

Kevin strolled slowly back up the palm-tree lined sidewalk, nearly overwhelmed by physical sensations. The trees shivered in the warm breeze, rustling the green fronds and drawing attention to the brown, untrimmed skirts of fallen branches. Birds chattered. Hibiscus bushes glimmered along a wall. Magenta and red bougainvillea engulfed a fence, shedding blossoms that sprayed across the walkway. *The smell of the air, even the smog . . . wonderful. The intensity of color and sound. I've almost forgotten.* Even as he marveled at his surroundings, Kevin Forester's familiar memories overlaid his childlike sense of wonder; *air, smog, birds, bushes, so who gives a good goddamn?*

His '90 Mustang convertible was parked in the garage beneath the apartment building. Sitting behind the wheel, Kevin adjusted the rear-view mirror and wondered about his attire; a white T-shirt, black cotton sport coat, Levi's, and white running shoes. As Alistair Alexander he had always worn exquisite suits. But of course Alistair Alexander of St. Louis Park, Minnesota, was dead, and Kevin Forester of Woodland Hills, California, was very much alive. And without a single suit in his limited wardrobe. *I don't even own a black pair of shoes or socks,* he thought as he twisted the key in the Mustang's ignition.

The assistant manager at the local branch of Wells Fargo Bank was working the Saturday morning shift. With the banker's help, Kevin examined his credit history. *Pathetic.* Then he made arrangements to forestall repossession of the Mustang and catch up on all his debts, which amounted to $5,300. A paltry amount to Alistair Alexander, but an overwhelming figure for addicted Kevin Forester who made $380 a week before commissions and taxes as a stationery-store clerk in Topanga Plaza.

Saturday afternoon he pawned or sold outright everything of value in his apartment: the stereo system with surround-sound speakers, the nearly new 27-inch Sony television set and VCR, a seldom-used set of weights, a .308

automatic handgun, and a Martin guitar he'd owned since he was 16. It was enough to pay the back rent on the apartment and leave him enough for a decent suit of clothes.

On the way home he stopped at a convenience store for the early Sunday edition of the *Los Angeles Times*. His body longed for a cigarette, a drink, some grass, cocaine . . . anything to ease the ever-increasing internal tremors. *No way! It's cold turkey. First things first.*

Trembling and sweating, he returned to his apartment. He stripped to his underwear and draped a towel around his neck, then sat blankly staring at the spot where the TV had been. One part of him was enjoying the physical sensations of being alive, no matter how bad he felt. Another part of him wanted to die and end the torment.

The apartment was a typical San Fernando Valley one-bedroom, with a kitchen and breakfast bar in a corner of the living room. The Navajo-white walls were decorated with framed posters featuring Kevin Forester's materialistic dreams. A naked woman lay on the hood of a fire-red Ferrari Testarossa. The words, "Living Well Is The Best Revenge" were reversed out of the night sky above a blue Lotus. Another poster invited him to "Ski Aspen."

The apartment furniture was right out of an Ikea catalog with a little Pier One and Pottery Barn thrown in. Simple designs constructed of metal and plastic, cushioned in black, white or red—take your pick.

Kevin padded to the balcony and stared down at the pool, two floors below. Palm trees grew out of terraced grass mounds surrounding the pool deck. Two bikini-clad women reclined in lounge chairs, absorbing the day's last rays. A girl of seven or eight played in the shallow end, watched by her father who sat in shorts, his bare feet dangling in the water. Kevin observed the little girl for a moment, shivered violently, and repressed a moan.

Clutching his stomach, he hurried into the bedroom, sat in the middle of his unmade bed and wrote a note: "THIS IS A NOTE FROM KEVIN FORESTER TO KEVIN FORESTER. WHEN I FIND IT, I MAY NOT REMEMBER HAVING WRITTEN IT, AND I WILL CERTAINLY QUESTION THE IMPORTANCE OF THESE WORDS. PLEASE REALIZE THAT THIS WAS NOT WRITTEN WHILE DRUNK OR STONED, BUT WHILE IN AN EXPANDED STATE OF AWARENESS THAT I MAY NEVER BE ABLE TO DUPLICATE. PLEASE DO NOT QUESTION. SIMPLY ACT, KNOWING THAT DEEP WITHIN THERE IS AN IMPORTANT REASON TO SEEK OUT MARY LOUISE ALEXANDER, 29, OF MINNEAPOLIS, MINNESOTA. HELP HER IN EVERY POSSIBLE WAY."

Placing the note in an envelope, he sealed it, wrote his name on the front and placed it in the bottom of his sock and underwear drawer.

Kevin spent the evening trying to ignore the demands of his body while he studied the business section of the newspaper. He couldn't believe a Dow of 3000, and that wasn't all that had changed in 12 years. Alistair Alexander's specialty was futures—a fast, dangerous way to make or lose money in the stock market. It looked to be a new game and he had a lot of studying to do.

"I don't know what's come over you the last few weeks, Kevin," said the stationery store manager, a balding man in his sixties. "Your commissions have started running more than your paycheck. I want you to know I appreciate your efforts." He handed Kevin his pay envelope.

"Sorry it took me so long to get the hang of it, John." Leaving the shopping mall with dozens of other store employees, Kevin spotted his friend Danny who worked in Nordstrom's.

"Hey, Kevin, join us for a drink." Danny, accompanied by a pretty young woman, reached him as he was about to cross the street to the parking lot.

"Sorry, I have a date."

"This is Kathy. What's going on, man?"

Kevin smiled at the attractive woman. "I'm cleaning up my act."

"Does that mean giving up your friends? Nobody's seen you. Pam says you've 'turned weird.' "

"Sobriety is weird to Pam."

Danny laughed. "Not even one drink?"

"Some other time, Danny, I've taken a night job to catch up on my debts."

Nine months later, dressed in a Brooks Brothers' suit, and wearing black wingtips, Kevin used his lunch hour to open a $2,800 account in a Woodland Hills brokerage house. $2,000 of this amount was used to control 15,000 pounds of frozen orange juice on the futures market. In three weeks he had parlayed the $2,800 into $8,700.

"Dad, this is Kevin." His hand trembled, holding the phone.

"Why the hell are you . . ."

"Please don't hang up, Dad. I know I haven't talked to you in a long time, but I'd like to patch it up if we can. I want to see you again." He listened to the hum of the long-distance line.

"You still up in L.A.?"

"Woodland Hills. Can I come see you?"

There was another long pause. "You know where I am."

"Tomorrow, okay?"

"Sure." The line went dead.

Kevin's father lived in a trailer in Yucaipa, California—a small desert community between Redlands and Palm Springs. The drive south was filled with bad memories—fights mostly. His parents had divorced when he was eight.

He had lived with his mother until she died when he was 15. The court sent him to Yucaipa to live with his drunken father.

"I may just kill you," Kevin had screamed one night, punching his father in the face, breaking his nose.

The older man crumpled to the floor, holding his face in his hands, blood oozing from between his fingers. "Get out and don't ever come back," whimpered his father.

Kevin bounded out the trailer door, 17 years old with no money and no place to go. When he reached the highway he stuck out his thumb. Los Angeles was two hours up the road.

Although he'd occasionally heard about his father from an uncle, Kevin had not returned to Yucaipa or talked to his old man in 16 years.

The exit off the 10 wound under the freeway in the direction of the rolling brown hills. Santa Ana winds bent the trees and tossed dust and debris across the blacktop. He drove through the few businesses that passed for the town and followed a gravel road five miles to the Shady Rest Trailer Court.

The only thing that had changed was the height of the palm trees, which still offered no "shady rest." He maneuvered the Mustang through the narrow third lane to his father's trailer. The front door of the mobile home was open. As Kevin climbed out of the car, Hank Forester stepped out onto the porch. Kevin hardly recognized him. Years of heavy drinking were etched on his face; he was stooped and carried an oxygen bottle connected to a nose mask.

"Dad." He walked up the porch steps.

"Kevin."

They shook hands and Hank motioned his son inside.

"You get the breath knocked out of you or something, Dad?"

"Emphysema."

Kevin sat on the sofa. Hank slid into an armchair facing his son. The living room was as Kevin remembered it. The old worn-out furniture had been replaced with newer worn-out furniture, but the pictures on the wall were the same—pastoral scenes his father hadn't looked at since they were hung. A few slats were missing from the picture-window blinds. In the silence, Kevin noticed the Santa Ana winds gusting against the side of the trailer, producing a chorus of creaks and groans from the structure.

"I'm sorry," Kevin said.

"How's that?"

"I'm sorry I hit you, and ran away, and never came back."

Hank Forester stared at his son. Finally, he said, "I wasn't ever the best father, but you already know that."

Kevin shrugged. "Tell me what's happened."

"I never remarried. Had enough of that with your mother. The V.A. over in Loma Linda takes pretty good care of me. Liver's shot to hell. Got my pension. It's enough to get by." He shut off the oxygen bottle leading to his mask, slipped a cigarette out of a pack and lit it. Exhaling, he said, "Gave up the hard stuff, but can't shake the coffin nails. I made us some coffee."

At first, conversation was difficult, but as the two men shared remembrances, they began to laugh about old angers. "What is, is," Kevin said. "We can't change it, but can rise above it." Before leaving, he gave his father $5000. "I hit it lucky in the stock market." He promised to return the next month.

Six months of buying and selling futures generated over $100,000, fulfilling Kevin's first monetary goal. He quit the stationery store job and moved into a two-bedroom apartment that served as both home and office.

It was while rebuilding his wardrobe—replacing old white athletic socks with new black dress ones—that he noticed a sealed envelope with his name on it in the dresser drawer. Trying to remember what the envelope contained, he opened it and read the contents. His expression mirrored his confusion. *Mary Louise Alexander, 29, of Minneapolis, Minnesota. Help her in every possible way.*

It was ridiculous. Why would he write such a thing about someone he didn't know? And when did he write it? *Minnesota for chrissake. Igloo land.* The phone rang while he was rereading the letter for the fifth time.

"You have to be the sharpest trader"—his stockbroker could hardly contain his excitement — "in the San Fernando Valley. Soybeans have gone through the roof." He related the figures.

"Sell," Kevin said, hanging up the phone and taking the Yellow Pages Directory out of his desk drawer. He thumbed through the thick volume to "Investigations." *Danner Detective Agency. Fast, Accurate, Local, National, International Investigations.*

Aboard a Northwest Airlines 727, somewhere above Colorado, Kevin opened the investigator's report. He looked again at the photographs of Mary Louise Alexander: a driver's license picture and two black and white 8x10's taken with a hidden camera on a downtown Minneapolis street.

She was not pretty. Five-eight, 135, freckle-faced with red hair. Her lips were too thin and her nose too big. But there was something about her that touched Kevin's heart. *Why?*

He reread the report: "Mary Louise Alexander (M.L.A.) attended the University of Minnesota, majored in marketing and graduated in the top five percent of her class. For the last two years she has worked as a marketing consultant for the Dayton Hudson Company in Minneapolis. She lives alone in a luxury apartment in Edina (a Minneapolis suburb) and drives a 1990 Mercedes 190E. Her mother died in 1972. Her father, Alistair Alexander, was a successful stockmarket speculator who died of cancer in 1980. From age 14, M.L.A. was raised by her aunt (Charlotte R. Alexander) who took up residence in the Alexander family home. There are no other known relatives. Upon graduating from college, M.L.A. inherited her father's five million dollar estate. She is an active investor in the stock market and manages her own portfolio. ENCLOSURES: Photographs of M.L.A., her address and auto license. The addresses of her aunt and employer."

Kevin tapped his pen on the report. *Poor little rich girl, her father a successful stock speculator.* He had done his own research on Alistair Alexander. What he found was a man who specialized in futures and whose buying and selling style mirrored his own. *What the hell is going on?*

The drive out of the airport overlooked the Mississippi River, swollen by spring rain. *Beautiful!* The green landscape, clean streets, and lack of graffiti were refreshing. As they neared downtown Minneapolis, the skyline came into view—*as contemporary as any in the West.*

The cab driver was a one-man chamber of commerce. By the time he reached the hotel, Kevin had a general awareness of the city, its cultural and recreational offerings, weather, politics and the best suburbs. In return, the driver wanted to know about L.A. gangs, freeway shootings and how often Kevin attended the Johnny Carson Show.

It was 1:45 P.M. by the time he had unpacked and changed clothes. After rehearsing the words, he picked up the phone and dialed the Dayton Hudson Company. "Mary Louise Alexander, in marketing, please."

"This is Mary Alexander."

Her voice was like a delicate wind chime on a warm

spring morning. Kevin shivered.

"Yes, Mary"— he hesitated — "my name is Kevin Forester and I'm from Woodland Hills, California. I'm in town on business and I have a most unusual request."

He waited.

"Yes."

For a flash, a millisecond, he was running through a field of yellow wildflowers, holding her hand.

"I'm an admirer of your late father. His buying and selling techniques mirror my own"—he hesitated again, fearful — "and I was wondering if you'd be willing to see me, talk to me about him."

"How do you know about me?" Her voice was cautious.

"In researching your father, I learned he had a daughter, although I know you were only 14 when he died. He had a remarkable ability. Do you have a pen?"

"Yes."

He gave her his California stockbroker's name and telephone number. "Please call him and ask about me. Then, if you're willing to meet me, I'm staying at the Whitney Hotel. I'll be in the lounge, wearing a dark suit with a red carnation in my lapel at six this evening."

Mary Louise Alexander was waiting in a shadowed corner of the hotel lounge when Kevin walked in at five-fifteen. He sat alone at a table with a clear view of the entrance. She watched him order soda water with a twist of lime. He wasn't what she'd call handsome, but he was attractive. For some reason that didn't make any sense at all, she wanted to run over and hug him.

"Mr. Forester, I presume," she said, approaching him from the side.

Kevin jumped, nearly spilling his drink. "Mary Louise." He stood.

She held out her hand. He took it. They both trembled.

"Please sit down." He pulled out a chair. *Running through wildflowers.*

They smiled at each other. Nervous. Her long hair was fire red, her eyes emerald green. She was wearing a navy blue double-breasted cotton sport coat, a white blouse and white linen pants. He observed her graceful movements and thought, absurdly, of a ballet dancer dressed in a pink tutu spinning across a stage and gliding onto a chair.

"Why do I have the feeling you already knew what I looked like?" Mary Louise said.

Kevin nodded. *She's much prettier in person.*

The waitress took her drink order. A glass of Chardonnay.

"Your broker thinks you're the best trader in Southern California. He said you've only been in the market for nine months." She felt dizzy.

"I did a lot of studying."

"There has to be more to it." *My God, he's gorgeous.* "Even most market professionals avoid the futures market."

"A knack, I guess."

"My father had the knack."

"I'd like to know more about him."

The waitress returned with the wine and another soda with a lime twist.

"Why did you really call me, Kevin?"

A look of desperation flashed across his face. Their eyes met, he looked away, back at her. "You wouldn't believe me if I told you."

"I think you'd better tell me."

"I do want to learn more about your father, but I'd rather get to know you better before I try to explain. Please?"

She looked at him for a moment without responding. "Are you going to try to sell me something?"

"Absolutely not."

"A confidence game?"

"Mary Louise, the only thing I want from you is the pleasure of your company for dinner."

She smiled. "All right. For some reason I feel I can trust you."

A candlelight dinner in the Whitney Grille was as impressive as the view of the garden plaza overlooking the Mississippi River. A champagne toast to friendship was followed with a main course of Great Lakes trout. They talked about their backgrounds, their approach to investing, their music and culinary likes and dislikes. They talked about Los Angeles and Minneapolis. And they talked about Alistair Alexander.

"And now you're going to tell me why you really called me, aren't you, Kevin?" She leaned back in her chair, sipping an after-dinner liqueur.

Nodding, he withdrew the note from his pocket and handed it to her. "Don't ask me to explain, because I can't."

She read and reread the words. Finally, she said, "But I don't need any help, Kevin."

"I realize that. Maybe it was a psychic way to get to meet you." He raised his hands in a gesture of futility. "All I know for sure, it that I'm glad I've met you."

She smiled shyly.

"Can I see you again?" he said.

"I'd like that," she said.

The following morning Kevin studied the market in a local brokerage before calling buy and sell orders to his California broker. At noon he met Mary Louise for lunch. She was more beautiful than ever, dressed in a tan cotton sport coat, white blouse and silky, pleated pants. It was raining and they snuggled under her umbrella for a two-block walk to a restaurant featuring Northern pike. "You'll never settle for Pacific Coast fish again," Mary Louise assured him.

"We'll see," he said.

"Here are the family photos"—she withdrew an envelope from her purse — "you said you wanted to see." While Mary Louise ordered for both of them, Kevin looked at the pictures. Alistair Alexander seemed so familiar; with his wife and daughter at a lake, in front of a stately home, laughing around a birthday cake with twelve candles, holding hands with his daughter in a field of yellow wildflowers.

"Where was this taken?" he asked, holding up the wildflower photo.

"It was a family tradition to spend my spring vacation at our family cabin near Brainerd. A fisherman took the picture of Daddy and me. It was a few years after my mother died."

Kevin nodded. He was experiencing an overwhelming sense of nostalgia . . . for something. *But what?*

Sharing Mary Louise's enthusiasm for the Northern pike, Kevin suggested they have lunch at the same restaurant the following day. That evening they ate fast food in a fifties-style diner. Afterwards, she took him on a tour of Walker Art Center.

On the third evening, she invited him to dinner at her apartment. The decor was as he'd imagined it, integrating elegance with informality. "American antiques and nineteenth-century English Naturalist," she said, "inherited from my parents' taste."

While Mary Louise cooked, Kevin looked at her family photo albums. *So familiar. So damn familiar.* He was fascinated by a photo of Mary Louise dressed in a pink ballet tutu. The caption said, "Age 12. Daddy's girl at her first public performance."

"I think about you all day." he said, helping her set the table.

"I think about you too, Kevin"—smiling as she lighted

candles — "I called a friend who's involved in metaphysics and told her about your note to yourself."

"And?"

"She didn't think it was unusual."

"She didn't?"

Mary Louise stepped into the kitchen and returned holding two plates—grilled chicken breasts with an onion marmalade, served on garlic open-faced French bread. Kevin opened the Chardonnay.

Seated next to each other at one end of the formal dining room table, they lifted their glasses in a toast.

"To us," he said.

She smiled, lovingly. "To us," she whispered.

"Tell me what your friend had to say about the note."

"She thinks you either received it in automatic writing because we're some kind of soulmates, or you're a walk-in."

"I don't understand."

"Neither do I, but it made perfect sense to her."

They laughed.

Kevin leaned over and kissed her on the lips. She hesitated only a moment before returning the kiss. Breaking away, they gazed into each other's eyes, then kissed again, more passionately, holding each other with a desperation neither understood but which both wanted to prolong.

"What's happening?" Kevin whispered as he released her. Tears blinded his eyes and choked his voice.

Mary Louise shook her head. "I think our dinner's going to get cold." Her eyes were bright with unshed tears.

Taking his hand, she guided him out of the dining room, upstairs to the bedroom.

There were no more words. Words were far too limiting for what they were experiencing. Their desire was beyond logic, beyond rational explanation. Standing beside the bed, Kevin's tongue explored her mouth, then trailed a path down her cheek to the moist hollow of her throat. Mary Louise lightly bit his neck, her arms solid and strong around him as she moved her hips against him in a suggestive body caress. In response, he pressed every inch of her body to his as they fell onto the bed and rolled over. He was above her, running his hands through a sea of long red hair. She whimpered, and he let her roll him over until she was on top, straddling him on her knees, bending forward, kissing him deeply, possessing his mouth.

Slowly, sensuously, silently, they undressed each other. Their bodies came together in reverence as they looked deeply into each other's eyes. They didn't move, didn't breathe. She shivered and cupped his face in her hands. "I feel like I've always known you." She moved against him.

"I know." He matched her movement.

At first their thrusts were slow and measured—a train inching up a mountain, the fires of expectation building as they climbed higher and higher. Finally, upon reaching the top, they released the brakes to cascade down the other side—a runaway, out of control, leaving the tracks on a dark curve in an explosion of physical sensation.

Afterwards, he held her, warm in his arms. Neither spoke as the orange glow of sunset filtering through the gauze curtains faded to darkness. Outside, the lights in distant windows glowed like faraway stars.

"Soulmates or a walk-in?" he said.

"I guess," she said, nuzzling her face into the chords of his neck, running her hand slowly down his chest, tickling, teasing, down, across his stomach, tickling, teasing, down . . .

Mary Louise took the rest of the week as vacation days.

"We have Thursday, Friday, Saturday and Sunday." She smiled at him with sleepy eyes. "What shall we do?"

"Make love for four days and nights."

"I won't be able to walk." She laughed. "What else?"

"Get to know each other. Show me the city; where you grew up, where you went to school, where you go to meditate about life."

Sitting together on a hilltop overlooking the Mississippi, they watched a barge work its way up river. The late afternoon sun tossed their shadows halfway down the hill. A fragrance of blossoms wafted on the spring breeze.

Kevin kissed her, looked in her eyes and said, "I love you."

"I love you too."

"Is this a dream?"

"Feels like a dream."

"I love it here"—he held her tighter — "but I don't know about the winters."

"We could winter in Los Angeles."

"Well, that solves the complications."

They were married six weeks after they met, the first weekend in June, in a small ceremony at the Edina Unitarian Church. Hank Forester flew to Minneapolis for the wedding. The reception was held at Aunt Charlotte Alexander's lake-side home, elegantly decorated for the occasion.

"I don't understand why you two aren't going to Europe or someplace wonderfully romantic for your honeymoon," Aunt Charlotte said.

"Mary Louise wants to stay at the family cabin in Brainerd." Kevin sipped champagne. "It's fine by me."

"Her most joyful memories are there," Charlotte said, looking across the room at Mary Louise dressed in a white bridal gown, talking with friends.

Aunt Charlotte was a petite woman whose blue eyes and dark hair belied the 66 years she claimed.

"She's not that old," Kevin had said after first meeting Mary Louise's only living relative.

"Charlotte's had a little face work, dyes her hair and does yoga. Plus, her excitement about life keeps her young."

"I like her."

"When I told her about you on the phone, she assumed you were a fortune hunter after my inheritance."

"And now?"

"She wants you for herself."

White balloons and crepe-paper bells were woven into the streamers that crisscrossed the ceiling of the living and dining rooms. Kevin watched his father mixing easily with the other well-wishers.

"Kevin, this is Kathy, my metaphysical friend." Mary Louise introduced her husband to a hazel-eyed blonde with a fashion-model figure.

"Right. Soulmates or a walk-in." Kevin extended his hand. "What's a soulmate and a walk-in?"

Mary Louise was called away by another friend.

"It's really romantic," Kathy said. "A soulmate relationship is a destined, idealized pairing of two souls who have known each other in numerous incarnations. They're totally happy together."

"Past lives?" Kevin drank the last of the champagne.

"A walk-in takes over someone else's body. It's like being reincarnated as an adult."

"That sounds like something out of *The Exorcist*."

"Oh no, it's very positive. Was there a time in the past when you were miserable or nothing was working, then all of a sudden everything started changing for the better?"

Kevin stared at the beautiful woman before him. "Yes. Almost a year ago."

Kathy nodded. "Well, then you're probably a walk-in."

"Wait, wait, Kathy. I'm not getting this."

She leaned into him and whispered, "You were dead, but you wanted to come back without having to go through childhood to get here."

"But wouldn't I remember?"

"For awhile, maybe long enough to write yourself a note."

"That's ridiculous."

"Is it?"

"Where did the real Kevin Forester go?"

"If you're a walk-in, his awareness is within you. His soul is on the other side."

"Then who am I, or who was I before I took over his body?"

"You had a reason for coming back, but there's no way to know what it is. This Kevin Forester is about to start a new life with Mary Louise, and your destiny will unfold naturally."

Kevin looked away, out the picture window at the lawn. "I'm not even religious. I'm sure not ready to accept something like this."

"It doesn't matter"—Kathy took his empty champagne glass — "if you do or don't. What is meant to be, will be."

Charlotte called from the dining room, "Kevin, the photographer wants to take pictures out on the lawn."

Kevin and Mary Louise danced together, across the lawn to unheard music, as if they were in a great ballroom. Everyone applauded. When they cut the cake, before placing a bite in Kevin's mouth, Mary Louise touched the white frosting to his nose. Everyone laughed.

While Mary Louise changed clothes, Kevin talked with his father. Aunt Charlotte had invited Hank to stay in Minneapolis for a couple of weeks as her house guest. She promised to show him the sights. He accepted.

"Mary Louise seems like a wonderful woman, Kevin."

"I'm the luckiest man in the world, Dad."

"You just don't seem like the same kid I used to fight with all the time"—he shook his head—"I guess it's true about people being able to change if they want to bad enough."

Showered with rice, the newlyweds ran down the drive-way to the Mercedes. Pulling away, in the rearview mirror, Kevin saw his father waving happily. He smiled and glanced at his wife. She was watching him, her face an expression of love. They held hands, driving silently into the warm evening, north, along a highway paralleling the Mississippi.

"It's a two hour drive," Mary Louise said. "I asked the caretakers to have the cabin ready."

"I hope the water line didn't freeze and rupture again," he replied. "It was a cold winter."

"How did you know about that, Kevin?"

"What?"

"The trouble we used to have with the water line."

"Didn't you tell me?"

"Twelve years ago, we buried the line deeper and insulated it better. There's been no problem since."

On the outskirts of Brainerd, Mary Louise directed him to turn right at the next crossroad. He already knew that but didn't tell her. He also knew they would arrive at the back entrance of the cabin, and that the picture window in the main room would look directly east, toward the lake.

Kevin carried his wife over the threshold into the kitch-en. They kissed and he told her she was beautiful. She lead him into the living room. The window framed a meadow of yellow wildflowers leading down to the lake, the last rays of sunlight turning the tranquil surface of the water into shimmering gold.

"The Cunninghams even prepared a fire. All we have to do is light it," Mary Louise said.

While she busily opened windows and checked the cupboards, Kevin explored the front porch. *The rocker's gone.* He descended the stairs to the meadow. *Good Lord, if I'm Alistair Alexander, I've married my own daughter. There has to be another explanation.*

They made love, serenaded by crickets and a mournfully hooting owl. They talked about having a large family, learning to ski together, and buying a home in Edina. "Mary Louise Forester," she said over and over, as if her new name was a spiritual mantra. The moon had nearly completed its pass across the night sky when they fell asleep.

The next morning they drove into Brainerd to shop for groceries and supplies to stock the cabin. Mary Louise purchased a large bottle of liquid antacid. "I think preparing for the wedding gave me an ulcer," she joked when Kevin asked her about it.

She tried to get him to go fishing. He said he didn't want to murder the fish in the lake. He prefered to run back into town and purchase more Northern pike. "We could open a Northern pike restaurant in Los Angeles and make a fortune," he said.

Taking turns reading aloud, they often used the chapter breaks as excuses to make love. They went swimming, boating, hiking, and took hundreds of photographs of each other. And they ran hand in hand through the yellow wildflowers.

"I don't want to go back." He fell exhausted into the flowers.

"We've been here three weeks." She picked a flower and used it to tickle his nose.

"We can make a great living right here, buying and selling futures with a computer, a modem and a fax machine."

"You won't like it in the winter."

"That's six months away."

"Okay, but we need to go home for more clothes, and I want to see the doctor about my ulcer. The pain is still there."

"Cancer? It can't be cancer," Kevin cried, biting his lip and clamping his wife's perspiring hand. Mary Louise sat in the chair beside him, unable to speak. On the other side of the desk, the doctor presented his prognosis and explained the treatment options. They listened without hearing, as if in a nightmare from which they would soon awaken.

Kevin insisted that the tests be rerun at the Mayo Clinic. The clinic doctors concurred with the original diagnosis.

"We'll fight it with every ounce of our combined energy," Kevin said.

"As far along as the cancer is, I don't think that will do any good," Mary Louise said. "Maybe we should just enjoy our time together."

Kevin insisted on fighting, as if his desire alone could defeat the unseen enemy attacking his beloved wife. He mounted the battle in the same way he had taken on the futures market, reading everything that had ever been written on the subject and calling specialists around the world.

Mary Louise started chemotherapy. It made her nauseous, tired, and caused her beautiful red hair to fall out. Kevin remained at her side, night and day, comforting, guiding her through healing visualizations. In response to the pain, he directed altered-state pain control sessions. When she could not keep her food down he gave her Compazine.

The wildflowers were gone when they returned to the cabin in August.

"I wanted to see them again," she said.

"Next year," he said.

"Yes," she said.

Kevin barbecued Northern pike on the front porch while she lay beneath covers in a lounge chair, watching the man she loved. In the afternoons the mosquitoes drove them inside, where he read aloud, and they played board games. When she lost her concentration at chess, he purposely missed opportunities.

Mary Louise was hospitalized in September. Kevin sat in the chair beside her bed, watching the IV drip, drip, drip into her arm, telling her it would be all right, that they'd lick it, and that he loved her more than life itself.

She returned to the Edina apartment in a wheelchair, armed with drugs: dacarbazine, doxorubicn, and vinblastine. As she got weaker, Kevin strained to hear her words. While rubbing her back he noticed that her skin was losing its elasticity, but he didn't tell her. Instead, he told her of the places they would visit when she was in remission, and that someday they would have two girls and a boy with freckled faces and flaming red hair.

The first snowfall of the season arrived two days before Thanksgiving. "We were supposed to be in Los Angeles by now," she said.

"I like it here," he said, sitting beside the bed, stroking her arm as they watched snowflakes flutter past the window. "We'll be going to California soon enough."

"I'll never see California," she said. Tears welled up in her eyes.

"That's not so," he countered.

"You have to face it, Kevin, I'm dying. I don't want to leave you, but I don't have any choice."

"You're not dying," he cried.

"It's as if you came into my life just to see me through this. It wasn't fair to you." Tears ran down her cheeks.

Closing his own tear-filled eyes, they were running hand-in-hand through yellow wildflowers. Opening his eyes, he leaned across the bed, kissed her on the cheek and laid his head on her pillow. "We'll always be together," he whispered.

She didn't answer.

He felt for a pulse that wasn't there.

Closing his eyes, they were running hand in hand through yellow wildflowers.

THE CHAIR

My wife cried when I told her she couldn't have the chair.

"I don't ask for much, do I, Paul?" she said, dabbing her eyes with a tissue.

"We don't have an extra $1,500. You know that, Peggy."

She caressed the hand-carved wood on the high back of the chair. A stern-eyed male head in an oval was entwined with flowering swirls encompassing smaller male heads at each side. The second tier of carving consisted of a crest, a crown, and a cluster of arrows. Massive arms curled down into elaborately carved legs and cross braces.

The antique dealer was a kindly man with a white beard. He wore a string tie and a baggy brown wool suit. "It's Spanish," he said. "Dates back to the late seventeen-hundreds."

"Can I just spend a little time with it?" Peggy asked.

"Of course. Let me know if I can help you."

He disappeared into the rows of antiques—tables, chairs, desks, buffets, carved arches and stained-glass windows, all stacked carefully in long rows with the space between so narrow customers had to walk sideways.

"It doesn't match our other furniture," I said.

"I'll get a job to pay for it," she said, sitting down in the chair and placing her arms on the great wooden arms. She closed her eyes and took a deep breath. Her lips quivered and she made a funny little squeaking sound before saying, "Evelyn understands the importance of remaining faithful, but she is not unlike a moth drawn helplessly to Garth's flame."

"Peggy!" I said. "What on earth are you talking about?"

"What?" Her eyes were glassy.

"Why did you say that about Evelyn?"

Peggy stood up, shook her head and looked into my eyes. "I was Evelyn," she said, trembling. "I mean it was like I was inside Evelyn's head. Oh, Paul, that was weird."

"Who the hell is Garth?"

"I don't know."

"Neither of us have had much sleep on this trip."

"Paul, I have to have the chair. I know it's ridiculous." She snuggled into my arms, nuzzled her nose into my neck and said, "Please. We'll find a way to pay for it."

I nodded, knowing from the moment she said she wanted the chair that we'd be taking it home. "Do you think it will fit in the back of the station wagon?"

The owner of the antique store took my check. I asked him to give me two days before he deposited it. He copied my driver's license number on the back of the check. Through the window I watched Peggy excitedly directing two young men on the positioning of the chair in the back of the station wagon. Peggy was nearly forty, but when she was excited she looked twenty-five. Smiling, she stood with her hands jammed in the pockets of her black ski jacket, worn open over her black wool slacks and bulky white sweater. Light snow swirled into her short dark hair.

"Thank you," she said, leaning over to kiss me on the cheek as I climbed behind the wheel. The chair was tied securely, so it couldn't move if we stopped fast or turned sharply.

"At least we don't have room to buy anything else." I started the car.

The sky was shrouded with flat, menacing storm clouds; the snowflakes were still light enough to be called flurries. Peggy unfolded the road map and traced her finger down a red line as I swung the big Ford wagon back onto Interstate 15, out of Utah. A road sign said Las Vegas 212 miles.

"We could have dinner at the Stardust," Peggy said.

"Appropriate. We stayed there on our honeymoon, and we return after visiting our first grandchild."

"I have a problem with 'grandma,' " Peggy said. "I think I'd rather be called Nana."

"You did wince every time Amanda used the G word," I laughed.

"It's not funny, Paul! How do you like being a *grandpa*?"

"Fine, but Salt Lake City is so far away. You don't just fly up from Los Angeles to watch your grandson play little league."

"Well, at least Evelyn still lives in L.A. She and John want a baby next year."

"Unless she runs off with old Garth," I said.

Peggy didn't answer.

The sky grew darker and slushy, wind-driven snow began to splatter the windshield. I turned on the headlights and let my thoughts drift to other things.

"We can't stay at the Stardust," Peggy said as the lights of Las Vegas appeared on the horizon. "Someone might steal my chair out of the car."

"Oh, I don't think . . ."

"We can't take a chance, Paul. If we stay in a motel on the edge of town, we can take the chair into the room with us."

"A motel on the edge of town?"

"We have to, don't you see?"

"You pick it," I said, and sighed.

"But once the chair is safely locked in our motel room, let's go to the Stardust for dinner."

"Okay," Peggy said, not sounding as if she liked the idea.

It was dark when I registered at the Purple Paradise Motel, and asked for a ground floor room. There were only two other cars in the slump-block complex, whose main attraction appeared to be a tired-looking swimming pool adorned with a few square yards of grass. I backed the wagon up to the door of unit 124. Peggy untied the chair and together we grunted and groaned to get it into the room. The back of the thing was nearly as tall as me, and it had to weigh two hundred pounds.

I was nearly out of breath from the exertion. "Well, as long as we're willing to crawl over the bed to get in and out of the room . . ."

Peggy finished my sentence. "The chair is safe."

"Honey, no thief is going to run off with your chair. No thief is that strong."

The Utah snow had turned to Nevada rain, and I watched Peggy carefully drying off the wet spots on the chair with a towel.

"We should get more exercise," I said, lying down on the bed. The wall air conditioner jutted ominously over a portion of the bed. Beneath it, brown water stains streaked the flowered wallpaper in a zigzag pattern that wound like a river through a meadow of daisies.

Peggy was looking at a tent card on top of the television set. It promoted X-rated in-room movies. Dropping the tent-card behind the TV set, she sat down in her chair facing me, looking like a queen ready to have court with her subjects. The neon motel sign shimmered in the rainy night outside our window, casting an unearthly glow over the chair.

"Why, why, why?" Peggy said, mechanically. "Why would Gilbert cast his lot with Sanchez?" She slammed a fist down on the arm of the chair.

"What are you talking about?" I asked, too tired to care.

"Pass the bread," she shouted, in a deep, raspy voice.

I jerked to attention like a marionette.

"Peggy, what are you doing? Are you flipping out on me?"

"I expect a little more respect than I receive around here," she shouted at me, a deep scowl creasing her brow, her eyes glassy.

"Respect? You know I respect you," I stammered.

"The cows were not milked until midday," she roared.

"Oh, for gawd's sake," I took two quick steps to the chair and bodily lifted Peggy to her feet.

"Paul, what?" She looked at me, then turned and looked at the chair. Pulling out of my arms, she backed away from the chair.

I shook my head and walked into the bathroom to splash cold water on my face.

"Paul, where are you going?" Peggy asked in a fearful whisper.

"To milk the cows," I said.

"Paul, I was inside the head of a big man sitting in this chair at the head of a long wooden table. A woman and two teenagers also sat at the table dressed like . . . ." She hesitated.

"Like what?" I asked, emerging from the bathroom, wiping my face with a towel.

"Like they probably did back in eighteenth-century Spain."

"So this is a haunted chair?" I laughed. "Peggy, you're tired. We've been driving all day. You're so enchanted with the chair, you're letting your imagination carry you away."

"It wasn't my imagination. It was real," she said. "You sit in it."

"Oh, come on."

"Paul, you sit in the chair."

"Okay." Easing my six-foot-one frame into the chair, I was surprised how comfortable it was. The back and seat were padded with embossed leather.

"Do I look regal?" I asked.

"What do you feel?"

"Like I need to milk a cow."

"Paul, please."

"Honey, I feel hungry."

She stood with her hands clasped looking at me in expectation.

"Sit down and tell me what happened," I said, sitting back in the chair and crossing my legs.

Peggy sat on the edge of the bed, her knees together, her hands clasped in her lap. She took a deep breath and said, "The motel room just faded away and I was sitting at the head of a table in a beautifully tiled dining room. Through an open arch I could see a fountain. The family was being served dinner. I think they were wealthy. I could draw a picture of the room it's so clear in my mind." She sighed. "I know I was upset at our neighbors about something."

"You were inside the man's head?" I asked. "Like you were inside Evelyn's head?"

Peggy wasn't listening. She pointed at the chair. "It was his chair. He loved it."

"Maybe his ghost came along with it," I said, patting the massive wooden arms.

"Don't say that. Joyce is always talking about weird things like that."

"Joyce is a loon," I said.

"She's just interested in metaphysics."

"Like I said, a loon."

"Paul, don't talk like that about my friends."

"Why don't you call Evelyn?" I suggested. "Ask her who Garth is."

Peggy nodded, and walked to the phone. She punched the numbers. "Hi, honey." There was a pause. "Daddy and I are in Las Vegas, we'll be home tomorrow. Yes, I took two rolls." Peggy laughed. "We're going to the Stardust for dinner, just like on our honeymoon." Peggy crossed and uncrossed her legs. "No, we're staying someplace else. It's a long story. I'll tell you later. Listen, honey, I need to know something. Who is Garth?"

I watched Peggy's face flush and her eyes widen. "No, I swear we haven't been spying on you. No, I haven't talked to John. Evelyn, please. This isn't like you." Peggy shot a terrified look across the room at me. "Of course you have a right to happiness. I didn't know you and John were having problems. Evelyn, please don't cry."

It took me awhile to calm Peggy down. I assured her that the chair had nothing to do with it. "It was mother's intuition, that's all. You and Evelyn have always been connected."

Peggy insisted on calling Joyce, her loony friend in L.A. I sat in the chair with my stomach growling for twenty minutes while Peggy related the story.

When she hung up the phone, Peggy said, "Joyce thinks the owner of the chair is still attached to it on the other side."

"You mean his ghost is here?" I rolled my eyes.

"She calls him an earthbound spirit. My brain waves probably match his. The chair is the connecting touchstone."

"Matching brain waves? Connecting touchstones? Come on, Peggy!"

Her eyes narrowed as she spoke. "Before we got to the antique store, I was thinking about Evelyn. A ghost can tap into anyone. My concern linked the ghost, Evelyn and me in a kind of psychic telephone conversation."

"Absurd," I said.

Peggy continued, "Tonight, I was tired, my mind was blank, and I simply drew a memory from the ghost. You may be sitting on him, Paul."

I stood up. "Peggy, Peggy. This is absolutely ridiculous. Intuition is one thing, but psychic links with dead people is for looney tunes who read about UFOs and attend seances."

"No, it isn't, Paul."

"Yes, it is, Peggy. If you really believe psychic links are possible, you sit down in this chair and tell me something about me that you don't know. What was my golf score at the club last week. What did I have for breakfast at the Jaycee meeting?" I gestured for her to sit.

Peggy scowled, got up, walked to the chair and defiantly plopped down into it. She closed her eyes, took a deep breath and slumped as if her bones had melted.

Silence.

I sat on the bed and thought about food.

Peggy made a couple of little squeaky sounds, then said, "Paul, you and your secretary, Annette, have been having an affair for six months. You usually go to her apartment on Fridays for lunch, but you also favor the Pier II Restaurant. Annette calls you the lecher when you're making love and she . . ."

At ten-thirty the next morning the manager of the Purple Paradise received a call from the maid, requesting that he come to unit 124. He arrived to find a very large, hand-carved chair sitting in the room.

"All their other things are gone?" the manager asked, looking around the room.

"Si," the maid replied. "Who would leave such a chair?"

The manager shrugged.

"Maybe they come back for it," the maid wondered, as she began stripping the bedding.

"You don't forget something six feet tall," the manager said, running his fingers over the beautifully carved wood. "Have Ramon carry it up to the front desk. It'll add some class to the place."

SOULMATE LOCATION SERVICE

"Women want me to predict when they will meet Mr. Right. Either they're single and want to know if the next guy will be Mr. Right, or their marriage is going bad and they want to know why." Dancer sipped his Manhattan and gestured for the waiter to bring another.

"Don't they want advice on how to save their relationship?" Casey asked, checking the volume meters on her tape recorder.

"To the contrary, they're looking for an excuse to end it. After the divorce they come back and want me to predict when they will meet Mr. Right."

"Do some of these women see you as Mr. Right?"

"I let them think I'm gay."

"Can I say that in my story?"

"You can even tell them I'm a fraud, but they'll still line up to pay $75 an hour to learn their romantic destiny."

"Do you find women that predictable?"

"Only in this regard."

"Do you manipulate women?"

"Does your newspaper manipulate liberals?"

"What?"

"You turn minor stories about police brutality and environmental infractions into front page exposes."

"That's what *LA Reporter* readers are interested in."

"Women are interested in finding their soulmate." Dancer smiled with warm spontaneity.

The uniformed waiter arrived with the drink and a fresh bowl of cocktail crackers. Casey declined a mineral water refill. The reporter was young—in her mid-twenties—and Dancer thought she tried to appear more mature by hiding her attractiveness behind a veneer of feminist activism. She wore her brown hair in the frizzy style popular with the jeans and baggy sport coat set.

Casey flipped over the cassette and pressed record. "Okay, Mr. Dancer, let me check a few facts. Your full name is Tillman Douglas Dancer. You're 42, never married, and you've been a professional psychic for fifteen years. You counsel your clients from your Santa Monica apartment. Is that correct?"

"I'm also losing my hair and I'm about twenty pounds overweight. You probably think I'm pompous, but I do care about women. I love them."

He leaned back, smiling at the young reporter as he crossed his legs and clasped his hands in his lap. Late afternoon sunlight filtered through the stained-glass windows of the ocean-front restaurant, tossing multicolored reflections across the happy hour crowd.

"You realize the reason I'm interviewing you is the ad you placed in our paper?" She pulled a copy of the throwaway tabloid from her briefcase, opened it to display the classified ads and laid it in front of Dancer. The ad read,

SOULMATE LOCATION SERVICE
All singles and those unhappily married
are invited to inquire. I will help you
find the one person on earth with whom
you will find total happiness.

GUARANTEED RESULTS.

Fee: $5000.

Write Box 254C at this newspaper.

"It's a new service I'm offering," Dancer said. "I think it will be very popular."

"Come on, Mr. Dancer. How can you guarantee to find someone's soulmate?"

"It's quite simple, really, but that doesn't mean it's easy."

Casey smiled sarcastically and pointed at the microphone sitting on the table between them.

"You wouldn't understand," he said.

"Try me."

Dancer sighed. Removing the maraschino cherry from his drink, he popped it into his mouth. He chewed slowly and swallowed before saying, "Everyone has a unique vibrational tone on a specific frequency." He looked into Casey's interested brown eyes. "The trick is, while in the astral body, to project to the person whose vibrational tone is closest to your own. They are most likely to be your twin soul."

"How do you do that?"

"By learning how."

"And you teach people how?"

"Yes."

"For five thousand dollars?"

"Yes."

"Why haven't you found your own soulmate?"

"I'm quite content living alone."

"Does it bother you that I think you're a con man?"

"Does it bother you that your boyfriend's sexual appetite is waning?"

Casey felt her face flush.

"He's sharing his favors with a short blonde who lives in the apartment next door."

"Rebecca? Oh, come on, you're just . . ."

"Giving you a sample psychic reading."

Casey stared at Dancer without expression. She looked at the microphone on the table. She looked out the window at the sliver of sun sinking into the sea. She looked back into Dancer's indigo eyes. "If you're right, you really are psychic and . . ."

Dancer finished her sentence, "I could help you find your soulmate, which would make a more interesting story."

After the interview, Casey planned to return to the *L.A. Reporter* offices. Instead, as if in a trance, she pulled out of the parking lot, down Ocean Avenue in the direction of Marina del Rey and her apartment—their apartment—a third-floor one bedroom with a deck overlooking the beach. She thought about Alan, sitting on the deck holding her hand, sipping wine as they watched the sun set. They'd lived together nearly two years and had often talked about getting married. They got along all right—great in bed. She knew she loved him and realized she probably took him for granted. The thought of Alan making love to Rebecca stabbed her mind as her grip tightened on the steering wheel.

Ocean Avenue changed to Speedway in Venice. The light changed from amber to red. A transient, bent over, pushing a heavy-laden shopping cart with a broken wheel, crossed the street in front of her car. He moved slowly, as if underwater. Turning his grime-covered face to look at her, their eyes met. He scowled.

Casey didn't respond.

He gave her the finger as he passed.

She didn't respond.

The light changed, and she hit the accelerator so hard the tires of the Subaru XT6 squealed as the vehicle leaped forward.

She took a deep breath of salt-sea air. Usually, she enjoyed driving this four-mile stretch of bizarre street, but today Dancer had turned the tables on her. Ms. up-and-coming investigative journalist shook up the people she interviewed—she found their Achilles heel and got them to say things that were best left unsaid.

But without so much as a strained look, Dancer shook her to the core by focusing in on the one troubling factor in her life—Alan's waning sexual interest. Crissake, he knew a short blonde lived next door—Rebecca—*their* friend. Alan had certainly never shown any outward interest in her, but maybe that should have been a clue. Rebecca was, to put it simply, gorgeous. *Prettier than me? Far prettier than me. A better body? Yes. We're both 29 so age isn't a factor. Mind? No contest. The deepest thing Rebecca ever talked about was the need of more starring roles for women in film. And an* Entertainment Tonight *interview probably inspired that. But Rebecca is fun—she makes us laugh. And she makes no secret of her appetite for sex.*

They had been drinking beer, watching the Super Bowl together. Rebecca intently followed one particular player. Finally in the third quarter, she said, "I'd love to add him to my stable of sex poodles."

Alan laughed. "Define sex poodle."

"Sexual playthings," Rebecca said. "You enjoy them for what they can give you, but the thought of a serious relationship could ruin your day and turn you gay."

Casey hit the brakes at Washington Avenue as the light changed, screeching to a stop just as the eclectic stream of humanity filled the street going to and from the pier. Swimsuit-clad people, clutching coolers in one hand and deck chairs in the other, mingled with surfers, boogie-boarders, fishermen, and tourists. A tall black man in a suit and tie cut the corner walking two Samoyed dogs. He was playing the harmonica and doing a little quick-step shuffle as he disappeared into the lengthening shadows of the beach buildings. Casey smiled.

Schooner Street was a continuous row of apartments on the beach side, and one of the last Venice canals on the other. Turning into the parking entrance of her apartment, she punched the entry code, the gate slid away and she drove into the basement level of the building. Alan's car was parked in his place, next to Rebecca's.

Chill out, Casey.

The elevator took her to the third floor, and she listened intently in the hallway. *What do you expect to hear? Orgasmic moans coming from 327?* Quietly opening the door to 329, she slipped inside. Alan's briefcase was not sitting by the breakfast bar where he normally left it. She crossed the room to the bedroom. Empty. She looked at the half-open bathroom door.

"Alan, I'm home."

Silence. She scanned the living room, neatly furnished in Sante Fe-style decoratively painted woods with festive-looking pillows. The deck door was closed. She slid it open and stepped out into the sunshine and the sound of breaking waves and rustling palm fronds. Rebecca's deck was eight feet away. And there was bikini-clad Rebecca sitting on Alan's lap, drinking beer. They all noticed each other at the same moment.

Casey's hand shot to her mouth, and she darted back into the apartment.

A moment later the apartment door opened and Alan bolted in wearing swim shorts. "It wasn't what it looked like, honey."

She didn't respond.

"I got off early, came home and decided to sun. Rebecca was sunning too, so . . ."

"Those aren't your swimming trunks, Alan."

"I couldn't find mine. Rebecca loaned me some."

Casey walked into their bedroom, opened the second drawer and found his swim shorts on top of his tennis shorts. She walked back into the living room carrying them on her index finger.

Alan shrugged.

"Where's your briefcase and suit?" Casey asked. Before he could answer, she said, "Obviously over at Rebecca's."

"Screw you, Casey." He swaggered past her into the bedroom, emerging a moment later pulling a T-shirt over his head, as if somehow a layer of clothing could shield him from what was to come.

"No wonder you haven't been interested in sex with me."

"Christ, Casey, leave it alone."

She looked at him in disbelief as he walked past her into the kitchen, opened the refrigerator and took out a can of Coors. With the breakfast bar between them, he said, "You're always so damned involved with your work, you never have any time for me. When I try to talk to you about something, all you want to talk about is whoever or whatever evil you're currently investigating, or how your writing style is improving."

"I'm always interested in your work." Casey's voice was as flat and as cold as an Alaskan plain.

"Well, I'm not," he said. "Not when I get home."

She nodded. "You want to talk about football or baseball or basketball. I'm sorry, Alan. I can't relate to any sport but tennis."

"See," he said as if he'd won.

"Alan, you've been having sex with Rebecca for who knows how long, and you've got me on the defensive about not sharing your enthusiasm for the Raiders?"

"You're always so damned serious," he replied.

"And you're always so damned frivolous. So what? We knew that about each other before we leased this." She gestured with a sweep, encompassing the living room.

"You don't love me, Casey. You love your job. I'm just

someone to satisfy your needs and pay half the rent."

Tears trembled on her eyelashes. "That's not true. Sure, I'd love you to be more interested in . . ."

He slammed the beer can down on the counter. "I'm moving in with Rebecca."

The tears rolled down her cheeks. "It's taken us three and a half minutes to get from, 'It isn't what it looks like, honey' to 'I'm moving in with Rebecca.' "

"I'll move my stuff out tomorrow, while you're at work. You can have the furniture we bought together because I don't have any place for it anyway. But the stereo and TV are mine. You can keep the bedroom TV."

"Got it all worked out, huh?"

He tipped the beer can at her, then walked out of the apartment and slammed the door.

"Goodbye, Alan," she whispered, sinking to her knees in the deep-pile carpeting.

Casey waited for two weeks to call Dancer. "Can I take you up on your offer?"

"You want me to help you find your soulmate?"

"If you can understand that the way I feel about men right now, I doubt I'd be attracted to a soulmate, if there is such a thing."

"Come to my apartment tomorrow night at seven." He gave her the address.

Monday night: Dancer lived in a typical three-story complex built around a swimming pool. Nice enough, but nothing special. He buzzed her through the security system and she bypassed the elevator to take the stairs to the second floor. The apartment door was open. She paused in the doorway and called, "Dancer."

"Come in and close the door, Casey."

She walked carefully into the dimly lit living room, to

find Dancer sitting cross-legged at a low table in the dining area. Three white candles burned on the table beside a pot of steaming tea.

"Take off your shoes and come sit down," he said. He was wearing a white robe and as he bent forward to pour Casey a cup of tea, the flickering candles reflected on his bald head.

Casey kneeled to untie her Nikes.

"I hope you like tea."

"Thank you."

"The boyfriend is gone?"

She nodded, sitting on the floor in a yoga posture—a difficult position in tight jeans.

"The parting was for the best."

"I've been checking you out all over town," Casey said, picking up and sniffing the mug of tea.

"And they told you I was a good psychic, a dependable character, and gay."

She laughed, nodded, and sipped the tea. "What kind of tea?"

"My own special blend. I've never given it a name."

"Will it turn me wild with lust or just into a fairy princess?"

"It will mellow you out so you're more receptive to an altered state of consciousness. Have you done any trance work?"

"I take yoga. The class usually ends with a guided meditation."

Casey started to relax in response to Dancer's casual manner. He dimpled mischievously when he smiled, like a little boy. *Women probably want to squeeze his cheeks and mother him.*

Scanning the room, Casey found the decor tasteful and metaphysically correct. Zen scrolls hung on the dining alcove walls. The large living room appeared to be set up to conduct seminars with as many as a dozen people seated comfortably. The multi-unit sofa and matching chairs were unobtrusive, in a neutral off-white palette. This, Casey assumed, was to focus all attention on the speaker and the people themselves. Human beings provided living color for the room. Even the visionary paintings on the walls were rendered in soft pastels. White candles were everywhere—on the glass coffee table, mounted on the walls and in candle stands.

"How do we proceed?" Casey asked.

"One step at a time. This week you will learn to astral project. This is necessary to find your soulmate," Dancer said. "We'll meet every other night. At the third meeting I'll help to free you from the bonds of physical reality."

"I've read that we all astral project at night while sleeping."

"Yes," he said, "but to find your soulmate, you must consciously project while in an altered state so you can control and remember the experience."

Casey sipped the tea. She slipped off her sport coat and laid it on the carpet beside her.

"What was his name?" Dancer asked.

"Alan."

"Soon, he'll leave her and want to come back to you."

"The apartment had a waiting list of people wanting an oceanside apartment. They let me out of the lease. I moved to a studio in Brentwood."

"He'll ask you to take him back."

"When?"

"In a few days."

"I won't."

"I know."

Casey met Dancer's eyes. "Since you're so good at forecasting the future, why don't you just tell me who my soulmate is?"

"I'm not *that good*." He paused. "Even if I were, you still need the psychological assurance that comes with self-discovery. Are you ready to begin?"

She nodded.

"Good. I'll explain the first step, then you'll lie down on the couch." He pointed to the living room. "And I'll induce an altered state and conduct a remote viewing session."

Casey took a notebook and pen out of her purse.

Dancer continued, "You're going to mentally project to someone you know well. You'll need to capture their essence in your mind—to vividly imagine how they look, how they move and talk."

Without hesitating, Casey said, "Alan."

Dancer scowled.

"Alan fills my mind, Dancer. Sometimes I hate him. Sometimes I love him, but he just doesn't go away. Even if I thought of my mother, Alan's presence would probably intrude."

"Good point, considering the circumstances. All right, Alan it is." He pushed his empty tea mug aside and rested both arms on the table. "Close your eyes, Casey, and imagine your new apartment."

She did. Dancer was silent.

When she opened her eyes, Dancer said, "You were seeing impressions through the blackness of your closed eyes. Perceiving is probably a better word than seeing."

"I could imagine the apartment clearly, right down to the stack of unpacked boxes by the front window."

"Good." Dancer uncramped his legs and stood up. "Let's go into the living room."

Casey made herself comfortable on the couch, unsnapped the top of her jeans and adjusted a cushion behind her neck. Candlelight flickered in her peripheral vision as she began to breathe deeply. Dancer sat in a chair beside her.

"Just completely relax, and allow the quietness of spirit to come in." His voice droned rhythmically, soothingly.

She closed her eyes.

"When outside thoughts come into your mind, simply brush them aside, and return your concentration to the sound of my voice."

She felt herself letting go.

"And I'm going to begin to relax your body, one part at a time . . ."

She was beginning to float.

Dancer directed the progressive relaxation, and counted her down into a deep hypnotic sleep.

Remaining focused upon his words, she felt detached—awake and asleep at the same time—adrift in a blue-black sea.

"All right, Casey, in a little while you are going to project your mind to Alan. But first, I want you to capture his essence in your mind. Do this now."

Casey thought about her ex-lover. She could see him vividly with her inner eyes, above her, making love. She could feel his arms around her. The image flickered like a candle and they were holding hands, walking along the beach, talking about . . . what? About getting married, buying a home up the coast in the Palisades or Topanga. She turned to him, but he was gone. A feeling of panic shot through her until she heard Dancer say, "All right, Casey, project your mind to Alan. Trust every thought, every visualization, feeling and emotion. On the count of three you will mentally project to Alan and see what he is doing right now. One, two, three."

For a moment there was only the blue-blackness, but it began to get lighter and lighter and details began to form. A large shape here, a solid mass over there, and Alan's voice, yelling. The fantasy-like images turned into Rebecca's apartment. Alan was standing with his hands on his hips, glaring at Rebecca who was sitting on the couch. "What am I to you, Rebecca, just another sex poodle?"

She laughed at that. "No, no, dear Alan, I wouldn't live with a sex poodle. But I won't live with a male chauvinist either."

"Is it chauvinistic to ask you not to sleep with other men?"

"Yes. To me, outside sex is like scratching an itch. It doesn't mean anything more than that. You need to put it in perspective."

Casey realized she was standing in the northeast corner of the room. She knew she wasn't, but she felt like she was. Then she heard Dancer whispering to her. "Can you perceive Alan clearly?"

"Yes."

"Then attempt to capture his tone. If you listen very, very closely, you will sense a tone, a sound, a vibration."

Casey listened, but all she could hear was the fight going on between Alan and Rebecca. Alan was infuriated as he always was when challenged. Rebecca was light, almost enjoying the confrontation without being affected by it. No, not *almost* enjoying. She *was* enjoying seeing Alan suffer.

"Dancer, I can't sense any tone or vibration."

"Yes, you can. Just tune out the words you're hearing and sights you're seeing, and be open to perceiving only the tone."

She tried again, telling herself, "I let go of everything but Alan's tone." She listened intently, at first with her ears, but that didn't work, then with her mind. She sensed something.

"Dancer, does it sound something like a never-ending musical chord on a synthesizer?"

"Yes, a perfect explanation. Everyone on the planet has a different vibrational tone. Listen to Alan's tone until you sense you've absorbed it—that you know it and could almost hum it."

She did.

Dancer then directed her to mentally return to her own body and to concentrate upon someone else. She chose her mother and the experiment was repeated. When she had visited six different people and perceived the vibrational tone of each, he asked her to perceive her own vibrational tone. She did it easily. He then awakened her with positive suggestions.

She opened her eyes to find him looking at her.

"You're a good subject," he said. "Tomorrow night, I want you to practice this on your own, targeting different people you know. Also, spend at least a half hour in an altered state, focused upon your own vibrational tone. Develop the ability to literally hum your tone. You must know it here and here." He touched his head and heart.

"I'll see you Wednesday evening at 7:00 P.M."

The following evening Casey practiced as instructed, asking herself, "Do you really believe you're going to find a soulmate this way?"

An inner voice came back to her, saying, *Of course not. I don't even want a soulmate. But it will make a good story either way, and you're keeping yourself busy so you don't think about Alan.* She shook her head. *But you think about Alan anyway.*

Between altered-state sessions, she stood by the front window of her new apartment, drinking a can of diet cola and watching the traffic in the street below. The phone rang.

"Casey?"

"Alan."

"How you doing?"

"Fine."

"I hope so. I miss you, you know."

"Alan, you and Rebecca will get along fine if you'll let

147

her screw other guys. I don't know what's wrong with you."

"Wha— Did she talk to you?"

"Goodnight, Alan."

She hung up the phone.

"Maybe I *would* like to find my soulmate," she said aloud, lying down to do another altered-state session.

Wednesday night Casey worked with Dancer for the second time. He intensified the mind projections and hypnotically programmed her with one-word commands to be used if needed while astral projecting.

Awakening from the trance, Casey sat up and rubbed her eyes. Dancer was watching her from his chair beside the couch, his hands steepled over his stomach. He sighed and said, "Unlike mind projecting, while out of body you can encounter frightening things in the nonphysical realms. Novices tend to panic. That's why I gave you the commands."

"What kind of frightening things?"

"Blocks. Maybe you're trying to get back to your body and you encounter a wall that stretches miles into the sky and runs both ways for as far as you can see."

"But it wouldn't be real?"

He shook his head. "It would be a manifestation of your own fear, but it would appear real. Rather than panic, just say the programmed word, 'return.' It will override such obstacles and bring you back to your body."

"What else might I expect to run into in my astral body?"

"Nothing you need to worry about," he said, smiling. "On the first trip, I go out with you."

Thursday, from after work until midnight, Casey practiced self-hypnosis and repeated the post-hypnotic commands until 3 A.M. Even then she couldn't go to sleep, so she mind projected to Alan. He was asleep in Rebecca's bed. Rebecca wasn't there. She tried to project to Rebecca but either didn't succeed or she drifted off to sleep in the middle of the session.

In the *L.A. Reporter* offices Friday morning, Casey prepared for an interview with a man suing the city over a skin problem he contracted in polluted Santa Monica Bay. As she was about to leave, the receptionist buzzed her phone. "It's Alan on line three, do you want to take it?"

She hesitated before saying, "Thanks, Marge, yeah."

She picked up the receiver. "Hello, Alan."

"Please have lunch with me, Casey. It's really important."

"What is there to talk about?"

"Please."

She didn't reply.

"Same place," he said, hope in his voice.

"Twelve-thirty," she said, hanging up.

The interview took longer than she planned, and Casey was thirty minutes late when she arrived at the White Rose. Alan sat at a table in the dining patio of the trendy restaurant, drinking his usual Herradura margarita, L.A.'s answer to New York's Manhattan.

"Hi, Casey," he said, standing unsteadily as she approached. "I didn't think you were coming." The words were slurred.

"Sorry. The interview ran long."

"Your interviews always run long."

"How many of those have you had?"

"Jus' three." He said it belligerently, defying her to make an issue out of it.

She nodded and scanned the patio. It was full of laughing customers chatting at the redwood picnic-style tables. The brick walls of the patio were covered with climbing ivy.

"I miss you," Alan said.

Casey noticed two gay men holding hands under the neighboring table. Two tables away, a longhair in leggings and a sport coat waved his hand excitedly at the waitress. The customers were primarily intellectuals and creative types from Venice and Santa Monica.

"I want to try again," Alan said.

Casey looked at him, but didn't reply.

"It would work, I know it."

"Nothing's changed, Alan. I'm still the serious bore and you're still the . . ."

"You could change if you wanted too," he said, banging his drink down. Margarita slopped over the edge and trailed down the side.

The waitress appeared, pen poised.

"Linguine with bay scallops and a cup of coffee, please," Casey said, smiling at the woman.

The waitress looked at Alan.

"Jus' another one of these," he said, lifting his drink.

"You've had enough, Alan."

"Oh, we're back to telling me what to do, huh?"

"You're drunk."

"Because of you."

"It's my fault you're drunk?"

"Damn right."

"And it was my fault you turned to Rebecca?"

"Damn right, but I forgive you. Can't you forgive me?"

Casey nodded and looked slowly around the patio before saying calmly, "Don't ever call me again, Alan." She found a ten-dollar bill in her purse and placed it beneath the ashtray. She met his eyes for a moment, then stood up and walked out of the restaurant.

By the time Dancer completed the induction, Casey realized her body was spinning. She knew she wasn't really moving, but it felt real. From far away, Dancer's voice reminded her of the post-programming commands and then began to instruct her, one step at a time, to leave her physical body. By the time his words became fuzzy she seemed to be floating. The realization scared her until she saw Dancer off to her left. He was floating like her, talking to her without talking, yet his words exploded in her mind as if he were yelling.

"You're out of body, Casey, floating free."

He was right. *Oh my God, I'm doing it.*

"I can't take your hand but you can follow me right up through the roof of the building." He pointed up, then drifted toward the ceiling and seemed to dissolve into the plaster and disappear. "Just imagine yourself rising up to the roof of the building."

She did, and instantly joined him on the rooftop. *I'm really on the roof, good God, I'm doing it.* In one direction there were more apartments just like Dancer's. Turning, she could see where Santa Monica met the sea. In the other direction a plane was taking off from LAX.

"Now, see down there," he pointed to a lighted building on the busy street a half block away. "It's a restaurant. I want you to imagine standing in front of it."

She did, and instantly found herself on the sidewalk in front of the store. Dancer was there beside her, smiling. Then a customer bounded out of the restaurant doorway and walked right through Dancer. *I don't believe it. I don't believe it.*

Dancer read her thoughts. "Believe it."

"Can cars run through me without hurting me?"

He nodded in the direction of the street.

Warily, Casey stepped off the curb. She wasn't sure if she stepped or floated, but she found herself between two parked cars, ready to move out into traffic. As she thought about it, she was there, and a city bus zoomed right at her. Panicking, she yelled "Return" and found herself instantly back in her physical body, trembling terribly. She opened and closed her eyes several times.

A moment later Dancer opened his eyes and said, "Be relaxed and at ease. Wide awake, wide awake."

Casey sat up. "I'm sorry. I blew it."

"No, you successfully astral projected. The bus couldn't have hurt you, but that's a lot of programming to overcome in an instant."

Dancer served tea. They talked small talk.

When the tea was gone, Dancer asked, "Do you want to astral project again tonight?"

"Yes."

"Good. But this time, once we're on the roof I want you to project to someone you know well. I'll come with you if I can, but it's not unusual to get separated if both people don't know the projection subject."

"My mother, in Phoenix," Casey said. "I know her tone."

"Let's do it."

When they were both once again on the roof of Dancer's apartment building, he said, "Now imagine your mother and hear her tone."

Instantly, Casey was in the living room of a slump-block house in central Phoenix. Her mother was sitting in a lounger chair watching TV and petting the calico cat in her lap. Casey looked around trying to orient herself to the surroundings. The experience was like mind projection only better. This was a matter of being there, which she assumed she was.

She looked around for Dancer and didn't see him, so she decided to experiment on her own. When she tried to touch her mother's arm her hand went right through the woman. *Jesus Christ. I'm sorry for doubting you, Dancer.* As if her thoughts projected his manifestation, Dancer appeared in the middle of the living room.

"Thanks," he said. "I needed that boost to find you."

"It really works, Dancer."

He nodded and raised his hands. "This time let's return to our bodies a little slower. I slammed in a bit too hard after the bus incident."

"How?" she asked.

"Just imagine the roof of the building again. Ready?"

"Ready." She imagined the rooftop, or thought she did. For a second she was moving in a blur of surrounding lights, then all hell seemed to break loose, and she was tumbling through blackness, down, down, down into infinity. *What's happening?*

"Gotcha," cackled a hideous voice that echoed from every direction. Something jumped on her back, slowing her descent until she floated to the ground.

"Nhe-nhe-nhe-nhe."

Whatever was on her back hurt. She tried to knock it off but couldn't reach it with her hands. "Nhe-nhe-nhe-nhe-nhe." She trembled and realized she felt cold. *How can I feel cold when I'm out of my body?* The ground squished beneath her. She strained to see in the eerie half light— there was no color, only shades of grey. Skeletal trees on the horizon reached ghostly fingers skyward, illuminated by a grey glow beyond.

"Nhe-nhe-nhe-nhe-nhe-nhe."

Whatever was on her back felt like it was burrowing into her. Casey cried, *Stop it! Stop it!* and tried to remember what Dancer had told her to do.

She almost had it when she heard a hideous, blood-chilling shriek—high pitched and feminine. Hearing it again, she turned to see the silhouette of a woman running along the horizon, through the trees. *What?* The woman turned in her direction.

"Hello there," Casey yelled, or thought she yelled.

The woman ran straight to Casey and stopped five yards in front of her. She was naked and plump with sagging breasts and a protruding stomach. Casey strained to see her face in the dim light.

"One of them's on yer back," cackled the woman. "They got ya now."

"One of what's on my back?"

"Croakers. Hideous, huh? They'll eat yer soul, you know." The woman stepped closer.

Casey strained to see, and when she did, wished she hadn't. The woman's face was a hideous distortion of reality—a crone from the pits—red eyed, hooknosed, her smile exposing toothless gums. Her foul breath made Casey gag.

"Where am I?" Casey asked.

"Where am I?" the crone cackled. "Where am I? That's a good one."

"But where?"

"Here, you're here. Where else could you be?" The woman crooked a long finger at Casey. "And here you'll stay."

Fire. Casey remembered Dancer's command. *Say the word "fire" and imagine yourself surrounded with cleansing flames.* "FIRE!"

The crone screamed in surprise and beat her hands in the air as she backed away. The flames leaped and crackled around Casey—cold fire of ferocious intensity. She was a pillar of flame, illuminating the bizarre landscape.

The thing on Casey's back began screeching shrilly and flapping what sounded like leathery wings. She began to feel the thing withdrawing—as if from deep inside her—in a desperate effort to escape the flames. When it went, it took her breath along with it. Casey fell to her knees, struggling to suck air into her depleted lungs. Turning, she saw the thing . . . the croaker.

NO, NO, NO, NO, NO. It was something out of a nightmare—half bat, half demon—a winged monstrosity with red eyes, a snout nose and long, long fangs. The wings were ten times the size of its body. And it was trying to fly, flopping like a crippled bird, screeching, wings pounding against the marshy ground.

Casey stumbled to her feet, still fighting for breath. She took one last look and bolted into the grayness, running as if the hordes of hell were after her—as indeed they appeared to be—toward the skeletal trees on the ridge. Upon reaching the trees she moved to brush a branch out of her way and found her hand went through it.

Oh, my God. Dancer, where are you? "RETURN!" she yelled and was about to yell it again, when her eyes fluttered and she opened them to see the candle-lit living room. Her breath came in deep draughts and she was trembling again.

Dancer sat is his chair. "Take a detour?" he asked. "I got back five minutes ago."

"Five minutes? You mean I was only in that terrible place for five minutes?" She pulled her arms tightly across her chest, took a deep breath and explained what had happened.

"The lower astral plane," Dancer said. "Somehow your own negativity pulled you down."

"You mean that place was real?" Casey sat up and shook her head.

"Real in the nonphysical sense. Certainly real to the souls and creatures who are trapped there."

"It was horrible. I don't want to astral project anymore."

He could see the fear in her eyes. "At death, hateful souls find themselves in the lower astral. They'll be trapped there until they accept the guidance of highly evolved entities who regularly visit the plane."

"Why wouldn't they accept help?"

"They're confused and closed off to anyone else knowing more than they do. The monster you called a 'croaker' was a thought form—the manifestation of twisted minds."

Casey leaned back into the couch cushions, looked

Dancer in the eyes and said, "Why did I end up there?"

"Your own anger. What were you upset about?"

Casey looked down at the candle on the coffee table and smiled to herself. "I had lunch with Alan. It upset me, but I repressed any outward display of anger."

Dancer nodded.

She brushed both hands through her brown hair. "Could that have pulled me down?"

"Probably," he said. "But now that you know about the lower astral, you won't be likely to get stuck again. If you sense a downward pull, surround yourself with white light and imagine yourself ascending."

"I could just say, 'return,' "

"But you'd have to come back and start the session all over again."

"Why couldn't I breathe when I was out of body, Dancer?"

"Old programming. You reacted the way you might react if something terrifying happened to you in this reality."

Casey shuddered.

"Tomorrow night you'll meet your soulmate."

She met his eyes.

He said, "Be here at five in the afternoon."

A tennis match on television distracted Casey for three hours Saturday morning. But by noon she was back to wondering if she should or shouldn't do the soulmate astral projection session. *Let's face it, Casey, you're playing an unfamiliar game. Until yesterday you'd never even heard of a lower astral plane, much less been trapped in one.* She decided that Dancer should have warned her. Then she realized that indirectly he had when he programmed her with the fire technique. He'd said, "Use it in case you ever feel attacked."

Damn. Why hadn't she asked him, "attacked by who or

what?" The memories of the crone and the thing on her back gave her the shivers so bad she decided to fight them by exploring the religious/philosophical aspects of her experience.

Sitting on a barstool at her kitchen counter, dressed in faded jeans and a T-shirt, she sipped black coffee and doodled on a yellow legal pad. "Purgatory." She wrote the word once in script and printed it in heavy black capital letters. She doodled a row of daisies that spelled out, "Catholics."

Turning on the barstool, she looked at the boxes of books waiting to be unpacked. At least they were marked by category. She opened the "reference" box and dug through the contents until finding a volume titled *Philosophy & Religion.* Opening the book to "purgatory," she found only a six-line entry. It read, "From the Latin word *purgare* — meaning to purify. According to Roman Catholic belief, a place where the souls of deceased sinners must make atonement. A place of suffering intended to cleanse or purge. Offerings of prayer and of the Mass are held to aid those in purgatory."

Good God, if the lower astral plane is purgatory, I'll never sin again. But when she thought about her sins she couldn't come up with many. Was living with a man out of wedlock a sin? Probably, according to the fundamentalist loons. *Surely that wouldn't get me sent down there?* The shivers crept up her arms again. She wanted to write an expose'story for the *L.A. Reporter,* alerting the world to the underworld.

Great, Casey. They'll give you the Pulitzer for cosmic foo-foo story of the year.

By 3 P.M. she'd decided three times to go ahead and do the soulmate session and three times to forget it. Sitting on some unpacked boxes by the apartment window, she ate an apple and watched people on the street two floors below. A breeze rustled the palm fronds and rippled the curtains. Faintly, from another apartment, she could hear the Indigo Girls latest hit. Below, an elderly couple walked by holding hands. A four or five-year-old boy played in the bed of a pickup parked at the curb, while his father waxed the truck.

Casey remembered her own father saying, "There's nothing to be afraid of, Casey." He had opened her closet doors to show that no monsters lurked behind the doors. Her dresses and play clothes were hung neatly on a rod. Below them was her toy box and shoe stand.

"But I heard them in there, Daddy," she cried, rubbing her eyes.

He sat on the edge of her bed and held her in his arms as they talked about the power of imagination. It was a conversation they'd had many times as she grew up, and he encouraged her to follow her dream of becoming a journalist. He died of cancer the year she graduated with honors from UCLA—four years ago.

What would you think of me now, Daddy, sitting here afraid to follow my story to completion because of the monsters that wait in the dark? Or is that it? Maybe I'm afraid I might really find my soulmate and be forced to deal with all that it means.

She remembered her dad opening the closet doors and standing there smiling at her. And she knew she'd be at Dancer's apartment at 5 P.M.

Lying on the couch, Casey listened to Dancer provide her with last minute instructions. "When you're out of body, you must hear your own vibrational tone in your mind. It must be crystal clear. Then vary it ever so slightly and hold the tone for several seconds before projecting to where it takes you."

"I wish you were coming with me."

He shook his head. "If you haven't returned in a half hour, I'll bring you back."

"How?" Casey asked.

"Don't be concerned with logistics," he replied and smiled.

Casey closed her eyes and breathed deeply as Dancer directed the hypnotic induction. When she was in her astral body and floating near the ceiling, she looked down to see her physical body lying comfortably on the couch. Dancer sat in his chair drinking tea.

Closing her astral eyes she concentrated on her tone. It was easy. Then she varied the pitch and willed herself to follow it, "to another person now living on the earth."

For a moment nothing happened, then she sensed movement, a blur of lights, and momentary fear. The next thing she knew she was in a large, high-ceiling living room. Logs blazed in a fireplace; seated in a leather chair before the hearth was an elderly woman. She was reading a newspaper. *Today's news. A London paper.*

Casey concentrated on the tone and realized immediately that it belonged to this woman. *Obviously, you're not my soulmate,* she thought, looking at the woman's intelligent face. *But I'll bet we'd be great friends if we had the chance to know each other.*

Wondering what to do, Casey realized that she'd raised her own vibrational tone to vary it. Concentrating again on her own tone, she lowered it just a little—so little she wasn't sure if she'd varied it at all. *Follow it.* The living room faded away like a slow dissolve in a movie. There was momentary blackness before another scene manifested around her.

She was standing directly in front of a good-looking man in his middle thirties who seemed to be looking right at her. "What the hell is going on?" he bellowed.

Casey gasped and said, "I'm sorry, I didn't think you—"

"The senator is going to push it," said another voice from behind Casey.

"Damn," said the man standing in front of her, tossing a file folder down on the desk.

Casey realized the man did not know she was there, and that she was in the city room of a newspaper a lot bigger than the *L.A. Reporter.* A few people sat at desks in what she assumed to be the reporters' pool. The morning edition had obviously been finalized or the room would have been a hotbed of activity.

She watched as the man loosened his tie with a sigh of resignation, then pulled out a chair, sat down, and snapped on a desk computer. He looked at his phone and hesitated before picking it up and pushing a precoded phone number. When the computer signalled ready, his fingers fleeted across the keyboard and a story appeared on the monochrome monitor.

"Hello, honey. I'm going to be stuck here for awhile. The Moranna story is breaking wide open." He was scowling. "I know that, but you know my business. I can't walk away from a story like this." As he listened he punched more keys and a picture of popular Senator Jason Moranna appeared on the monitor. Casey caught a glimpse of the headline—something about government contract kickbacks. "Sonia, you've got to be more understanding if . . ." He listened for a moment, his full attention on the conversation. "Damn it, don't hang up on me again. Sonia, if . . ."

He took a deep breath and hung up the phone.

Casey decided this frustrated man sitting at his desk in front of her was probably the handsomest man she'd ever seen. Six-one, raven haired, and not quite thin enough to be called skinny. He had a square stubborn jaw, his face was dark with beard stubble, and his blue eyes sparkled with intelligence.

"Are you my soulmate?" she asked aloud.

Almost as if he'd heard her on another level of mind, he sat back in his chair and smiled to himself. Then another man ran up to his desk, saying, "Paul, here's what Jimmy just called in." Together, the two men read the notes.

Paul. So your name's Paul. She moved around to his in-basket and looked at an envelope sitting in the tray. It was addressed to Paul Conway at the *New York Gazette*, New York City.

Paul Conway. She looked at him. Beyond Paul, on the other side of the room, windows ran along the wall. She thought about looking out and found herself instantly standing by the glass. In the reflection she saw Paul and the other man, behind her. Her own reflection did not register in the glass. Beyond the glass was the Manhattan skyline. *Oh, my God, is this really happening?*

She turned and wondered, *Was he wearing a wedding ring?* Instantly she was beside him looking down at his left hand. *No ring.* She tried, unsuccessfully, to push the idea of soulmates out of her mind. *Paul Conway. Mrs. Paul Conway. Casey Conway. Paul and Casey Conway. STOP IT! Good Lord, get a grip on yourself—you sound like a high-school girl. Talk about ridiculous. Talk about lack of objectivity. Talk about . . ."*

One second Casey was standing beside Paul Conway, the next was a blur as she ascended up out of the altered state of consciousness to open her eyes and see Dancer's eyes looking anxiously down at her.

"Good," he said.

"Good, what do you mean good? Did you jerk me back here?

Dancer tapped his watch. "Thirty minutes."

"Oh, Dancer. I met someone."

He nodded and smiled.

"I think he's a writer, or a reporter for the *New York Gazette*. And . . ."

Dancer interrupted. "He has a green dot between the second and third toes of his left foot."

"What?"

"A green dot. Remember it. I don't know why that's important, but it just came to me like bolt out of the blue."

Casey looked at the psychic quizzically. "He probably has a girlfriend."

"I didn't guarantee you that when you found your soulmate he wouldn't be involved."

"If I were to meet him, would he recognize me?"

"Did you recognize him?"

"I thought he was beautiful . . . handsome . . . powerful . . . but . . . I don't know."

"In other words, you were attracted to him."

"Oh, yes."

"Usually there's an instant attraction. But everyone over sixteen is so cynical, it usually takes us awhile to let down our defenses. Maybe more so in New York than elsewhere."

"What shall I do now, Dancer?"

He shrugged and smiled.

She pointed to the telephone on the end table. "May I?"

He nodded.

She dialed directory assistance for the number of the *New York Gazette*. It would now be 10:10 P.M. in Manhattan. She direct dialed the number, when the operator answered she said, "Paul Conway, please. I believe he's still working."

"One moment, please."

Casey covered the mouthpiece of the phone and whispered to Dancer, "There is a Paul Conway."

"Conway speaking," said a deep voice on the other end of the line.

Casey's eyes went wide. "Ah, are you working late on the Senator Jason Moranna story?"

"How did . . . Who is this anyway?"

Casey hung up the phone. Her heart was beating like a schoolgirl who'd just experienced her first kiss.

Dancer chuckled to himself.

Casey leaned back into the couch cushions, still holding the phone on her lap. "Oh, great. Do I spend the little money I have in my savings account to go to New York?"

"You will," Dancer said, matter of factly.

Casey looked at her psychic benefactor and knew he was right.

Sunday morning Casey called her boss at home and asked him if she could have the week off to pursue a story in New York City. "I'll pay all the expenses, unless you decide to run the story," she said.

He tried to get her to further explain, but she refused. "Okay," he finally said. "Well, I don't have a lot to lose, and maybe you'll come home with a Pulitzer nomination."

She laughed and returned the phone to its cradle, relieved and more scared than she could ever remember being, except on the lower astral plane, and that didn't count.

The Delta red eye from LAX to Kennedy saved her hundreds of dollars. Arriving in New York before dawn, it was 6:30 A.M. by the time she'd claimed her suitcase and was settled in a cab. "The Roosevelt on Madison and Forty-Fifth, please." The cab driver didn't understand her any better than she understood him, so she wrote the address on a piece of paper.

"Ya, ya, ya," he said, waving his hands. The ride was the next best thing to an amusement park, and she wished the cab was equipped with a seatbelt as the driver careened through the heavy traffic on the expressway. The fare was $33. She gave the man two twenties. "Ya, ya." He said from behind the wheel, bowing and offering no change.

The hotel doorman took her suitcase and pointed her up the stairs toward the registration desk. She wondered if she would remember the hotel. She did. Her high school graduation present had been a trip to New York, and she'd stayed in a suite here with her mother and father.

What the hell am I doing here?

When Casey was settled in her small room, she looked out the window at the dirty-brick walls of an office building. *And now that I'm here, what do I do?* She'd dozed fitfully on the plane and was exhausted, but she knew she wouldn't sleep. She dressed in tan slacks, a crisp white blouse and a blue Liz Claiborne jacket, to take a walk up Fifth Avenue.

The sidewalks were crowded with people rushing to work. At 46th Street an early-bird hustler tried to sell her a fifteen-dollar imitation of a Cartier watch. Cabs honked angrily. Homeless people slept on sidewalk grates hissing steam from the bowels of the city. Between 47th and 48th, a black man was running a shell-game on the top of an upturned cardboard box. A crowd gathered around the action and the man's buddies stood ready to warn him of approaching police.

Casey thought of the Venice Boardwalk at home, and decided it probably outdid the streets of New York, even at 8:00 A.M.

The aroma of fresh-baked pastries wafted along the sidewalk. Casey's mouth watered until she inhaled a nauseating blast of bus fumes at the street corner. Purchasing a cup of coffee from a street vendor, she turned left on 49th Street and strolled up the long block to Rockefeller Center.

The spring morning was a lot colder than anything Casey was used to in Los Angeles. The promenade and walkways surrounding the plaza blazed with a rainbow of blooming tulips. People were already skating in the ice rink. Standing in the exact place where she had once stood with her mother and father, she sipped her coffee and watched the graceful skaters circling below.

Now what, Casey?

Walking back to the street, she hailed a cab stopped momentarily at the curb. "The *New York Gazette*," she said, trying to sound as detached as the locals.

Without responding, the cabbie wheeled into traffic and eight minutes later pulled to an abrupt stop in front of a block-square building. As the cab pulled away she stood for a moment, observing the stone carving on the face of the structure. She wanted to look up at the towering presence, but knew that to do so would mark her as a tourist. In the lobby, to the left was a newsstand, to the right a coffee shop. Straight ahead, the elevators were beyond a security check point.

"Can I help you, miss?" asked a tall uniformed black man.

"Mr. Paul Conway, please. My name is Casey Garrett."

"Is Mr. Conway expecting you?"

She shook her head. "But I have a story I think he might be interested in."

The security man talked for a moment into a phone, then handed the receiver to Casey. "This is Ms. Friedman. She's Mr. Conway's secretary."

"Hello," Casey said, tentatively. "I was hoping I could see Paul Conway."

"Exactly what is this about?" asked the woman.

"A story I think he might be interested in."

"Political information?"

"No, a personal story."

"Maybe you'd like to talk to a reporter."

"Isn't Paul Conway a reporter?"

"No, he's the Gazette's political analyst, and I'm afraid he's very busy. Today he's in Washington D.C." The woman paused. "Can I have someone else help you?"

"No, but thank you," Casey said, handing the phone back to the security man. Her heart sank.

Serves you right, Casey. What did you expect? She walked out of the lobby and down the steps to the sidewalk. *Did you think he'd rush you right up to his office, instantly recognize your soulmate status and kiss you passionately? Maybe then you'd have had lunch together at the Plaza and when you were done, you'd have discreetly taken an elevator to a penthouse suite for an afternoon of lovemaking.* She stood quietly on the street till she got her bearings, then set off toward the Roosevelt Hotel. *Maybe a long walk will clear your foggy head.*

She slept all afternoon, then awakened to have dinner in the lobby restaurant. Back in her room she called her mother in Phoenix and talked for a few minutes. Next, she called Dancer and told him what had happened.

"It will work out," he told her. "Stop worrying."

It didn't work out on Tuesday. Ms. Friedman told her Paul Conway was still in Washington and that it wouldn't do her any good to keep calling. She spent the morning at the Museum of Modern Art and the afternoon browsing in a huge bookstore.

Gee, I can spend my week in New York reading. And that's exactly what you're going to end up doing if you don't get creative about meeting Paul Conway. That's when she got the idea.

In an electronic store on Fifth Avenue, she bought a small cassette tape player/recorder, and a blank tape. Back in her room at the Roosevelt, she rough drafted the statement, rejected it and tried again. *You've got to get his attention immediately.* She rewrote it four more times before inserting the blank tape in the recorder and pressing the button.

"Hello, Paul Conway. To get your attention I will first remark about the green dot between the second and third toes of your left foot. Are you listening? I hope so. I'm an investigative reporter for the *Los Angeles Reporter*, a weekly tabloid with a circulation of a hundred thousand. Although my paper is nothing by comparison to the *Gazette*, we've won our share of journalistic honors. I flew to New York for just one reason, to meet you. You're part of the most bizarre story I've ever investigated. You, and only you, can give me the ending I need to wrap it up, one way or another. My name is Casey Garrett, and I'll be staying at the Roosevelt Hotel until Saturday morning. Sorry for the misleading label—I wanted to be sure of getting this directly to you. Thank you for listening."

On the tape label she wrote, "Important Political Information For Paul Conway's Ears Only."

Wednesday morning the hotel concierge had the tape delivered to the *New York Gazette*.

To take her mind off Paul Conway, Casey spent Wednesday morning shopping for clothes. When she didn't find anything she liked in the uptown stores, she took a cab to Greenwich Village and found shops more to her liking.

In a kicky walk-down boutique, she purchased a new sport coat and a pair of unique black boots from a crewcut woman wearing neon earrings. She ate lunch at a sidewalk Italian restaurant. Four men in robes and turbans chattered in a foreign language at the table next to her. At another table two lesbians couldn't keep their eyes off of her. Casey felt at home. As different as New York was from Los Angeles, the two cities were alike in so many ways, and they were both unique to the rest of the country.

You'd better like it here. When you become Mrs. Paul Conway you'll live here. She choked on her salad. *Good God, Casey will you stop with this ridiculous fairy tale.*

One of the lesbians caught Casey's eye and nodded. In response, Casey smiled and shook her head, declining gracefully. The other woman smiled too, and wrinkled her nose in a gesture indicating disappointment.

It was after six when Casey walked up the stairs to the Roosevelt lobby and checked for messages at the desk. "Oh yes," said the female desk clerk. "There's a man waiting for you." The woman raised her hand to the bellman.

Casey's face flushed and her heart hammered. *Run to the restroom and check your makeup.*

The bellman strolled to the registration desk and the woman handed him the slip of paper. "He's waiting in the lobby bar, Ms. Garrett."

The bellman led her across the lobby, up the stairs to the bar, and directly to a table where a man was sitting alone having a drink. He wasn't Paul Conway.

The man stood up and extended his hand to Casey. "I'm Walter Ennis, Paul Conway's researcher, Ms. Garrett." He handed a folded bill to the bellman. "Please sit down." He pulled out a chair.

Casey placed her shopping bags on a spare chair and sat across from Walter.

"Would you like a drink?"

"Mineral water with lime, thank you."

A waitress appeared. Walter related Casey's order and requested, "Another Gibson."

"You expected Paul?" Walter asked.

Casey said, "I didn't expect anyone. I'd hoped to have a few minutes to talk to Paul Conway, yes."

Walter nodded. "Well, Paul is anxious to talk to you. When he couldn't reach you on the phone, he asked me to come here and wait for you."

Casey squeezed her hands in her lap.

Walter continued, "Paul had to attend an important reception. The Vice President is there. But he'll be free by ten. Can he see you then?"

The waitress arrived with the drinks.

"Why, ah, yes. Of course," Casey stammered.

Walter seemed to relax. "Where are you from, Casey?"

She broke into a big smile. "From the other side . . . ah, of the country. Brentwood, California."

Walter nodded. "Do you know the Reagans?"

"I . . . haven't had the pleasure," she replied and repressed a laugh.

When she stepped out of the elevator, Paul Conway was waiting for her. He was formally dressed, with his top coat over one arm. Casey was glad she'd worn a black evening dress and cloak.

"Casey?"

"Hello, Paul." She extended her hand and he took it, holding it longer than necessary as he looked in her eyes. His touch was electric and she hoped her reactions didn't show.

He said, "I know a quiet place nearby where we can talk. They have the finest coffee and cheesecake in the city."

"I'd like that."

He extended his arm, she took it, and he led her across the lobby, down the stairs, through the revolving door to a waiting limousine. The driver climbed out of the car and quickly opened the passenger door.

As the car pulled away from the curb, Casey realized he was looking at her. "You're very good," he said.

"What?" She met his eyes.

"You're a very good investigative journalist."

"But how do . . ."

He laughed. "Even your editor doesn't know the nature of the story you're pursuing. He must trust you a lot."

"You checked on me?"

"You've certainly been checking on me," he replied.

The limo eased to a stop in front of a small restaurant with a quaint cottage-like exterior that looked like it belonged in a fairy tale. The maitre d' recognized Paul and led the couple to a candlelighted table in the back.

"You probably think I'm crazy," Casey said, looking into his intense blue eyes.

"No. Not after reading your pieces on pollution in the bay, the homeless revolution, and LAPD corruption."

"How?"

"Your editor faxed them to me. I think he's afraid the *New York Gazette* might hire you away. I hope they do."

Casey shook her head, confused.

"You could hold your own with any reporter on the *Gazette.*"

"Thank you, but . . ."

"But now you're going to tell me how you know about the green dot between my toes."

"There really is a green dot?"

"Yes, and no one on earth knows about it. My mother was afraid I'd be kidnapped, so she had the dot tattooed for identification purposes when I was six years old. My parents have been dead for ten years. I'm sure they never told anyone about it, and I certainly haven't. Even my ex-wife didn't know it was there."

Casey shivered. "It's a long story, Paul."

"I hope so," he said. "I hope it takes all night to tell."

Dancer had just said goodbye to the last of his psychic development students and was brewing a fresh pot of tea when someone knocked. He padded to the door, smiling.

"Casey!" he said warmly. He wasn't surprised.

"I came in as your students were going out. Is it all right?"

"Of course it's all right, stranger."

"You got my message? The one I left on your answering machine."

"Oh, yes," he laughed. "Let's see, that was three weeks ago, wasn't it? "

She nodded, sheepishly.

"Come in. Sit down and have tea."

"I've been living a whirlwind, Dancer."

"I know, I know. Did you think I wouldn't check on you?"

He poured the tea. Casey laughed.

Dancer continued, "I loved it in the restaurant when he told you he'd already read your stories. You should have seen the look on your face."

"You were . . ."

"Of course. I got you into it, didn't I?" He smiled. "I've even looked in on you a couple of times when you were, ah, let me say, intimately involved. Whew!"

"That's terrible." She laughed and had to put down her cup to avoid spilling the tea.

"He's quite talented, isn't he?" Dancer quipped.

"Dancer!" She scowled at him.

"The answer is, yes."

"What's the question?" Casey asked, laughing.

"Will I give the bride away? Yes. If I remember correctly, the wedding is scheduled for June tenth."

She nodded and lay back on the couch cushions. "We haven't been apart since that first night."

"I know, I know," Dancer said. "And you'll have three sons who will all go to Harvard. Ain't love grand?"

GUARDIAN ANGEL

Marina was pretty enough, smart enough, and young enough to attract the right man. But she was too shy, according to her mother, her friends and the people she worked with.

"Stop being so shy about Aaron, Marina."

"Easy for you to say, Libby. You don't have a shy bone in your body."

Marina tightened the reins as they crested the hill a few yards from the road. Her buckskin quarter horse tossed his head in protest and stepped into the path of Libby's smoky Arabian. Marina stroked the gelding's lathered neck, talking to him in a calm, gentle voice.

The rolling California hills, once lush and green, were now a sea of golden grass that ebbed and flowed like waves in the dry October wind.

"Devil winds," Libby said. "They make the horses as spooky as they do me. But they don't affect you, do they?"

Marina shook her head, her long cinnamon-colored hair shimmering in the afternoon light like strands of lustrous glass. Her mouth was full, her nose Grecian, her eyes as green as polished jade. A red bandana headband, plaid western shirt, worn jeans, and roughout cowboy boots set off her suntanned features.

"We were talking about you being too shy—too shy to talk

to Aaron," Libby said, brushing wisps of blond hair out of her eyes. "He's perfect for you. He's single, he owns the riding academy, and he practically drools every time he sees you."

Marina swung her slender body out of the saddle and looked up at her friend. "You really look like Goldie Hawn today," was her offhand remark.

"And you're changing the subject again."

"Let's walk the horses for awhile."

"Subject changer."

"Libby, I'd love to talk to Aaron and a lot of other men but I can't. I freeze. I clutch up and make a fool of myself."

"I'd like to kill the guy that raped you," Libby said, disgustedly.

"That was a long time ago, Libby."

"You use horses to hide from men."

"I understand horses."

They continued along the macadam road for a few minutes until they came to a trail leading through the scattered trees to the stables. Although less than a mile from the endless traffic spilling in and out of Los Angeles on the Ventura Freeway, Marina and Libby rode through countryside as rural in appearance as central Montana.

"Hi, Aaron," Libby waved as they entered the stable area of the Thousand Oaks Riding Academy.

"Hi, Libby, Hi, Marina," Aaron called from the back of a sorrel Arabian. His dark eyes dominated a handsome square face. He smiled at Marina. She looked away.

"Aaron, do you have a minute?" Libby called.

Before Marina could react, Aaron trotted his horse toward the two women.

"I'm going to get in a lot of trouble for this, Aaron, but here goes. Marina is terribly shy, but she's very attracted to you."

Marina turned on Libby, shocked surprise rapidly giving way to seething anger.

Aaron said, "Marina, I'm shy too. I'm nearly forty and I still

173

can't . . ."

Marina jerked the reins to the right, snapping her horse into a twist as she threw her heels into the animal's flanks. The buckskin leaped forward as Marina whipped the long end of the reins on his rump. Bolting straight for the fence separating the stables from the parking area, they jumped the barrier, cleared it easily, but barely missed a sports car pulling out of a parking place.

Libby called after her. Marina could hear hoofbeats following her into the foothills but when she reached the ridge and looked back, Libby had given up and was returning to the stables. Marina eased out of the saddle and watched, one hand holding the reins as she wiped the tears from her cheeks with the other. The raw fury had been replaced by a sense of shame, humiliation and deep sadness. Turning, she walked the buckskin along the ridge, higher into the hills.

On the crest of a hill overlooking similar hills with no signs of civilization in sight, Marina lay beneath an oak tree looking up through the barely swaying boughs. The hazy orange sun slipped slowly behind the western hills, painting the sky in pink and purple.

"Please, God, why does it have to be so difficult?" she wondered aloud. "Please help me."

She closed her eyes and saw Aaron's smiling face and she blushed at what he must think of her now. She forced the image from her mind. It was replaced by the familiar picture of herself walking across a shopping mall parking lot, and placing her purchases on the roof of the car while searching for her keys. The man grabbed her from behind, clamped her mouth and stuck the knife to her throat.

"But I was shy before that," Marina's conscience reminded her. She opened her eyes. After remembering the horror countless times it had lost its edge. Today, it was more like recalling a scary movie from her high school days.

Laughter.

Maria leaped to her feet, spooking the hobbled buckskin grazing a few feet away. She looked around her, puzzled. She was on the crest of the hill and could see for miles in every direction. No one.

I heard it. I know I did.

She sat down nervously, pulling her knees to her chest. A nearly full moon appeared in the darkening sky near the eastern horizon. The grass rustled in the wind, sounding like distant murmuring voices. She closed her eyes and again heard the laughter. She descended the Forum steps clad in a white toga. No, *he* descended the steps. He had expressed his ideas, good ideas, and they were not only rejected, they had called him a fool.

Marina felt a tightness in her throat and a shortness of breath as her husband, a British Captain, rejected her pleas for forgiveness. She was lying on a great four-poster bed, crying. Reeling in confusion Marina tried to open her eyes, as the old Chinese man hit her on the side of the head, saying, "Never raise your eyes or your voice again. You are worthless." Head down, she shuffled away.

"What the hell is going on?" Marina shouted, her eyes flying open.

"Just a few past-life memories," said the man, seated comfortably in the grass in front of her.

Marina started to rise and stumbled backward, too scared to scream. She fell against the tree trunk and froze.

"I'm a guardian angel," he said. "If you'll look closely, you can see that I even glow a little."

He was dressed in a white robe; in the semi-darkness, he did appear to glow. *A trick of the light.* She pressed her back against the tree.

"Some people expect angels to have wings, but we don't. See?" He turned enough for Marina to see his back. When she didn't reply, he shrugged his shoulders and said, "Remember when you were five years old and you put your hand up in

175

class?"

Marina remembered but did not respond.

"The teacher got mad and told you to put your hand down. The other children laughed at you. That was the last time you ever put your hand up."

Marina decided that was true.

"Maybe you can't talk to men, Marina, but I'm an angel, so you can talk to me."

He faded away and Marina breathed a sigh of relief. She looked to both sides and behind her before emerging from the safety of the tree.

"Will you talk to me if I come back?" a voice said.

Marina looked around, saw nothing and shook her head.

"Please. I'll get into trouble."

Marina worked up the courage to ask, "Why?"

"Tonight, for the first time, you asked for help. It's my duty."

"I didn't ask for your help," she said.

"You said, 'Please, God, why does it have to be so difficult? Please help me.' Don't you remember?"

Marina nodded.

"Will you talk to me if I come back?"

"Okay."

The angel reappeared about five feet in front of Marina. He was definitely glowing now. He appeared to be in his thirties, of medium height and build, with golden hair, and a handsome baby face.

"This is a dream, right?" Marina asked.

The angel shook his head. "The past-life memories were like a dream. Vision is a more accurate term."

"Those were my past lives?"

"I can show you a lot more."

"No, thank you."

"I wanted you to realize that you have many reasons to repress your emotions. But an awareness of the cause can help you to let go of the effect."

"Can we sit down?" Marina asked.

They sat cross-legged in the long grass, facing each other beneath the star-splattered sky. Marina was no longer fearful, but she doubted the reality of what was happening even as she experienced it.

"You're really a guardian angel?"

"Well, I . . ."

"Do you have a name?"

"You'll laugh."

"No, I won't"

"It's Bartholomew."

Marina laughed.

Bartholomew nodded. "I have a plan. I'm only an angel, not a Master. But I can conjure up small miracles when called upon. I can take away your shyness for twenty-four hours, I think."

Marina laughed. "And then I turn back into a pumpkin?"

"And then you realize that your shyness is nothing but a groundless fear you have the power to release."

She looked at him. A flicker of a smile rose at the edge of her mouth and she nodded.

"What do I have to do?"

"Just sit there. Look at the moon. I'll stand behind you and perform the ritual. When it's complete, you'll be confident and self-assured for twenty-four hours." He pushed up the sleeves of his robe in preparation.

Bartholomew's fingertips on her temples projected a soothing vibration. It felt like a silent internal hum—what she thought the roar of eternity and the essence of purity must be like. She looked at the moon. Her eyes drooped and closed. When she opened them the moon had traveled across the sky.

"Bartholomew!"

She stood up. The buckskin was grazing below the crest of

the hill, but if there had ever been an angel he was gone now. Turning slowly to survey the scene she noticed something glowing in the grass. The sash of a robe.

Picking it up, she ran the corded sash through her fingers and smiled. *Twenty-four hours.*

The lights were still on in the offices of the riding academy. After she brushed down the buckskin and put him in his stall, Marina walked across the empty arena to her locker. In the women's room she showered and changed into fresh jeans and a sweater. Standing before the small mirror, she carefully brushed her hair and applied fresh makeup.

She hesitated a moment at the office entrance, then boldly walked past the empty reception area and down the hall. The door to Aaron's office was open and he was working at his desk. Trophies, ribbons and photos filled the walls of the room and a Western show saddle sat on a stand in the corner.

He looked up. "Marina."

"I'm sorry, Aaron, for my childish behavior."

"No," he stammered, surprised that she was talking to him. "But I would have sent a posse out if you hadn't gotten back pretty soon."

"A posse?" She laughed, leaning against the door frame.

"Of course I knew you could outride and elude anyone I sent after you."

She smiled directly into his eyes.

He continued. "As I started to say earlier, I'm shy too. I still have a hard time working up the courage to ask a woman for a date."

"Really?"

He nodded. "Do you have any idea how much I admire your ability with horses?"

She shook her head.

"I've tried to talk to you so many times . . ."

"I know," she said, slipping both hands into the pockets of her jeans.

"Marina, would you have dinner with me?"

"Now?"

"I know you haven't eaten."

"That would be nice."

Aaron locked the offices and they walked together past the jumping arena, lighted by a ring of sodium vapor lights. Several teenagers were patiently watching their instructor demonstrate jumping procedures. The instructor waved at Aaron and he waved back.

Aaron opened the door for her and Marina climbed into the T.O. Riding Academy crew-cab pickup. "What kind of food do you like?"

"Mexican is my favorite."

"Is El Torito all right?"

"Great."

Aaron wheeled the big pickup into traffic and they drove down the familiar street lined with palm trees. On the radio Willie Nelson sang, "Wake Me When It's Over." The Santa Anas, hot desert winds, blew through the open windows of the cab. Marina brushed her long hair out of her eyes and smiled to herself. *Aaron is even more nervous than I am,* she thought. *Thank you, Bartholomew.*

"What do you do, Marina?"

"I'm a copywriter at a Westlake ad agency."

"You should train horses. It's a shame to waste talent like yours."

"I'd love it."

"Do you want to? I'd be glad to hire you tomorrow."

"Really?"

"Really."

Twenty-four hours later Marina was on the crest of the hill where she had met Bartholomew. She looked at the moon, the glowing sash in one hand, the reins of the buckskin in the other. Bartholomew slowly shimmered into view a few feet away.

"You forgot your sash," she said, handing it to him with a smile.

"Thank you, Marina."

"Thank you, Bartholomew. I'm not afraid anymore. I know now that I can go back down into that city and communicate with people. Your miracle worked." She put her arms around him and kissed him on the cheek. "I have a wonderful new job, and Aaron really likes me, and . . ."

"It wasn't really a miracle," Bartholomew interrupted. "I just let you . . ."

"It was a miracle," she corrected.

On the other side, Bartholomew materialized on the sixth astral plane. Tiered fountains and willow trees were scattered between the colonnades and courtyards where souls in glowing robes clustered around teachers or walked together through the landscaped grounds. It was here that souls prepared to be angels—a long and arduous process of schooling and apprenticeship.

Bartholomew was on his way across the lawn to class when he heard a deep, rich, commanding voice.

"BARTHOLOMEW."

"Yes, Father," stammered Bartholomew.

"YOU HAVEN'T BEEN PRETENDING TO BE AN ANGEL AGAIN, HAVE YOU?"

"Well, ah . . ."

"YOU'LL NEVER QUALIFY FOR THE ANGEL PROGRAM IF YOU TELL LIES AND PRETEND YOU CAN PERFORM MIRACLES, BARTHOLOMEW."

"Yes, Father."

GREATER GOOD

"The planets will be perfectly aligned at the stroke of midnight on the vernal equinox," he said, licking his lips. Lowering his voice mysteriously, he added, "This will be the first time in 827 years."

"Really?" Amanda said, snapping her gum several times before asking, "So what?"

"So," he threw his head back and extended his arms toward the sky, Messiah-like. "So, something incredible is going to happen."

"Like a high tide or an earthquake?"

"No, like the arrival of the Pheladians." His voice crackled with aliveness.

Not knowing what a Pheladian was, she didn't comment. She studied him out of the corner of her eye. Twenty-eight, handsome as hell with long, dark hair, dark eyes, high cheekbones and dressed to kill in a baggy black suit, Mitchell idealized the L.A. club scene's self-image. He was "bad," which meant "good," even if he was weird. She was his female counterpart, but her hair was several inches longer and her body several inches shorter. She wore jeans, a red T-shirt and a black sport coat.

They sat side by side on stools at the counter of a Hollywood Boulevard diner. At 1:30 A.M. the place was full of pushers, hookers and loaded kids from the clubs. The odors of fried onions and coffee melded with the reek of individual hookers passing by on their way to and from the restroom. Roses. Lilacs. Some grade-B grass floated past, clinging like perfume to an 18-year-old wearing a mini-skirt that didn't quite cover the bottom of her buttocks.

"I've triangulated all known sightings from historical times up to the present, and I found a pattern. There's absolutely no doubt about it," he said, tapping his coffee cup with a spoon. "At midnight on March 21st, they'll appear at three places on earth. The closest is above Camelback Mountain in the Phoenix Valley."

"Arizona?"

"Arizona."

"The Pheladians?"

"No doubt about it."

The waitress refilled their coffee cups, then plopped two hamburger platters and a grease-splattered check on the counter before them. On the jukebox, Elvis Presley wailed "Heartbreak Hotel."

"I think they might take us on board," Mitchell said.

"On board what?" Amanda asked.

"Their ship, UFO, flying saucer, you know."

"Like in *E.T.*?"

He nodded and took a bite of the hamburger.

"Jeeze, Mitchell, you're really weird. I've only known you two weeks and I think you're the weirdest guy I've ever been with."

"The Pheladians aren't as weird as Hollywood Boulevard," he said, turning on his stool to observe the action on the street. Outside the diner windows, two cops detained a guy on roller skates wearing bikini briefs and a boa constrictor wrapped around his neck. Beyond them a row of bikers hooted at the hookers, and a guy stood on a curbside box playing a dobro guitar.

"I'm driving to Phoenix in two days. You should come with me."

"In hopes of boarding a spaceship?"

"Yeah."

"Why would I want to do that?"

"To meet a highly advanced race."

"Maybe they'd eat us."

"Don't be ridiculous."

"We eat everything dumber than we are, and what we don't eat we put in zoos. Why would Pheladians be any different?"

"They're too advanced."

"Because they're capable of space travel?" she asked.

He didn't say.

"We're capable of space travel," she said.

Hair whipping wildly in the wind, they flew down Interstate 10 in Mitchell's black, one-eyed Pontiac convertible with nearly bald tires. A three-quarter moon illuminated the car's red interior. The vanity license plate read GR8R GD—greater good. Amanda was wearing her purple and gold Los Angeles Lakers jacket over a black T-shirt and jeans. Mitchell, attired in a black leather jacket, white silk shirt and baggy grey pants, sang along with a rock song on the radio. "I'm headin' up the hill to get my thrills." Amanda harmonized on, "It's a long way home and I'm going alone."

When the song was over, Amanda had to shout to be heard over the radio, wind and rattle of the car. "Blythe is two miles."

Mitchell nodded.

"If the Pheladians take us aboard, what will you ask them?"

"For solutions to the world's problems: Crime, drugs, AIDS, hunger, how to attain world peace, and how . . ."

183

He was interrupted by a siren and red lights swirling in the rearview mirror. Mitchell slowed and pulled to the side of the road.

The California Highway Patrolman, hat cocked low over his eyes, climbed from his cruiser in slow motion and swaggered to the driver's door of the Pontiac.

"License?" he said, looking down at Mitchell, one hand resting lightly on the butt of a big-bore revolver, the other on his hip.

"I wasn't speeding, officer."

The chisel-faced patrolman didn't answer. He scrutinized the driver's license, looking from the photo in the lower left-hand corner, to the real-life Mitchell sitting below him. "Growed a lot a hair in nine months," he snarled.

"It was in a ponytail when DMV took the picture."

"Yeah?"

"Yeah."

"You being smart with me, boy?"

"No, sir, I'm agreeing with you."

The officer sauntered slowly back to the patrol car with its swirling lights and hiss-crackling radio.

"We have to be on top of Camelback Mountain by midnight," Mitchell said, frustration lacing his voice.

"Six and a half hours," Amanda said. "We're only about four hours from Phoenix."

"We've got to find the place and climb the mountain in the dark. That's cutting it pretty close."

The patrolman returned. "I'm issuing a ticket for the busted headlight. You get it fixed in Blythe before you come back out on this here freeway. I catch you back out here and it ain't fixed, I'll see you sleep in jail, you hear?"

In the door mirror Mitchell watched the officer return to his cruiser. "If the world loses the opportunity to resolve its major problems because of a 1975 Pontiac headlight, I'll never recover," he said.

As they accelerated back onto the highway, Amanda watched the CHP car behind them. "He's following."

"Shit," Mitchell mumbled, taking the first Blythe exit. He turned right onto a street of gas stations, fast-food restaurants and liquor stores, each trying to outdo the other with rotating, flashing or neon signs, some spiraling 60 feet in the air.

"He's following us," Amanda said. "Pull into any gas station."

Sitting in front of the bay doors of a Chevron station, they watched the patrol car slow down, then roll on past and disappear into the next block.

"How far are we from the border?" Amanda asked.

"About 10 miles. Let's go for it," Mitchell said.

Wheeling the great whale of an automobile back onto the street, Mitchell jammed the pedal to the metal, fishtailed, corrected, and ran for the freeway entrance. Taking the corner on two wheels, he pounded the steering wheel with his fists as if that would increase the rate of acceleration.

Cannonballing up the ramp and back onto the Interstate at 75 miles per hour, Amanda spotted the swirling red lights of the patrol car pulling onto the entrance ramp.

"He's on us already. Go, Mitchell."

Mitchell war-whooped and pounded the steering wheel a few more times. Eighty. Eighty-Five. A shimmy and thumping sound started at 93. It went away at 100, but came back at 110. The old gas-hog was doing what its creators intended it to do. One hundred twenty.

"Seven miles to the border," Amanda screamed, bouncing up and down in the passenger seat. "Look at this sucker go."

"He's gaining on us," Mitchell yelled, "Probably radioed ahead to stop us."

"What's at the border?"

"The Colorado River and the Arizona Fruit Inspection station. Sometimes they man it, sometimes they don't."

"Fruit inspection?"

"They don't want any California bugs in Arizona."

Behind them, the late-model patrol car lost traction for a few moments, drifting over the center line as if it were trying to go airborne. Amanda watched the cop fighting the wheel.

"Five miles to the border," she squealed.

The siren wailed like a banshee, its wild, red eyes spinning balefully in the desert night. Ahead, at a truck stop, a semi jockey started to pull out onto the macadam, spotted the road race, and changed his mind. The 120 miles-per-hour wind whipping around them, Mitchell and Amanda shivered almost as violently as the lumbering vehicle. A vibration thundered somewhere beneath them, accompanied by a bang-clang-rattle that sounded like an artillery attack.

"Two miles. Go, Mitchell."

The highway patrol car was five car lengths behind and the officer was shouting over the loudspeaker. "PULL OVER, IN THE NAME OF THE LAW. YOU'RE UNDER ARREST. PULL OVER NOW."

"One mile, Mitchell."

Mitchell stood on the gas pedal. Amanda pumped up the radio volume to hear Bon Jovi screaming about riding a steel horse. Sirens wailing, lights swirling, the desert shooting past in a blur, the two cars screamed neck and neck down the highway toward the Colorado River bridge.

"PULL OVER, YOU'RE UNDER ARREST, AND YOU'RE GOING TO JAIL."

"He's trying to do his job, but you're trying to save the world. Go, Mitchell, go." She pounded the dashboard and howled.

The highway patrol car swerved out of its lane and nearly sideswiped the Pontiac, amid the garbled roaring of "LONG-HAIRED FRUITCAKE. UNDER ARREST, YOU SON OF A . . ."

Amanda was standing up in the passenger seat, giving the officer the finger when the road dipped as it met the bridge. The Pontiac's cushiony shock absorbers stretched to the limit with a snap-shudder as the vehicle vaulted into the air, catapulting Amanda up into a somersault and slamming her down, spread-eagled on the hood, as the car careened onto the bridge at 124 miles per hour.

Her face pressed into a twisted distortion against the windshield, Amanda desperately grasped the windshield wipers and clamped her feet into the folds of the hood. As her Lakers jacket flapped like bumblebee wings, they shot across the Colorado River and through the empty Arizona Fruit Inspection station to freedom.

By the time Mitchell pulled off onto the shoulder of the road, the sound of the siren had faded beneath Bon Jovi's plaintive cry about being a concrete cowboy.

Mitchell stood up behind the steering wheel and leaned over the windshield to take Amanda's hand. "You were great!"

She mumbled something unintelligible and nodded.

He popped open the glove compartment, grabbed the flashlight, and vaulted out of the car.

"Muffler and tailpipe came loose," he yelled.

Amanda slid off the hood and landed on her butt in the dirt. She leaned back against the fender with a sigh.

Mitchell slid feet first under the vehicle and began kicking off what remained of the muffler system. When the job was done, he slid out, kissed Amanda on the lips, and said, "Let's go."

"Can I throw up first?" she asked.

Interstate 10 was a flat, straight, macadam line across the

Arizona desert, nothing on either side of the divided four-lane but sagebrush and cactus, coyotes and rattlesnakes. The barren stretch was hot in the day, cool at night, and frigid during the winter and spring.

Amanda cuddled into Mitchell for warmth, pulling her Lakers jacket tighter around her neck as they roared noisily down the highway, the open exhaust sounding like the souped-up machine Mitchell had dreamed of owning when he was sixteen years old.

Mitchell fantasized about writing a book on his Pheladian triangulations and the alien encounter he was going to experience. It would be a New Age bestseller, no doubt about it. He'd call it "Extraterrestrial Solutions." On the cover he envisioned his photo superimposed over a star map. The *National Enquirer* would probably buy serialization rights from the publisher. He wouldn't like that, but there was probably nothing he could do about it, and it would sell more books anyway. Maybe he could go out on the lecture circuit and conduct some seminars.

"I could be the next Shirley MacLaine," he yelled.

"What?" Amanda said, shivering.

"I'd put up the ragtop if I could, but I can't," he shouted.

"Why is the temperature needle laying over on hot?" Amanda yelled.

Mitchell pulled to the side of the highway and threw the shifter into park. He jerked the hand release beneath the dashboard, leaped out and popped the hood. A vaporous cloud of steam sizzled angrily into the air like a malevolent ghost. Mitchell jumped back.

"What can we do?" Amanda was standing up in the front seat, trying to peer around the massive, dented hood.

"Wait for it to cool down," Mitchell said, returning to the driver's door. "Then add fluid. What kind of liquid do we have on board?"

"A thermos of coffee and a six-pack of beer."

A car passed, momentarily flooding them in its high-beams, before disappearing into the moonlight shadows. An owl hooted. The desert wind moaned like fearful murmuring voices warning them not to go on.

"We could pee in it," Mitchell said.

"You're kidding."

"No, I'm not."

"It would be easier for you," she said.

They waited 15 minutes before removing the radiator cap and adding the coffee and beer. Mitchell personally contributed to the liquid level, but Amanda refused. "You'd tell everybody," she said.

At 20 miles per hour, it took them 30 minutes to reach Quartzsite, a town famous for its rock-hound swap meets and little else.

A generic gas station was open and a big, short-haired, barrel-chested man was working on a Harley in one of the bays. He was in his thirties and wearing a lumberjack shirt and Levi's.

Mitchell approached him cautiously. "My car was overheating out on the freeway."

The attendant didn't look up. "Could be the thermostat." His voice sounded like the bottom of a well.

Mitchell waited.

The attendant searched for a wrench, found it, loosened a bolt, whistled and said, "Could be a clogged core."

Mitchell waited.

The man patted the bike and sighed, then said, "Could be you were low on water."

As he stood up, he looked at Mitchell for the first time — a long intense look as if perceiving an alien species. "You from L.A.?"

"West Hollywood."

The attendant shook his head. "Well, let's take a look at your problem."

The problem turned out to be the thermostat. But the attendant didn't like the idea of beer and coffee in the cooling system. He insisted they flush the radiator and refill it with coolant. They didn't tell him about the pee.

Mitchell and Amanda sat on cases of motor oil, drinking Classic Cokes.

"Nine teaspoons of sugar," Amanda said, tapping the can. "I'm gonna be climbing the walls."

He nodded as he looked at the Pontiac up on the rack, dark fluid pouring out of the radiator into the catch pan.

"Do you really think the aliens could help resolve earth's problems?" Amanda asked.

"Sure," he replied. "If they've been monitoring us since Biblical times and before, they've been highly advanced for thousands of years. They've had time to find out what works and what doesn't."

Amanda nodded.

The hydraulic hoist hissed like a punctured balloon as it lowered the Pontiac slowly to the garage floor. The attendant poured several yellow plastic jugs of fluid into the radiator and took another ten minutes to figure the bill.

At 7:43 P.M. they were once again eating up the highway, roaring eastward through the desert night. The moonlight etched the lines of Mitchell's handsome cheekbones. Amanda studied his face. A palm-reading friend of hers called high cheekbones "the sure-fire sign of a flake." But Amanda's face-reading book said they signalled an adventurous personality.

She thought of Mitchell as a New Age Don Quixote, rushing madly at a twirling spaceship astride a 1975 Pontiac convertible. Weird? Sure. But cool weird. He not only cared about mankind's problems, he was doing something about them. The other guys she dated were only interested in sex, drugs, rock 'n roll, or the next football game. Hell, Mitchell had been an extra in five MTV videos. He had potential. He also talked a lot about writing a book.

When the right front tire blew out a half mile from the Tonopah exit, Mitchell pounded the steering wheel and shouted about negative forces trying to keep the world in darkness. They rode the rim the last few hundred yards to a 76 station.

"Ruined the rim," said a watery-eyed, pot-bellied attendant. He had thinning red hair and an alcoholic nose, and wore bib overalls and a sweat-stained T-shirt. He spit.

"I've got to get to Phoenix," Mitchell pleaded.

"Don't you have a spare?" asked the man.

"I don't remember. Trunk doesn't open."

The man ambled to the back of the car, looked and grunted. He walked into the garage bay, picked up a crowbar, and sauntered back to the trunk. *Scrunch-h-h-h.* It popped open. "There's your spare," he said, and spit some more. He felt the spare.

"Flat," he said.

"Can you fix it?" Mitchell asked.

"Five dollars."

"Fine."

Sitting on the cement island between the unleaded and super unleaded pumps, beneath the eerie illumination of the sodium-vapor lights, Mitchell and Amanda watched the attendant work on the tire.

Amanda said, "You don't really believe evil forces are working against us, do you?"

"Seems like it."

"But your headlight was already out, the radiator thermostat was rusted shut, the trunk lock was broken, and the tires are bald."

"Considering our mission, the positive powers of the universe should be helping us to rise above such trivial concerns."

"Does it work that way?"

"It should."

"You mean when your intentions are pure, the universe is supposed to support you?"

"Yeah."

"Then why did the universe let Christ get nailed to a cross?"

Mitchell looked at her blankly. "I guess it works in mysterious ways."

The attendant freed the repaired tire, lifted it and let it bounce to the pavement.

Amanda looked at her watch. "We still have time. We're going to make it, Mitchell."

They arrived at the Black Canyon Freeway on the western side of Phoenix at 10:47 P.M. Studying the map, Amanda navigated them through the city streets into Scottsdale.

"There it is," Mitchell said in awe, looking at the black outline of the camel-shaped mountain against the purple, star-splattered sky.

Amanda plotted a route through neighborhood streets, past multimillion-dollar homes, up the north face of Camelback.

"We'll have to hike from here," she said as they came to the end of the road.

Mitchell jerked on the emergency break, snapped off the ignition and leaped out. "How much time?"

"Twenty minutes," Amanda yelled. "Rock-and-roll!"

Carrying flashlights, they began to climb the well-marked trail. The moonlight tossed oily shadows across their path, exaggerating distances and projecting grotesque shapes.

Leading the way, Mitchell climbed through a crevice and stepped off the path into cactus.

"Ah-a-a-a."

"What?" Amanda shrieked.

By the time she was through the crevice, Mitchell was crouched over, trying to resolve the painful mistake. "Oh-h-h-h, shit," he bellowed, standing up with clumps of cactus dangling from his hands.

"Don't move, Mitchell," she waved the flashlight back and forth. "It's cholla—jumping cactus."

"Jumping? It attacked when I tried to get it off my shoes and pant legs."

"Probably a manifestation of the evil forces that are trying to stop us," she laughed.

"Amanda!"

"Do you have a handkerchief?"

"In my right hip pocket."

Amanda found the handkerchief and lightly wrapped it around the cactus on his right hand. "Hold still," she said, jerking the clump free.

"Jeeze," he moaned as it came off.

Amanda placed the cactus on a rock, the flashlight on top of it and freed the handkerchief. "Other hand."

"I've never seen anything like this in my life," he said, trying to bite the remaining spines out of his hand. "Do they really jump?"

"The spines are needle thin with tiny hooks that attach at the slightest touch."

"How do you know all this?" he asked, wincing as she freed the clump from his other hand.

"My mother's dog got into it in Mexico."

At 11:58 P.M. they reached the crest of the mountain, gasping for breath. Mitchell was still pulling cactus spines from his hands.

"We did it. We did it," they screamed in unison, hugging each other and dancing a little impromptu quick-step. Below them lights spread out in every direction, bordered by the blackness of the mountains circling the valley. Above them was the three-quarter moon and a million stars.

193

11:59.

"I don't see anything," Amanda said.

"They'll be here," Mitchell assured her.

12:00 midnight.

"Oh. Oh. Oh, shit," Amanda whispered as a huge circular object shimmered into view several hundred feet above the mountain.

"Wave your arms. Shine the flashlights," Mitchell yelled at Amanda. At the top of his lungs, he bellowed, "We're here. We knew you were coming. Take us aboard."

"Bullshit, Mitchell. Shut up. I don't want to be taken aboard," Amanda shouted, her eyes big and fearful. Her heart hammered, and she was holding her breath as the taste of vomit crawled up into her throat.

"It's why we're here, you ninny," Mitchell sputtered.

"But I didn't believe it was going to happen," Amanda whimpered. Doing her best to assume a fetal position on the ground, she looked through the crook of her raised arm at Mitchell and the ship above him. "I just wanted an excuse to be with you, Mitchell."

A huge, whining, spinning, circular monstrosity suspended above them, the ship was as big as a city. It was like every science fiction movie Mitchell had ever seen—a massive interstellar spaceship hovering over a tiny earthbound man. And woman.

Stepping over Amanda, Mitchell flailed his arms, spinning the flashlight beam in circles, calling out to the aliens to be taken aboard.

Small white lights lined the outer rim of the craft, while on the base two great blue lights appeared as eyes, watching. Then a beam of light sizzled out of the center of the spaceship, bathing the mountaintop in intense illumination. One moment they were looking at the wonder above them, the next they were encased in a clear, swirling circular chamber that slowed and stopped before a group of unusual-looking beings.

Amanda quivered at Mitchell's feet, pallid, wild-eyed and trembling. Her arm over her face, she peeked at the aliens and said, "I'm going to throw up."

"Don't puke, Amanda. It might piss them off," Mitchell's voice was resolute as he smiled at the aliens, an exaggerated, ass-kissing grimace that appeared frozen on his face.

The aliens' color was ivory and they had no hair. Their eyes were large, feral orbs that glowed in reflected light. They had no discernible noses; they had holes for ears and their mouths were thin slits. They were dressed alike in olive-green robes, each collar of a different color.

In the top of the chamber something clicked, whirred, and hissed. A blue cloud of translucent steam swirled into the capsule. Amanda started to scream and decided instead to hold her breath.

"I think they're just decontaminating us, Amanda," Mitchell said, when he saw her face turning red. He helped her to her feet.

"With what, DDT?" she muttered.

The walls of the cylinder parted and buzzed as they slid open. One of the aliens said, "Step out, please." A weird wheezing sound accompanied the words.

"You speak English?" Mitchell said, stepping into the kaleidoscope of lights and screens, dials and buttons.

One of the aliens bowed in response.

"We knew you were coming. We were waiting for you."

"This way, please," said a blue-collared one.

They followed him through a doorway, into a room that looked to Mitchell like an operating room or medical laboratory.

"Undress, please," said the alien, pointing a long bony finger at Mitchell, then at Amanda.

"Why?" Amanda demanded. "What are you going to

do?"

"Undress, please."

Amanda leaned forward and looked into the alien's glowing eyes. "No," she said, calmly but firmly.

The alien shuffled to a cluster of instruments mounted on a panel, extracted something resembling a dentist drill, and pressed a button that shot a sizzling blue needle of flame five feet across the room. "Undress, please."

Mitchell and Amanda undressed and stood holding hands awaiting the next directive. "They probably just want to run a few tests to see what makes us tick."

"Why us?" Amanda tried to control her quavering voice.

"Because we were the ones who were smart enough to figure out where they would appear," he said proudly.

Three more blue-collared aliens entered the room and motioned Mitchell and Amanda to lie down side by side on two examining tables.

Mitchell figured they were probably blood tested, brain scanned, tissue sampled, and X-rayed. Each of the four examiners had in turn scrutinized Mitchell's penis; picking in up, letting it flop over, squeezing it. When he started getting an erection, it caused quite a furor among the aliens. But then Amanda said, "For crisssake, Mitchell," in a disgusted tone and it shrank back to normal. He could tell the aliens were disappointed.

They were communicating amongst themselves in their own language, which to Mitchell and Amanda sounded more like wheezes and grunts than words.

"Mate," said one of the aliens.

"Huh?"

The alien tickled Mitchell's penis with one hand and Amanda's vagina with the other.

"Not in front of you guys," Amanda said, sitting up on the examining table. "There's a limit."

"Mate," said another, picking up the flame-throwing dental drill.

"Jeeze, Mitchell. We better do it."

"I don't know that I can," he replied, fear in his voice for the first time.

"Come on over here, I'll help," she said.

Mitchell climbed off his examining table and sat down beside Amanda on hers. She placed her hand on his penis.

"We could be at the China Club right now, Mitchell, listening to heavy metal, getting loaded, maybe slipping out to the parking lot to do this. This is only the fifth time we've done it, you know?"

"The talk isn't helping," Mitchell said, looking at the four aliens gathered in a semi-circle around them, watching intently.

"But no," Amanda continued. "Instead we're probably somewhere between Mars and Jupiter putting on a sex show for extraterrestrial perverts." She stopped and looked at his penis. "You're not trying, Mitchell."

"I'm too nervous," he whimpered.

"Oh, cripes." She climbed off the table. "Close your eyes and pretend we're someplace else," she said.

The aliens wheezed and grunted. Mitchell sighed.

"Now that's more like it," she said, climbing back on the table and lying down. "Show time, big boy."

Without looking at the aliens, Mitchell quickly lowered himself into Amanda with a pleasurable moan. She smiled, winked and thrust her hips, driving him deeper into her body. "Intergalactic kink," she said, holding him tightly, burying her face into his neck, biting his ear lobe, matching his thrusts and rhythm.

Mitchell came with a joyful moan, and the aliens applauded. After collecting samples of his semen from his spent penis, and running a test on Amanda, the four exited the room leaving the couple alone.

"Mitchell, do you think they'll let us go?"

"I think they admire us," he said.

"Yeah, but will they let us go?"

The door opened and an orange-collared alien stepped into the room. "Get dressed, Toseka wants to see you." He bowed slightly, then stood at attention, waiting.

Mitchell and Amanda followed him through a series of hallways, down a metallic walkway, and into a cone-shaped device. The alien then touched a light on the wall panel and they accelerated upward in an extended whoosh. The doors opened into a small circular room, ringed with round, porthole-like windows—the apex of the spacecraft.

"Welcome," said a figure seated in a throne-like chair in the center of the room. "My name is Toseka." He looked like the others but the collar of his robe radiated a shimmering golden light.

"I'm Mitchell. This is Amanda, my girlfriend." Mitchell raised his hand in greeting.

"Please sit down," Toseka said. "I am the starship commander." The other alien stepped back into the elevator and the doors slid closed.

Couches lined walls that emitted a pale illumination. Mitchell and Amanda sat facing Toseka.

"Tell me how you knew we would be arriving at this precise place, at this precise time?" Toseka asked.

"Yes, sir," Mitchell beamed, and began to explain the complicated procedure of triangulation, using historical sightings and ancient writings as reference points.

Amanda remained silent, unable to stop trembling.

"Yes, yes," Toseka said. "You have no idea how much we value such intelligence. I travel the universe in search of this kind of intelligence."

"Thank you, sir," Mitchell said, before nervously saying, "I wonder if I could ask you some important questions?"

"What kind of questions?"

"How to resolve earth's primary problems."

"We are an intellectual race," Toseka replied. "We attempt to resolve all problems as quickly and efficiently as possible."

"For the greater good?" Mitchell asked.

"How do you define greater good?" Toseka asked.

"As promoting humanitarian harmony and serving the needs of the planet," Mitchell said.

"Serving the masses," Toseka said. "Yes."

"Yes," Mitchell nodded, his expression euphoric.

"We're in agreement, then," Toseka nodded. "What is your first question?"

"Amanda and I are from Los Angeles. Crime is out of control. People live in fear. The prisons are overflowing. No matter what the authorities do, it gets worse. How can we resolve it?"

"Terminate all criminals."

Mitchell looked at Toseka, then at Amanda, then back to the alien. "No, I mean . . ."

"I assume you currently protect the rights of the individual?" Toseka said. Mitchell nodded. Toseka continued, "But eventually most civilizations realize that this doesn't serve the greater good. You must protect the masses from the few individuals who threaten their security."

"But you can't just kill them," Mitchell protested.

Toseka tilted his head to the side and looked at Mitchell. "Don't assume crime is a disease to be treated. It must be prevented. When released from prison, criminals become repeat offenders, so it isn't logical to return them to the streets. And why should a society drain its wealth to support prisons? Some planets mentally neutralize wrongdoers, but then they have to support the husks that remain. Termination is the best deterrent to crime, and it serves the greater good."

Mitchell's mouth dropped open. He decided to pursue

another line of questioning. "We have a terrible drug problem on earth. How can we resolve it?"

"Terminate the dealers and users. The problem will be resolved in six months. It's the only logical way."

"No, no, we couldn't do that," Mitchell protested.

"I thought you were concerned about the greater good," Toseka said.

"Yes, but . . ."

"The logical, intellectual approach to a problem is to resolve it quickly and efficiently. The moment you realize one solution isn't working, move to a more extreme solution. Hesitation compromises the greater good. You can waste decades unsuccessfully trying to rehabilitate those addicted to their poisons. Instead, resolve the problem by simply eliminating those who cause it."

"What about the innocent people who would be killed along with the guilty?" Mitchell stammered.

"Why worry about a few in proportion to the greater good of the masses?" Toseka asked, apparently unable to relate to Mitchell's concerns. "It isn't logical."

"Well, what about AIDS?" Mitchell asked. "It's a sexually transmitted plague. Now don't tell me you'd terminate incurable AIDS patients?"

"Will your people stop fornicating indiscriminately?"

"No."

"Then the logical solution is mandatory testing of everyone on the planet and isolation of all carrying the disease."

"Like a leper colony?" Mitchell said.

"That way the masses can only fornicate with healthy beings," Toseka replied. "How long does it take for the disease to run its course?"

"About ten years."

"Then in ten years the problem will be resolved for the greater good."

"Your solutions are inhumane," Mitchell sputtered.

"No. To put the well-being of the many above the interests of the few is most humane. Maybe ten thousand are served and one isn't," Toseka said. "Your way, no one is served but the perpetrator of the problem. Everyone else lives in fear." He slowly shook his head. "Pheladians have no problems with crime, drugs or plague."

Mitchell responded with anger. "Maybe sometimes an individual's needs should come before the greater good."

"I agree," Toseka said. "As a Pheladian starship commander I increase my intelligence by ingesting the most intelligent species in the universe. Their wisdom then becomes my own. It may detract from the greater good of your planet, but it serves the greater good of all Pheladians by assuring a wise individual commander."

"Ingesting? You mean eating?" Mitchell stammered, his voice clotted with fear.

"For the greater good," Toseka said, smiling. "But don't worry. We'll release Amanda to share this wisdom with the others of your planet. And she now carries your seed so in time your intelligence, embodied in your child, will continue to serve the greater good of your people."

The alien pressed a button on the arm of his chair and the floor directly beneath him began to open like a giant lens. "I'll give you time to say your goodbyes," Toseka said as he descended. The lens closed and they were alone.

"Oh, Mitchell," Amanda cried, throwing her arms around her lover. "Maybe the positive powers of the universe were using your car to try to save you," she said, sadly.

Holding each other tightly, they looked out the window of the great starship to see the heavens shooting past. Mitchell realized they were in deep space, hurtling toward some distant planet in the Pheladian system he wouldn't live to see.

"Tell the world and tell our kid," he whispered bravely,

blinking back tears gathering in the corners of his eyes.

"I promise," she said.

They held each other, crying. They wondered about the karma of it all. He asked her to memorize goodbye messages to his parents and friends. He gave her the keys to the Pontiac.

As he waited for Toseka to return, Mitchell imagined the headline on the front page of a supermarket tabloid:

**"Aliens Propose Plans
for Greater Good Before
Eating the Father of
Her Unborn Child!"**

AURIC LIGHT

Relentlessly driving rain rattled the window casings. Lightning sizzled out of the cloud-plated sky. Mortar-like explosions of thunder rumbled along the main street of Clammet Cove like an enemy invasion.

Denton awakened remembering Vietnam. He stared at the grey film of rain rippling down the window, blurring the November morning. He closed his eyes, saw the firefight, felt the shrapnel pierce his head, felt the blood-wet grass, and watched the greyness seep into a black void.

He opened his eyes to escape the impressions. His eyes wouldn't focus.

The alarm clock read 66:4488AAMM.

He blinked and shook his head to clear his vision. His head felt as if something had come loose inside. Nausea forced him out of bed and into the bathroom where he crouched over the toilet in queasy expectation. Nothing. He stood up and leaned against the medicine cabinet, wincing at the reflection in the mirror. He shook his head again to clear his vision. The image didn't change. Around his shoulder-length dark hair was a shimmering aura of yellow light that faded into a vivid pink as it neared his neck. Behind him was an intense white light. Denton looked over his shoulder to see where the reflection was coming from but saw only the shower stall and a towel hanging over the door.

He looked into the mirror again. The nausea and dizziness were diminishing, but the light around his head seemed to be intensifying. He splashed cold water in his face and stood up to look sideways into the mirror. *Yellow and pink.*

Clean shirts were hanging in the closet. He rented the room from Katrina Rennell and paid her teenage daughter, Alicia, fifteen dollars a week to wash and iron his clothes.

Tucking his shirt into his Levi's, he padded barefooted down the stairs. The enticing aroma of baking biscuits and fresh-brewed coffee led him into the kitchen. Katrina was sitting at the table in the center of the room, preparing breakfast.

"Katrina, look at my head. Do you see anything strange?"

"Did you get a haircut?" Katrina looked up from peeling potatoes. She was a stocky, middle-aged German widow, grey-haired and stoic. She and her daughter lived on the room and board from five guest rooms in the Victorian house by the sea.

"I'm not glowing or anything, am I?"

"At the Surf Club last night, Denton?" she asked and smiled. "Better sober up." She pointed at the coffee urn.

He took a mug from the cupboard, filled it and sat down across the table from his landlady, curling his feet under him in the chair. The cozy kitchen was a warm contrast to the cold rain splattering heavily against the windows. On the counter sat a vase of purple blossoms that would later be used as a dining room table centerpiece. Somehow, even in November, Katrina managed to display fresh flowers. The kitchen reminded Denton of his childhood; he felt comfortable here. The cherry cabinetry and wainscoted cupboards offset the stripped maple floors. The windows, bracketed with blue and white swag curtains, looked out on the rain-swept garden.

"You don't look too good, Denton," Katrina said.

He smiled meekly.

"Hi, Denton. Hi, Mama." Alicia said, hurrying into the kitchen, adjusting a bulky white sweater over her black wool skirt. Dropping her school books on the table, she crossed the room to the counter and popped two slices of bread into the toaster. "I heard you typing away on your book until the wee hours," she said to Denton, as she sat down at the table with a carton of milk in one hand and a glass in the other.

"Hope I didn't keep you up," he replied.

"I was studying for my math test." She finished pouring the milk with a flourish and set the carton on the table. For the first time she looked closely at Denton. She squinted her eyes and looked again. "I swear, your aura's showing." She stood up, leaned across the table and waved her hand back and forth about six inches above his head.

"Alicia!" Katrina snapped.

"Well, look at him, mom. Yellow on top and all pink down here." She fluffed the ends of her blonde shoulder-length hair.

"You see it, too?" Denton asked, relief in his voice.

"I don't see a thing," Katrina said, squinting at Denton. "I think you're both a bit blippy this morning."

"I can't usually see auras," Alicia said matter-of-factly as she buttered her toast. "But my friend Buffy can. Her mom's a psychic and she taught her how."

"You act like this is normal," Denton said.

"Everybody has an aura, but most people can't see them. You must be real spiritual today or something."

Denton looked blankly at the teenager.

"Buffy's mom could tell you about it. She runs the health food store at Temple and Main."

"You're both nuts," Katrina said, shredding potatoes for

hash browns.

"If you're spiritual, how about making my headache go away?" Alicia joked. "I didn't get enough sleep."

Denton laughed.

"No, Denton. Do it. Touch my head and make it go away."

Quiet footsteps approached the kitchen. Ruth Foster, a retired schoolteacher, entered the room, hands tucked into her quilted bathrobe.

Denton put his left hand on Alicia's head and made a silly buzzing sound. "E.T. says your headache is healed," he said.

Alicia swooned drunkenly in her chair. "Jeeeze, man." She shook her head and looked at Denton as if he were a stranger.

"Alicia," her mother chided. "Quit playing games and get ready to go to school."

"No games, Mom." She started to get up and fell back into the chair. "My headache's gone but he zapped every ounce of energy right along with it." On the second try she stood up, gathered her books, and again looked at Denton warily. "Thanks. I mean it." She kissed her mother on the cheek and was gone.

"Take an umbrella," Katrina called after her.

"Well, if you have healing energy, Denton, I would certainly appreciate a shot in my knees," Ruth Foster said, sitting down in the chair Alicia had vacated. A tall, thin woman with short grey hair and a warm personality, her presence assured lively mealtime conversations about world events rather than idle gossip. Denton liked her.

"Alicia was just horsing around," Denton said, shrugging his shoulders.

"Maybe, maybe not," Ruth said, sipping her coffee. "Please."

"Miss Foster, I'm just a detective story writer, I can't

heal anybody."

"Please," she said. "They hurt so much all the time, anything's worth a try."

He looked into her pleading eyes and noticed her trembling hands. He shrugged again, smiling sheepishly, and placed both hands on her knees. This time he did not make a silly noise, but instead concentrated on Ruth's knees. He imagined a healing warmth building up within and sent it racing down his arms into his hands.

"Oh . . . oh . . . my, oh, my," Ruth moaned and fell back in the chair. She held one hand to her forehead. Her eyes glazed. "Oh, thank you, God."

Katrina shook her head, stood up, walked to the gas stove and turned it on. Still watching Denton and Ruth, she poured oil into a cast iron skillet. When the oil hissed and popped, she added the shredded potatoes.

"Are you all right, Ruth?" Katrina asked casually as she cracked eggs into a bowl.

"The pain is gone. It is. Oh, blessed be." She held her hands to her chest and took a deep, disbelieving breath.

"Oh, come on, Ruth. You're not serious," Denton said.

Tears spilled out of Ruth's eyes and Denton knew she was. "Ten years. That's how long they've been hurting. Ten years." She smiled at him as if he were the savior himself.

Denton shivered as though chilled by the November rain. He got up slowly, smiled at Katrina and Ruth and hurried out of the kitchen, back up the stairs to his room.

The windshield wipers snapped back and forth at the highest speed in a vain attempt to provide a clear view of the roadway. Denton hunched forward over the wheel of his Bronco II, berating himself for coming out on a day like this.

Main Street ran parallel to the beach for twelve blocks.

He stopped at the red light. CLAMMET COVE—POPULA-TION 1828, said the sign arching over the street above the central stoplight. The quiet coastal town was Denton's hideaway. It offered the peace and seclusion that he couldn't find in Los Angeles, 300 miles south.

He had written his two earlier novels at Katrina's boarding house, and both had sold well. The house was good luck. The third novel would be finished by Christmas.

Denton parked in front of Mother Nature's Health Food Store and turned off the motor. He hesitated before opening the door. What was he going to say to this woman? He knew little about psychics and cared even less. *So why are you here?* He finally decided to simply go into the store, browse around and see if she noticed his glow.

Entering the store set a windchime tinkling. Though the distance from his car to the door had only been a dozen feet, he was drenched. He stood in the entrance way and shook the water off his poncho. A woman studying a computer printout looked up from the checkout counter. Denton figured she was his age, thirty-five. A straight-haired blonde in a long, print dress, she was pretty in a natural sort of way. *Buffy's mom,* he thought.

"Hi," she said. "Can I help you?"

"Vitamin C?" he said.

"Second aisle, top shelf on the right." She pointed.

Denton was overwhelmed by the varieties and dosages of Vitamin C. After choosing a bottle of acid-free 1,000 milligram tablets, he strolled casually around the store looking at displays of herbs, grains, natural shampoos, and self-help books and tapes. He glanced out the window at the pyrotechnic display of lightning over the sea. A long roll of thunder rattled the walls of the store.

"Not many people out today," he said, setting the bottle on the counter.

"You'll probably be my only customer." Her penetrating

blue eyes crossed the distance between them. "Is this to fight off a cold?" she asked, tapping the bottle of Vitamin C.

"Ah, yes."

"It will be more effective if you take it with zinc and beta carotene."

"Really? Then I'll take some of those too. Thank you."

Buffy's mother left and quickly returned with two small bottles. She punched the cash register. "$13.28," she said.

He handed her a twenty dollar bill.

"Are you just passing through Clammet Cove?" she asked, counting out the change.

"I'm staying at Katrina Rennell's boarding house. Hiding away to work on a book."

"Really? What kind of book?"

"A novel," he said. "A fast-action thriller—cops, blood-and-guts."

She nodded. "My daughter goes to school with Alicia Rennell."

"Yes. Well, actually, that's why I'm here. Not that I didn't need the Vitamin C, but . . ." he stammered and felt his face flush. "Well, Alicia told me you're a psychic and you can read auras."

She smiled. "Yours is a beautiful yellow and fades into pink at your shoulders. I wouldn't expect a blood-and-guts writer to have such a nice aura."

"Do thriller writers usually have ugly auras?" he asked.

She laughed. "I'm sorry. I didn't mean it that way. It's just that if you focus your energy on writing about violence, I would expect a muddy aura." She shrugged.

"To tell the truth, I don't think I've ever had an aura before this morning. When I looked in the mirror, there it was."

"You've always had an aura, but if you've never seen it before and you can see it now, that is unusual." She looked at him differently, her piercing eyes seeming slightly unfocused as she stared at the bridge of his nose. After a few moments she said, "There's a darker area right here." She touched his hair a couple inches above his left ear.

"I was hit there by shrapnel, in Nam. The metal is still there."

She nodded. "I'm brewing a pot of herbal tea. Would you like a cup?"

"I'm not interrupting?"

"You're a welcome interruption." She flipped the corner of the computer printout. "Reordering is boring."

"I'm Denton Garret," he said, extending his hand.

"Joan McIntyre," she said, accepting it.

As they settled down comfortably, teapot on the counter between them, Denton told her about his morning—the dream, the dizziness, and the shock of seeing himself in the mirror. After explaining the unusual healings, he asked her about herself. She was divorced and had moved from Berkeley to the Cove five years ago. She lived with her daughter, three cats and a Great Dane named Lord Bowser in an A-frame in the mountains overlooking the town.

After she satisfied his curiosity, she asked her own personal questions.

"Never married. I attended UCLA on the G.I. Bill after the war and learned to write. Worked as a reporter for the *L.A. Times* for six years, until I'd saved enough money to devote a year to fiction. My first novel was made into a TV movie. I don't imagine you read cop thrillers?"

"Sorry," she said. "There's just too much violence in the world." She looked away for a moment. "Your first love is poetry. You've written a poetry book, but it hasn't been published."

Denton stared at her in amazement then shut his mouth and grinned. "I've never known anyone who was psychic."

"Are you willing to try an experiment?" she asked.

"Sure. What?"

"I'd like to test your healing ability, and maybe do some well-deserved good."

"Joan, I . . ."

"Come on. I'll leave a note on the door. A helper will be here in a half hour. She'll cover the store." Joan had on her raincoat and was belting it.

"Where are we going?"

"Up in the hills. It won't take long." She smiled warmly and nodded reassuringly.

Turning left off Main Street onto State Route 156, it took ten minutes to reach the tall pines in Denton's Bronco II. They had to speak loud to be heard over the roar of the storm. Rain drummed on the hood and roof of the vehicle. The windshield wipers whipped frantically. The tires hissed noisily, throwing water into the wheel wells. After nearly hydroplaning on a curve, Denton switched into four-wheel drive.

"I've never been up here," he said. "It's beautiful."

"I live up here," Joan said. "Turn left at the next cross road."

"Who are we going to see?" he asked.

"An old man who has devoted his life to serving the planet. Now he's sick and refuses to turn to traditional medicine."

"What's wrong with him?"

"I don't know. He won't say. He buys vitamins and herbs at the store. Buffy and I check on him regularly."

"Can he take care of himself?"

Joan nodded. "He's a vegetarian and grows all his own food."

Denton turned off the main road and onto a narrow access road that wound higher into the mountains.

"There," Joan said. "Turn there."

Hidden in a clearing in a tall strand of pine trees was a log cabin. Wood smoke curled out of the chimney into the downpour. Denton pulled up beside a vintage Ford pickup parked a few feet from the front porch.

"We'll jump out and run on the count of three," Joan said, her hand on the door handle. "One, two, three."

They leaped from the vehicle and bolted onto the front porch. Laughing excitedly, they shook the rain from their coats. They inhaled the exhilarating smell of the woods and the burning fireplace.

Lightning stabbed out of the cloud-shrouded sky and struck nearby. Denton had never experienced such an intense electrical storm. When the thunder exploded like a fragmenting hand grenade, he could feel the metal in his skull vibrate in response.

Joan knocked. When no one answered the door, she twisted the knob and pushed it open a few inches.

"Jacob," she called.

"Come in," said a frail voice.

The interior of the rough looking mountain cabin looked like a library. Floor-to-ceiling bookshelves lined two walls of the large main room. A stone fireplace covered most of the third wall, and glowing embers popped and crackled behind a screen. Above the fireplace hung photos and certificates, and on the mantel were several trophies. Colorful Mexican serapes featuring Aztec designs covered a comfortable-looking couch, and the coffee table was made of hand-hewn wooden planks. Two Adirondak-style wooden chairs with plump cushions sat side by side, facing the couch. In the corner of the room was a simple kitchen. A stained-glass Tiffany lamp hung over a small wooden kitchen table and four chairs.

"Wait here," Joan said. "Jacob?" she called again, stepping through a doorway in the wall of books.

Denton took off his poncho and hung it on a hook by the door, next to a man's jacket and raincoat.

Fascinated, he was drawn to the pictures above the fireplace. In the first photo a man stood beside John F. Kennedy. The photo was signed, "To Jacob, who makes me look good. Thanks, Jack." In the next 8 x 10 the same man was with Adlai Stevenson. A framed certificate said, "Humanitarian Award for outstanding service to the world community." Denton was about to read the small print when he noticed the gold medallion on the mantel. The Nobel Prize. He read the inscription. "Awarded to Jacob Levitz, 1968."

"Denton," Joan called from the doorway. "Please, come in."

Denton entered the small bedroom to see an old man with a mane of shaggy white hair, lying propped up in bed. A quilted comforter covered his legs. In his lap was a notebook on a clipboard. The open page was nearly filled with handwriting. A brass lamp with a yellowed shade sat on a small bedside table. On the other side of the bed was a wooden chair.

"Jacob Levitz, this is Denton Garret. Denton is a writer and maybe a healer. Jacob is . . ."

Denton interrupted Joan's introduction. "I know who Mister Levitz is," he said, smiling.

"I wish I could greet you properly, young man," Jacob said, feebly extending his hand. "But I'm afraid this isn't one of my better days."

"It's an honor, sir." Denton replied, taking the old man's hand and gently cupping it between his.

"Joan wants me to let you heal me. I've explained that I'm too far gone for such an ambitious undertaking. I do, however appreciate your willingness to go along with her. She can be quite persuasive." He smiled.

Joan touched Denton on the arm and gestured for him to take the bedside chair. She sat on the edge of the bed.

"Jacob is writing his eighteenth book. It's about education, and it will attract worldwide attention."

"Joan is my biggest fan. She's not very objective."

"Poppycock," she said. "Things won't change until all the children are educated."

"How's the book coming?" Denton asked.

"Slowly. My body is not cooperating."

"He spent four years gathering research," Joan said.

"I don't mean to be morbid, but you and I have to accept the fact that this book won't make it to print," Jacob said to Joan.

"Yes, it will. Denton is going to heal you."

Jacob started to protest, but Joan made a slicing motion with her hand, symbolically cutting off any further discussion. Denton's eyes met Jacob's. They smiled in mutual resignation. Joan stood up to make room for Denton to take her place on the bed. "I'll wait in the other room," she said.

Ten minutes later Denton joined Joan on the couch in the living room. "He's sleeping."

Joan looked at him in expectation. "Joan, I don't have the faintest idea what's going on. I don't know anything about psychic abilities, auras, or healings. When I healed Alicia's headache and Ruth's knees, it weakened them momentarily. The healing put Jacob to sleep."

"Could you use a drink?" she asked.

"Yeah," he said, smiling into her ultramarine eyes.

"Jacob's not much of a drinker, but he likes a nip of Scotch now and then." She took a bottle and a glass from the cupboard.

"How do you know him?" he asked.

"When I opened the store, he was my first customer. He walked in that morning and said, 'It's about time.' " She looked out the kitchen window and noticed that the rain was letting up.

"Tell me what you're not telling me," Denton said, as she handed him the glass of whiskey. He was surprised at how attracted he was to this woman.

"In the store, when you were telling me about the heal-ings, I heard Jacob's name so loud it sounded as if someone were screaming in my ear. I knew I had to bring you here." She shrugged. "That's it."

"A psychic message from beyond?" he questioned.

"From somewhere," she said.

"Where else could it have been from?"

"From my Higher Self—maybe yours, maybe Jacob's— or a spirit guide or a Master."

Denton shook his head. "I have a lot to learn."

"Not unless it's important to you," she said, taking a log from the box on the hearth and adding it to the dying fire. The thin cotton dress clung to her body, clearly outlining it against the firelight. Warmth flooded though Denton's body. She returned to the couch and curled up beside him.

"Events are not as random as they appear," she said.

"I don't understand."

"Everything that has happened to you today has hap-pened for a reason." She took his left hand in hers, and stroked it with her other hand. Neither said anything. Final-ly she whispered, "The power went away with the storm."

Denton looked at her in surprise.

"I don't know," she said. "Somehow, I think your healing power was related to the storm."

"That's okay," he said, sounding relieved. "I didn't really want to change professions."

She laughed, then her expression turned serious. "I also sense a sadness from long ago."

"An Englishwoman I met in Vietnam. We were engaged. She was killed. I wanted to die but couldn't."

Joan continued to stroke the back of his hand.

Denton looked into the fireplace to see the new log be-gin to flame. He said, "When you open to love, you're vulnerable. You can lose everything you care about in one mortar attack or one auto accident."

"But if you aren't vulnerable, you'll never experience your potential for joy and commitment." Joan said.

"My, my, what an attractive couple you two make," Jacob Levitz said, walking into the room. He wore tan duck pants, a wool sweater and loafers. "Thank you, my boy. I don't know what you did, but I haven't felt this good in months."

Joan leaped to her feet and threw her arms around the old man, kissing him over and over on the cheek. He laughed and said, "Enough of this emotionalism. I'll fix you lunch."

"You will do no such thing," Joan said. "Sit down." She directed him into one of the chairs.

Jacob looked at Denton and said, "She always knows what is best for everyone else. If you don't know that, I have a feeling you're going to find out."

"I just met Denton this morning," Joan said from the kitchen.

Jacob smiled knowingly and said, "Then this is a very important day for each of us, isn't it?" Neither Denton or Joan responded. Jacob looked at Denton. "I can tell by the length of your hair that you don't write for the establishment."

Denton chuckled. "Cop thrillers, and for the first time I'm embarrassed to say it." He looked across the room at Joan tearing lettuce for a salad.

"Why?" asked Jacob. "Don't your characters grow as a result of their conflicts?"

Denton nodded and said, "And the good guys win."

Jacob laughed. "I predict that within the year Joan will have you beating your characters' swords into plows and setting out to save the planet."

"Jacob, I'm going to put salt on your salad," Joan said, in a threatening tone of voice.

✦ ✦ ✦

In the days that followed, the people of Clammet Cove came to Katrina's boardinghouse in search of Denton. He always took the time to explain that the pyrotechnics of the storm had interacted with the shrapnel fragment in his head, somehow channeling the healing power for a few hours.

"But won't you try to heal me?" they would beg.

Denton would sit down with them and attempt to channel the power. When it didn't work he apologized, and they thanked him.

Joan said, "The community will soon accept that you're no longer a healer. But you'd better run for the hills the next time lightning strikes Clammet Cove."

Over a candlelight dinner on their fourth date, Denton said, "You realize that I can't get enough of you?"

She smiled, looking deeply into his eyes. "I feel like a schoolgirl."

The waiter arrived at the table with the wine. Denton tasted it, looked at Joan and nodded his approval. When the wine was poured he lifted his glass for a toast. "To our future."

"To our future," she said, clicking her glass with his.

"Are you sure you want a future with a psychic health food fanatic, a teenager, three cats, and a Great Dane?"

"The Great Dane is cause for some concern," he said. "He doesn't seem to like my intrusion into his life."

"Lord Bowser will adjust," she laughed. "Buffy and the cats are almost as enchanted with you as I am. Five out of six isn't bad."

He nodded, smiled and finished the glass of wine. "What would you like to do for Thanksgiving?"

"Fix you the most incredible vegetarian feast you've ever eaten."

"No turkey?" he asked.

"No turkey," she said. "You won't miss it, believe me. Let's invite Jacob. Maybe we can get him to stop writing his book long enough to sit down to a full meal."

Light snow dusted the mountain landscape around the A-frame on Christmas morning. Joan and Denton sat on the hearth to the side of the crackling fire. Buffy was curled up on the couch drinking eggnog. Jacob relaxed in the lounger chair with Lord Bowser's head in his lap.

"Has this overgrown excuse for a dog accepted you yet, Denton?" Jacob asked.

Joan answered for Denton. "Denton and Bowser have an understanding."

Buffy laughed.

"Yeah," Denton said, "I bring him bones from the butcher shop and in return he doesn't bite me."

Jacob chuckled and said, "Denton, Joan's always been beautiful, but never as radiant as she's become lately. I hope you're willing to take responsibility for that."

"Well, it just so happens," Denton said, pulling a small gift-wrapped package from his pocket, "that I'd love to take responsibility for that."

Joan looked at Denton in surprise, smiled shyly, took a deep breath and slowly opened the package containing an engagement ring. Buffy cheered, Jacob applauded, and Lord Bowser growled. Joan kissed her lover gently on the lips and whispered, "Oh, yes."

Jacob died on the fourth of July, three weeks after Denton and Joan's wedding, and a month prior to the publication of his eighteenth book. The funeral was attended by people from all over the world, and the media said that the timing of Jacob's death assured his new book bestseller status.

"You gave him the time to finish the book," Joan said

through her tears, snuggling into Denton's arms.

"Not me," he said. "God wanted that book published."

Jacob Denton Garret was born in Clammet Cove, California, on May 3rd of the following year, two weeks before the publication of his father's fourth novel. The book's hero was a radical environmental activist determined to make the world's corporations ecologically responsible. It was offered in the Sierra Club and Greenpeace catalogs, and went on to become a TV movie of the week.

BENEATH SEDONA

A mirage of spiraling towers and pillared pavilions shimmered into view above the erosion-carved buttes. Driving down the two-lane blacktop through the high desert, he saw it and slammed his foot on the brake. The tires squealed as the rented sedan slewed sideways, the rear wheels leaving the road in a cloud of dust and scatter of rocks. The undercarriage of the vehicle rattled and metal whined as the car shuddered and finally fishtailed to a stop.

"Kyle, for God's sake! What's wrong?" His wife clutched the arm rest, her other hand braced against the dashboard.

"Look, Jennifer." Unsnapping his safety belt, he threw open the car door and vaulted out into the hundred-degree Arizona afternoon. Shielding his eyes from the dust and sun he looked into the sky above the place where the road disappeared into the mountains.

"What, Kyle? What?"

"Don't you see it? Above the buttes. It's, it's a city, I think."

Jennifer got out of the car and looked where her husband was pointing. "Those are called clouds, Kyle."

"No. Overlaying the clouds, translucent, like a mirage. Strange buildings."

Kyle grabbed his 35mm Pentax from the front seat. He adjusted the focus and watched through the lens as the image of the city faded into the clouds. Lowering the camera he looked over the roof of the car to see his wife staring at him.

"You didn't see it?"

She shook her head.

He slid behind the wheel. His wife climbed back into the passenger seat.

"A city," he said. "It was there."

"Probably a trick of the sun." Jennifer brushed strands of long red hair out of her freckled face and wiped her brow with the back of her hand. "How about some airconditioning?"

The motor turned over and cool air spewed out of the vents. Kyle took a long look at the jagged skyline and surrounding terrain. The desert was dotted with scrub growth—chaparral, manzanita and Palo Verde trees. The air smelled of dusty sage. Sedona lay six miles ahead, in the middle of the unique red rocks clustered on the horizon.

"They look like temples, don't they?" she said.

"You think I'm nuts?" he said.

Jennifer leaned over and kissed her husband on the cheek. "Nope," she said. "A sexy romantic excited about visiting the energy vortexes, but not nuts."

He looked into her kelly-green eyes. "It could have been an hallucination."

"Starting a vacation with an hallucination is all right with me," she said and laughed. "Come on, let's go see the place."

They drove slowly through the town, past gift shops, a metaphysical book store, motels, a New Age center, restaurants, a crystal shop, more gift shops, and a camera store.

"The local economy is obviously tourist-based," Kyle said as the last signs of commercialism gave way to a sheer drop on one side of the road and red-rock walls and pine trees on the other. The first place to turn around was across a high bridge over Oak Creek. Cars were parked bumper to bumper along the road. Young people in bathing suits, some carrying inner tubes, scurried from cars, and darted in and out of the rocks on their way back into the canyon.

"Popular place," Jennifer quipped.

"Slide Rock, if I correctly remember my tourist guide," Kyle replied, turning the car back toward Sedona.

Los Abrigados Resort was nestled a few blocks off the main highway, on the banks of Oak Creek, amid giant sycamore and oak trees.

"El-e-gant!" Jennifer whispered as they drove around the giant fountain and under the pillared hotel entrance. Kyle went into the lobby to register. She watched her husband stride up the steps, two at a time. After ten years of marriage he was still all she ever wanted—a handsome, blue-eyed, black-haired six-footer, who didn't look quite right in a pair of jeans. She was too used to the Italian suits he usually wore. He was thirty-seven but was acting childishly excited about Sedona. Although she didn't share his enthusiasm for metaphysical explorations, she was enchanted by the idea of two weeks to relax and play without the kids.

"You have chosen well, oh great wise one," Jennifer laughed, falling back on the king-sized bed. The suite was appropriately furnished in Southwestern style, with dark woods accented by shades of orange, yellow, red, and brown. The large bedroom was separate from the living room and dining area that contained a stocked refrigerator/bar. French doors opened onto a patio with a hot tub. Beyond, the spectacular mountains surrounded them like a fortress.

"It's sure not Manhattan," Kyle said, looking at the view. "People actually live here and enjoy this year around."

"Not with your salary as a hot-shot magazine editor."

"Maybe there's more to life than being a magazine editor in an overcrowded, crime-ridden city," he said, turning to look at his wife. "Would you follow me anywhere?"

"You betcha, cowboy, especially to lunch. But first I want to call Mom, check on the kids and tell them our room number," Jennifer said, picking up the phone.

Dressed in shorts and polo shirts, they walked hand-in-hand through the resort grounds, past the pool filled with suntanned and sunburned people. Doors opening off the pool led to a long corridor past the ballroom, through the Spanish tiled lobby. Original paintings of Southwestern scenes covered the walls. Stepping in the doors of the restaurant, Kyle froze, jerking Jennifer's hand so hard she winced.

"Jennifer." He was looking at an oil painting hanging above a display of California wine. On the canvas, a beautifully rendered translucent city appeared above red-rock buttes.

Kyle stepped closer and read the brass tag centered on the frame. "LEMURIAN CITY By Lisa Augustine. 1990."

"The same city I saw above the buttes," Kyle whispered.

"Two for lunch?" asked a dark-suited young man holding menus. His warm welcoming smile spread from ear to ear.

Kyle turned to him and said, "Do you know anything about this painting?"

He shook his head. "Silly, huh? The artist probably just got tired of painting red mountains and cowboys."

"Does the artist live here?" Kyle asked.

"Maybe. There's a gallery next door in Tlaquepaque. I'm sure they can tell you."

"Next door?"

"Yes." The young man pointed across the parking lot at a large Spanish colonial structure. "Shops and galleries — the largest gallery is right on Oak Creek."

Kyle turned to Jennifer, "Can we go there first?"

She shrugged and said, "Sure."

In the gallery Kyle introduced himself to a white-haired

man who was dressed as if he'd just stepped out of a corporate board meeting. "I'm Kyle Dermont and this is my wife Jennifer. We're from New York City."

The man nodded approvingly. "I'm Randolph Hastings. Welcome." He handed Kyle his card.

"In Los Abrigados we saw a painting by a Lisa Augustine."

"We represent Miss Augustine," the man said proudly.

"Does she live here in Sedona?" Jennifer asked.

"Yes, but the gallery handles all her contacts."

"I'd just like to ask her about the subject of a painting titled 'Lemurian City.' "

Randolph smiled. "Come along," he said. "We have several of Lisa's paintings on display."

Kyle and Jennifer followed him through rooms of western and landscape art, into a room where they hung what Randolph called "the visionary pieces." Four Lisa Augustine paintings adorned one wall. In the first painting, titled "Our Heritage," the city was no longer a mirage, but a brightly rendered, bustling metropolis. Spiraling temples, fantasy-like pavilions, and glimmering fountains were situated among waterfalls, fruit trees and smiling people dressed in togas. There were no red-rock buttes in the scene.

Jennifer squeezed her husband's hand as they moved to the second painting, titled "Summer Solstice." It was an interior view of a beautiful temple where people were celebrating a festival. The third painting, titled "Lovers Of Life," showed nude people in a garden, some openly making love, other's feasting at a buffet or gathered in conversation around a fountain. In the background was a luminous pavilion. The fourth painting was quite different. It presented the same unusual structures but they appeared to be underground. Blackness replaced the blue sky, and the city was illuminated with great crystal clusters radiating an eerie glow. "Beneath Sedona, By Lisa Augustine.

1987," read the brass title plate.

"Some of the New Agers believe that Sedona is built over an ancient Lemurian city," Randolph said, rolling his eyes. Kyle didn't catch the gesture, but Jennifer did.

"A city that still exists?" Jennifer asked.

"Not very likely, now, is it?" Randolph said, politely disbelieving.

"How much is the painting in the restaurant?" Kyle asked.

"Twelve hundred dollars."

"If I were to buy it, could I talk to Lisa?" Kyle glanced at Jennifer. She nodded her approval.

"I can't say without consulting her," Randolph said. "Would you like me to call her?"

Kyle nodded. "Tell her I saw the city above the buttes as we drove into Sedona for the first time an hour ago. It almost caused me to wreck my car."

Randolph raised his eyebrows and left the room without commenting.

"Lisa wants to meet you," Randolph said, as he walked back into the room. "She is on her way. Maybe we can get the paperwork out of the way before she arrives. Would you like us to ship the painting?"

"No, I just want to look at it for a while," Kyle replied.

The painting was delivered from the hotel and Kyle was just slipping their checkbook back into Jennifer's purse when a dark woman in her late thirties or early forties stepped into the office. Her long raven hair was braided into two pigtails and adorned with coral beads. A white blouse, leather vest, jeans and kaibab moccasins accentuated her slender figure.

Everyone stood up. "Kyle and Jennifer Dermont, this is Lisa Augustine," Randolph said.

"Welcome home," Lisa said, extending her hand to Kyle. Accepting it, they looked into each other's eyes for what seemed to be a very long time. Lisa then turned to Jennifer and said, "Thank you for purchasing my painting."

"We were just going to have lunch," Jennifer said. "Won't you join us?"

At the resort restaurant, they were seated at a table by the window. Kyle took a chair between the two women. After ordering a round of drinks, Lisa was the first to speak.

"You saw the city?" she said.

Kyle nodded. "Why? How?"

"Because it is there for some to see," Lisa replied. "You saw a mental projection of an ancient city that still exists."

"How could that be?" Jennifer asked, trying not to sound skeptical.

"The image is mentally projected by dedicated souls who live beneath the surface of Sedona. Only those with a past-life Lemurian lineage can see it. If you are truly Lemurian you can know the secrets and accept the sanctuary."

"Are you the conduit?" Kyle said.

Lisa nodded.

Jennifer raised her hands in frustration. "What in the world are we talking about here?"

Kyle looked at his wife, then at Lisa. "Let me see if I've got it. Somehow, those with a Lemurian past are drawn to Sedona. Upon entering the area they see what appears to be a mirage. Then while touring the city they see one of Lisa's paintings and are shaken by the experience."

"The paintings are also on postcards and a book cover," Lisa added. "If I'm contacted by someone who has seen the projection, I check them for authenticity and then take them to the underground city for an orientation."

Kyle asked, "Don't the locals realize what's going on?"

"To them I'm just another talented New Age dreamer not to be taken seriously."

Jennifer was shaking her head when the waiter arrived with the drinks. Kyle and Jennifer ordered sandwiches.

When the waiter was gone Jennifer said, "Kyle, you simply accept this? An underground city? Mental projections? Sanctuary? Good Lord!"

Lisa stretched her hand across the table placing it upon Jennifer's hand. "Do you know much about Lemuria?" she asked.

Jennifer shook her head.

Lisa said, "Mu was the birthplace of the human race, a great continent that now lies beneath the sea. Easter Island is all that remains. Our cities were built of lava rock and metals unknown to modern science. We developed a civilization superior to any that followed."

Kyle said, "According to Colonel James Churchward, the Southwestern Indian tribes are direct descendants of ancient Lemurians. From what I've read Churchward was a member of British Intelligence serving in India. In a monastery he met an old rishi whom he described as a great master, the last surviving member of the ancient Naacal priesthood.' "

Lisa nodded and Kyle continued. "The rishi eventually led Churchward to a hidden cave and a cache of ancient clay tablets. The tablets were written in Naacal, the rishi explained, the oldest language of man. They told of the geology, history and religion of Mu the Motherland, and its final cataclysmic destruction over 12,000 years earlier."

"Yes," Lisa said, "Churchward learned to read the ancient writings. On Friday the 13th Day of Zac, devastating earthquakes caused the continent to sink. Sixty-four million souls were drowned, an end to over a hundred-thousand years of development."

"You really know all about this?" Jennifer asked her husband.

"Honey, you've never been very interested in anything metaphysical. I also studied Cerve's research. He claims the typical Lemurian was a tall, well-muscled vegetarian who was far advanced mentally and spiritually. In the center of his high forehead was a growth about the size of a walnut. This third eye was actually the Lemurian's sixth sense organ. Through it, he could see, hear, feel, and communicate over long distances. He was also capable of communicating with animals, and could see into the fourth dimension.

"The Lemurians possessed powerful magnetic stones or crystals, found in volcanic areas, which radiated energy and light. These crystals had the strange ability to repel water and were used to power the boats which ultimately brought the Lemurians to North America."

"How do you verify if Kyle is a Lemurian?" Jennifer asked, looking directly into Lisa's dark eyes.

Lisa looked down at the table, took a deep breath and said, "First, let me explain that if he is of Mu, I will guide you both to a secret tunnel where you will be taken to Legora, the city in the painting. It is Kyle's birthright and yours by love, Jennifer. You will be told of the secrets and then you may choose to stay or to leave."

"But what if we leave and tell the world?" Kyle asked.

"Who would believe you? You'd never find the entrance again."

"How do you verify if Kyle is a Lemurian?" Jennifer asked again.

"By making love to him," Lisa replied. Jennifer's face reflected her shock. "Please hear me out, Jennifer," Lisa pleaded. "Lemurian sexual attitudes are freer. If it were you who saw the mental projection, a Lemurian man would have to make love to you to authenticate your lineage. We are governed by strict morals, but they are unlike yours. Because Kyle is your husband, if I make love to him you must be present. I have nothing more to say. Here is my card. You can call me if you want to proceed."

Lisa stood up, smiled and hurried out of the restaurant.

"Don't look at me like that, Jennifer. I'm as shocked as you are."

"How long have we been in Sedona, Kyle? Less that two hours. In that time you've nearly wrecked the car, spent twelve hundred dollars on a painting whose artist has propositioned you right in front of me. This is going to be quite a vacation."

"Well, we've ah, gotten off to . . ."

"She wants to screw you while I watch. I don't believe it." Jennifer slammed her drink down on the table as the waiter arrived with the sandwiches. He looked at her uneasily, quickly set the food on the table and was gone.

"Honey, I don't think it means the same thing to her that it does to us. Different societies . . ."

"Kyle, do you really, truly believe that there's a city like the one in that painting beneath Sedona?"

"I don't know. Why did I see it in the sky?"

"It's probably some weird sex cult projecting pictures on the clouds or something."

"Honey, I don't think that's possible in broad daylight. And if it was, why would they go to all that trouble to get . . ."

"Do you want to make it with her, Kyle? Tell me the truth."

"No. No, I don't, but if there is a Lemurian city beneath Sedona I'd sure like to see it."

Jennifer's eyes narrowed, her breath coming in short staccato bursts. She picked up her sandwich and chomped on it with a vengeance.

Back in their room to change into bathing suits, Kyle handed Jennifer a book on the Sedona psychic energy vortexes. "Just read from here on," he said, marking a page with a pen and turning the corner. "Then we won't talk about it again unless you bring it up. Fair enough?"

"Fair enough," Jennifer replied, wiggling into her bikini.

Kyle stood by the bed admiring his wife's well-toned body. A quick wolf-whistle was followed by a quicker exit into the bathroom when she playfully threw a shoe at him.

They took turns applying suntan lotion to each other's white bodies, then nestled into side-by-side chaise lounges by the pool. Jennifer opened the book to the marked page. She scanned the earlier pages in the chapter and found they contained a lot of the information discussed at lunch. She began to read from the mark:

Lemurian religion was based on fact, as opposed to faith, containing no sects, theologies or dogma. All Lemurians were attuned to the Cosmic Mind or Consciousness, which permeates the universe.

Reincarnation, an established fact to the Lemurians, was the basis of their religion. In The Sacred Writings of Mu, *Churchward wrote, "We are told man's soul lives on until finally it reaches the source of its origin."*

About 70,000 years before the destruction of Mu, a colonial movement began sending groups of migrations westward to Asia and eastward to South, Central and North America. The first of these eastern migrations led to approximately the present state of Nevada at a time preceding the rising of our western mountain ranges.

"That the Cliff Dwelling tribes of Arizona came from Mu is certain," Churchward wrote, *"for every one of their pictures that are used for guideposts contains a reference to Mu. In fact, the rock writings and pictures of the Cliff Dwellers, except those drawn for artistic effects, are permeated with references to Mu, both before and after her submersion. In addition to this, they invariably used the symbols that were in vogue in the Motherland."*

Hopi Indian legend would seem to support Churchward's hypothesis. The Hopis believe that they originally came out of the west on bamboo rafts. Arriving at a wall of steep mountains, they climbed to the top and looked back; in the distance, they could see islands sinking. The continent of Mu consisted of one large and two smaller islands.

The Hopis are a deeply religious culture with many magic-oriented beliefs, as were the Lemurians. Beneath their dwellings, the Hopis dig kivas, underground rooms used for religious ceremonies. The Lemurians also used underground rooms for religious rites.

The Indians consider the Sedona red-rock country to be sacred ground; the home of the Great Spirit. Perhaps this is why so many people in search of enlightenment and inner peace come to this area, attracted, as it were, by some invisible force. Visitors from the ethereal plane are also said to linger here.

Amazing psychic occurrences have been reported as well: visions, telepathy, spontaneous past-life recall, precognitions, UFO sightings, poltergeist activity, enhanced automatic writing, spiritual healings and other psychic phenomena.

An ancient Lemurian city is said to be buried beneath the Coconino sandstone. Powerful talisman-like crystals are thought to be hidden underground. (Coincidentally, the Navajo Indians believe that they emerged from underground.)

Maybe the psychic occurrences and legends relate to the fact that Sedona is one of the world's three most powerful energy centers. Surrounding Sedona are four energy vortexes—two electric, one magnetic, and one electromagnetic—and they emit more energy from the earth than any other single place on the planet!

Jennifer closed the book and was about to lay it on the table beside the chaise when Kyle said, "Chapter Four is also about the Sedona/Lemuria connection."

Jennifer flipped through the pages and stopped. "Even I know about Edgar Cayce," she said.

"Read it to me," Kyle said.

"In Edgar Cayce's reading number 812-1, the sleeping prophet talked about a woman name Amelelia, a priestess in the 'Temple of Light,' who was an overseer of communications between various lands. The reading mentions Mu and a particular portion of Arizona and Nevada that are as a portion of the Brotherhood of those people from Mu."

"And now, my Lemurian husband, it's time to swim," Jennifer said, flipping the book onto the table and standing up. "Are you coming or do I splash you from the pool?"

Following dinner at a local Mexican restaurant, Kyle and Jennifer returned to the resort and made love. Kyle fantasized that it was Lisa beneath him while his wife watched from across the room. Jennifer imagined the same thing but tried to push the thoughts out of her mind. Neither mentioned it.

When they were done, Kyle opened the doors of the bedroom cabinet containing the television set and placed the painting of the Lemurian City in front of the screen. They fell asleep looking at it. Jennifer dreamed of walking hand in hand with her husband down a never-ending tunnel that became increasingly more fearful as she descended into the earth.

Finally, forcing herself to awaken, she found the room lights still on. Kyle was sleeping peacefully beside her and the painting still sat on its perch in front of the television set. Padding across the room to open the curtains, she saw that the eastern sky was beginning to lighten.

"Kyle." She shook him. "Let's go out and watch the sunrise."

"Sunrise? Are you crazy?" came the muffled reply from beneath the covers.

She tossed her pillow at his head.

On Airport Mesa, sitting with their arms around each other in the pre-dawn chill, Kyle and Jennifer drank coffee from cardboard cups. The sky melded from blue to pink to crimson before the sun rose from behind a craggy mountain and sent runners of light shooting across the valley below.

"Have we ever watched a sunrise in Manhattan?" Jennifer asked.

Kyle shook his head and snuggled his face into his wife's long red hair. "Gorgeous," he whispered.

"It sure is."

"Not it, you."

"That kind of talk will get you everywhere," she laughed and pulled away. "Kyle, I don't think I'm going to be very good at this meditation stuff."

"Nothing to it. You can't visit Sedona and not meditate in the vortexes."

"I can't?"

"It's not allowed. Let's do a sunrise meditation."

"I'd rather have breakfast."

He pinched her on the nose. "Now do it just like we've discussed."

They both sat erect, crossed their legs and rested their hands on their knees, index fingers touching thumbs to form a circle. Jennifer breathed deeply as she'd practiced on the drive from the Phoenix airport to Sedona. She began to relax and count down. The sun felt warm on her skin and clothing as she imagined herself walking down a steep hill that she remembered from her childhood. Upstate New York. Yes. Woods over there. A dirt road there. Yes.

I'm barefoot, she realized when she reached the road and felt the warm dirt between her toes. Crickets chirped in the waving grass. The day smelled like alfalfa hay and sweat, as she walked down the road around the bend through the trees to the spiraling towers and strange-looking pavilions. *No.* She began to run toward the city, hoping it would turn back into the creek and trees that belonged here. It didn't. Soon she was in the midst of people dressed in white togas. A lady wearing clown makeup tried to hand her something on a stick. *No.* She ran across a manicured lawn, past the garden with its fragrant aroma of roses, past an old man reading poetry, then a group gathered around a dancer, and a couple making love. The couple waved and invited her to join them. *No.* Running even faster, she dodged through the people and collided with a tall man. They both lost their footing and tumbled to the ground. Jennifer sat up and looked at his high forehead with a big bump in the middle. *No,* she screamed and opened her eyes, to find Kyle watching her.

"Isn't it great?" he asked.

"I'm hungry," she said, brushing her hair out of her eyes and wiping her moist palms on her jeans.

"Did you perceive visions or just mentally float?" he asked.

"You'll think I'm nuts."

"No, I won't."

"I saw your damned city beneath Sedona."

"You're nuts," he said, laughing. "Tell me about it on the way back to the car."

During their first six days in Sedona Kyle and Jennifer meditated in each of the vortexes and explored the town, including three metaphysical bookstores, two crystal shops and three New Age centers. They ate in all the best restaurants and even spent an afternoon at Slide Rock.

"We still have a week," Kyle said, sitting beside his wife in the patio hot tub outside their room. A quarter moon smiled in the sky like a Cheshire cat. Insects hummed and every once in a while, far away, a coyote's howl drifted on the wind.

"It's another world, isn't it?" Jennifer said, trying to position her body so the hot tub jet massaged her sore feet.

"Sedona or Lemuria?" Kyle asked.

"I was talking about Sedona. Do you still want to visit the subterranean city?"

"I haven't said a word about Lemuria all week," he said, defensively.

"No, you haven't. But I keep dreaming about the damn place, and every time I meditate, those spiraling towers and weird pavilions are part of it. It's haunting me."

Kyle kissed his wife and cupped one of her bare breasts in his hand.

"You're trying to change the subject," she said. "If the Lemurian city is real, Kyle, and my jealousy keeps us from experiencing it . . ."

"Jennifer." He touched her lips. "I love you. It's not right for me to make love to Lisa."

"I know you love me. And I doubt that you're attracted to Lisa beyond the idea of a little variety." She smiled and wrinkled her nose. "Right?"

He hesitated. "Well, ah, right."

"So the idea is interesting?"

"No. But, well. Jennifer, stop that."

"Kyle?"

"Jennifer. What man wouldn't want to make love to an attractive woman while his wife cheered him on?"

"Cheered him on?" She cupped her hand and splashed water in his face.

"Well, maybe you could join in. I certainly wouldn't complain about that," he said, laughing and ducking.

"Be serious," she said. "I've been thinking about it a lot. The dreams and visions keep me thinking about it. I'm pretty sure I don't like this psychic stuff, but the possibility of visiting a parallel world is just too much to resist."

"Jennifer."

She looked at her husband. "I think we should call Lisa."

Kyle interrupted. "Honey, if these people can send visual projections, have you considered that they might be able to send thought projections?" Kyle questioned.

She didn't reply.

He continued, "Your dreams and visions may have been projected by the Lemurians as a form of conversion."

"Brainwashing? My God, Kyle, have we crossed over into the twilight zone?"

"Tell me how the dreams have progressed," he said, wiping his face with a towel.

"They've become less fearful and more appealing. Maybe initially my fears were more powerful than their projections, but they're winning me over. Last night I dreamed about the structure of Lemurian society. It seems to run like an ideal community—no crime, no want, no injustice."

Kyle looked out at the jagged black mountains silhouetted against the purple, star-splattered sky. "I haven't had a single dream or vision about Lemuria."

"Because you were always open to the visit," Jennifer said. "They didn't need to sell you."

"But why, Jennifer? Do they need new blood? Are they expanding, and if so, for what purpose? There can only be so much room down there, if there is a down there."

"You're doubting?" she asked.

"I'm suspicious of anyone using conversion techniques."

"Well, let's look at our choices. One, you get it on with Lisa and we go for a visit and hope they don't eat us." She laughed, as he splashed water at her. "Two," she continued, "We go home and forget all about it. Three, we go to the authorities."

"I'm sure the authorities would buy right into the idea of a lost race of underground Lemurians," he said.

"They might if we didn't mention a city beneath Sedona. If we told them our children were kidnapped and Lisa was taking us to them, the FBI and a SWAT team would follow.

Kyle looked at his wife in surprise. "I'd never have thought of that."

"But if we're wrong and a peaceful society exists . . ." her words trailed off as she watched a shooting star fire across the sky and disappear behind the mountains.

"What do you think we should do?" he asked.

"Do you think they're dangerous or that anything subversive is going on?" she asked in reply.

"No. I think they just want the opportunity to state their case."

"Me too," she said. "That's why I'm going to get out of this hot tub and go in and call Lisa."

Without saying a word, Kyle watched his wife towel off, slip into a bathrobe and disappear through the French doors.

Thirty minutes later Lisa knocked on the door of their suite. Jennifer answered the door with a cheery "Hi, Lisa," and gestured for her to sit in one of the chairs by the couch. Lisa was wearing a long dress adorned with Indian beads, and her black hair hung almost to her waist. Kyle and Jennifer wore shorts and pullovers, and were barefooted.

Jennifer poured three glasses of wine. Sitting beside her husband on the couch, she raised her glass in a toast. "To Lemuria," she said.

"To Lemuria," they repeated. Kyle nervously looked from one woman to the other.

"Do you have any questions?" Lisa asked.

"What is the purpose of expanding your numbers?" Jennifer asked.

"We seek only to fulfill our responsibilities by offering you a better way to live."

"We have two children," Jennifer said.

"They would also be welcomed."

"How can it be better to live underground?" Kyle asked.

"It isn't exactly underground," Lisa said. "But I can't tell you any more than that."

"Why do you live in Sedona?" Jennifer asked.

"To serve the greater good. I'll soon be replaced by another volunteer."

"We think your people mentally programmed Jennifer's dreams and visions," Kyle said, looking directly into Lisa's eyes.

"That is correct."

"Why is it so important to you?" Jennifer asked.

"Only fear could keep you from visiting the city and making an informed choice. We're here on earth to learn to let go of fear." Kyle and Jennifer nodded their heads. "Jennifer feared losing you if I made love to you. That's a false fear."

"If I'm not a Lemurian, how could I have seen the mental projection?" Kyle said.

"There is always the possibility that you're extremely psychic and happened to tune into our frequency."

"And sex will tell you if . . ."

"Immediately," Lisa said before he could finish his sentence. "I will know here and here." She touched her heart and the center of her forehead.

"When will we go to Legora?"

"Right away."

Jennifer took a deep, exaggerated breath and stood up. She offered one hand to Lisa and the other to Kyle.

Kyle and Lisa arose but Lisa said, "You two go into the bedroom and make love. I'll join you in a little while."

Jennifer started to protest, "But I thought . . ."

"Make love to your husband," Lisa said, softly, smiling.

Jennifer, still holding Kyle's hand, walked into the bedroom, leaving the door open. The bedside lamp cast a warm glow over the bed. Kyle looked at his wife, shrugged his shoulders and raised his eyebrows. Smiling knowingly,

Jennifer unsnapped her shorts and let them fall to the floor. Kyle helped her take off the pullover, then she undressed him.

Standing together, naked at the foot of the bed, they looked out into the living room to see Lisa flipping through a magazine.

"Come on," Jennifer fell onto the bed pulling Kyle down on top of her. "Try to convince me this isn't exciting," she whispered in his ear.

"Naa," he purred.

"Then your body must have a mind of its own" she said, wiggling her hips.

He kissed her tenderly and blew on her cheek, nibbled her ears and buried his face in her hair as her body trembled against him. She moaned loudly as he entered her, and the gentleness exploded into thrusting of rapidly increasing intensity.

He locked his arms around his wife and rolled over so that she was on top, sitting up. She tossed her hair out of her eyes. Kyle grabbed her buttocks, squeezing and pumping her up and down. Then he was wildly massaging her breasts, pulling her down to his mouth, suckling, tasting her salty-sweetness.

Sweat covered his body. The lamp cast a giant shadow on the wall as Jennifer rose and fell in a kaleidoscopic swirl of rhythmic movement accompanied by the whimpering sounds of uninhibited pleasure.

He was making love with an uncommon fierceness when Jennifer slid away and Lisa took her place on top of him. Her long ebony hair swept across his face, as she snapped her head back and forth in response to their mutual thrusting. His hands groped her body—different skin, different breasts, different buttocks.

Jennifer was lying beside him now, whispering, "I love you, Kyle."

He closed his eyes and embraced the joy of spinning out of control, crazed, falling through the centuries, through darkness into light, twisting and tumbling into erupting volcanos, through fire and water, and the terrible birth trauma of his species as his body arched and released with such intensity the spasms left him weak and gasping for breath. He opened his eyes and saw only Jennifer's hair flowing above him like cascading lava, drowning him in its flame-red softness.

His wife's orgasm was as intense as his own. And afterwards, for a long time, she lay on top of him, her face buried in the corded muscles of his neck as she fought to catch her breath.

When she rolled away he whispered, "I love you."

She propped her head up on one arm and ran her fingers through his hair. "That was painless, wasn't it?"

"Was it?" he asked looking into her eyes.

She nodded and smiled lovingly. "It was beautiful."

"You weren't jealous?"

She shook her head.

"I wish I could remember it better," he said, shaking his head as if to loosen the memories.

"Lisa's waiting," Jennifer said, slipping out of bed.

Lisa drove. They sat three in the front seat of her Ford four-door. When five miles out of Sedona she pulled the car to the side of the road and said, "You'll have to put on these blindfolds. It's the rule."

No one talked again until the car came to a stop ten minutes later.

"I'll guide you," Lisa said, opening her door and getting out. A moment later the passenger door opened. "Jennifer, hold Kyle's hand. Kyle, take my hand."

They walked a dozen steps. "Wait," Lisa said.

An owl hooted. From far away came the bone-chilling

cries of frenzied coyotes fighting over a fresh kill. The desert was alive with sounds. Kyle and Jennifer could sense the slithering of snakes and the darting of lizards. The air smelled of dust and brittle brown things New Yorkers knew nothing of. Then with a sliding sound came a different smell—a damp underground odor that could have come from a tomb or a fruit cellar . . . or a stairway to another world.

"Step forward a few paces," Lisa said, guiding them.

The sliding sound repeated behind them.

"You can remove the blindfolds," Lisa said.

"Oh, my God," Jennifer gasped, looking down an eerily lighted stairway that seemed to descend without end. Ten steps down and a flat landing, as far as they could see.

Kyle touched the quartz crystal clusters glowing on the wall. There was no heat, just a bluish glow. He kneeled down and ran his fingers over the smooth white fresco that covered the stairs, the arched ceiling and walls. It reminded him of the surface on Mayan ruins he'd visited on a college trip.

"There really is an underground city," Jennifer said.

"Not really," Lisa corrected, as she began to lead the way down the stairs. "Legora exists in a different frequency, but the gate is beneath Sedona.

Kyle looked at her with a blank expression.

"You see," Lisa said, smiling. "It's a different world existing in the same space as your own. Much like many radio stations exist in the same air waves. When you twist the dial you tap into different frequencies and experience different programs."

"So we'll see the same red-rock buttes but without the town of Sedona?" Jennifer asked.

"Oh, no. Legora exists in a valley surrounded on three sides by rolling hills. On the fourth side is a hundred mile beach that looks out on the Celaro Sea."

The air got colder and their footsteps and voices echoed longer as they descended deeper into the ground. The stairway did not twist or turn, but continued steeply, straight down. On every landing was a glowing cluster of crystals to light the way.

"How long will it take us to reach the bottom?" Kyle asked.

"About ten more minutes."

"Is the Lemurian society as advanced as our own?"

"Depending upon your viewpoint it is more advanced or less advanced. There is no pollution, no crime. Everyone owns their own home. But we share few of the technological achievements you're used to."

"No computers?" Kyle said.

"No, and instead of powerful engines to propel transportation and shipping, we reverse gravity. Our airships are the UFOs sometimes observed in the sky over Sedona."

"How?" Jennifer asked.

"Psychic people capable of momentarily seeing through the veil. Sometimes an electromagnetic flux can momentarily allow it to happen, as when one radio stations bleeds through on top of another. In Legora we sometimes see your jet planes."

"How long have you been leading ex-Lemurians home?" Kyle asked.

"Five years."

"How many people in that time?" Jennifer asked.

"Over a hundred."

"How many decided to stay in Legora?" Kyle asked.

"All."

"No one declined?"

"No. No one has ever declined."

"How long has this been going on?"

"Seventy years that I know of," Lisa replied.

"And you don't know of anyone in all that time that has

preferred life in the United States of America?" Kyle wondered.

"No."

"Doesn't that seem strange to you?" Jennifer asked Lisa.

"It's a better way of life."

Far below they could see that the stairway ended in a large room with luminous walls and an oval-shaped door that shimmered like glowing metal.

"What do people do to keep busy, Lisa?" Kyle asked.

"Whatever they want."

"Life is all peace and harmony? There's no dissension?"

"Of course not."

"What about business? Commerce?"

"You are given what you need. Commerce is unnecessary."

"What about challenge?" Kyle persisted.

"Challenge?" Lisa said.

"Aliveness!" Kyle said, stopping three landings above the large room. "People need goals and challenges to keep life interesting."

"Kyle?" Jennifer said his name as a question.

"Honey, don't you get it? If no one has ever declined this invitation, there really isn't any choice. Either through mind control or because the society is that compelling, we'll succumb if we go through the gate."

"Succumb?"

"We won't be able to resist the Lemurian world."

Jennifer looked at Lisa, who was staring at Kyle.

He continued, "I'm reminded of the question about an orgasmatron if one is ever invented. What if we had a device that could give us continual orgasmic pleasure? Would we have the strength to turn it off long enough to eat and sleep and make a living, or would we just continue to come until we died?"

Kyle looked at Jennifer. "Are you unhappy with your

life, honey?"

"No," she said, "not at all."

"Do you want to say goodbye to your friends and family and lifestyle?"

"No, but if utopia exists . . ."

He interrupted. "Obviously it does. And if it doesn't, it can make us think it does."

Jennifer didn't reply.

Kyle said, "Sometimes I complain about things I have the ability to change. I hate New York's crime, congestion, and weather, but I'm free to move elsewhere. I also love the city for its creative potentials, so I stay. But, like everyone else, I'm only a value judgment away from changing my life." Pausing, he took a long look down the stairs at the room and strange door, then he said, "I don't think I'm ready to give up the excitement and challenge of the choices awaiting me."

Jennifer nodded.

Lisa looked at Kyle disbelievingly.

Then Jennifer laughed loudly, and the laugh echoed in the ancient stairway like a chorus of hopeful souls seeing the light.

Laughing too, Kyle took her hand and they turned and began the long walk back up to their world.

THE BEGINNING

She was naked when she met him. It wasn't him exactly, but a mental projection that had been freed by the extreme depth of his altered state of consciousness.

"Hello."

His voice echoed in her mind. Evelyn stared at the handsome man in his birthday suit, standing on the hillside overlooking a green valley.

"I've never met anyone here before," he said.

"I've never been here before." Her words weren't spoken, yet she knew he perceived them. "Where are we?"

He smiled at her attempts to cover her nakedness. "It's a trance place. I doubt it has a name."

"A trance place?"

"You're in deep hypnosis, aren't you?" he asked.

"Yes, in Calvin O'Conner's psychic development class."

"What part of the country?"

"The West Coast, in . . ."

He interrupted. "I'm in a therapy program back East. The doc's using me as a guinea pig, but it's a great break, touring other frequencies." He turned and gazed at a distant river winding through the pastoral landscape. The sun was high in the sky, and birds chattered in nearby oak trees.

"I don't understand." She shook her head.

The man sat down on an outcropping of rocks, brushed his hands through his dark hair and said, "I've read about O'Conner's psychic research. Very impressive. In the class, he was hypnotizing you, right?"

Evelyn nodded. "He said the induction would take an hour."

"And when O'Conner's voice faded away, you arrived here, right?"

"I think so. I don't remember."

"In plenary hypnosis they lose control of you. One minute you're responding to command, the next, off you go on your own."

Evelyn decided it was silly to try to cover her body and gave it up.

"You have a nice body," he said, smiling.

She felt herself blush. "So do you."

They paused to look into each other. She figured he was about 35, her age. "This place isn't real, is it?"

He raised his hands in a questioning gesture and shrugged. "It's as real as anywhere else. Every reality vibrates at a different rate."

"If I touched you, would I feel your flesh?" she asked.

He stood up, strolled the distance between them, and took her in his arms. "You tell me," he said, kissing her tenderly.

Evelyn was unable to respond.

"My name is Burward A. Kendall," he whispered.

She could feel his excitement pressed against her body.

"I know this is . . ." As his words faded in her mind, his body contracted, trembled and disappeared. "What? Burward?" Twirling in a circle, Evelyn found herself alone on the hillside with an empty feeling in the pit of her stomach. The afternoon breeze tossed her long brown hair and brushed the grass against her bare legs.

How can I feel bad about losing a man I met five minutes ago in an alternate reality? she thought. Circling again, she accepted her solitude and decided to walk down the hill to the valley floor. *I'll either wake up or they'll call me back before I get there anyway.*

As the hillside gave way to the flat valley floor, Evelyn found herself in a grove of oak trees. She pulled a leaf from a tree and crushed it to release its fragrance. She stepped carefully to avoid bruising her feet on the fallen branches. The trees soon thinned, and she emerged in a meadow—a sea of rippling, knee-deep grass. Strolling across the meadow she found fruit trees growing along the bank of the river. *Ripe peaches.*

Reaching above her head to pick a peach, the tree pulled away from her and the colors faded. *My God! No . . .* She was ten paces from the tree. Twenty. Everything was fading.

"Open your eyes and be wide awake. Number five, wide awake."

Evelyn opened her eyes to see Calvin O'Conner staring down at her. She lay prone on the floor of his living room, surrounded by six other students. Her friend Maria squeezed Evelyn's arm and asked, "You okay?"

Evelyn nodded, rolled to her side and sat up.

"Why didn't she want to come back?" one of the students asked.

"We'll have to ask her," Calvin said. He was a tall, thin middle-aged man with dishevelled chestnut-colored hair and hypnotic blue eyes that seemed to pierce the soul of everyone they gazed upon.

Evelyn moved unsteadily to a chair and sank into its overstuffed depths. She scanned the tastefully decorated living room that doubled as a class room on Wednesday evenings. Calvin sat in his regular chair beside a portable blackboard. The students lounged on the floor or sat in chairs. At the end of the living room was a large picture window that looked out on the ocean, tonight illuminated by a full moon.

"It was like an intense dream," Evelyn said. "I was on a hillside looking at a naked man."

The students chuckled. Calvin smiled.

"We talked. Before he disappeared, he kissed me and it certainly felt real."

One of the students said, "I wish I'd had an experience like that. All I did was float in a void."

Calvin nodded. "I wanted to see what each of you would experience in ultra-depth. No one fully understands it that well."

The students took turns telling what they had experienced. Jess and Charlie, both local college students, explained that they simply floated "as if on a black sea on a moonless night." Fred was a plump, balding insurance salesman who had participated in an American Civil War battle. "Probably a past life," he concluded. Mary, a middle-aged woman who wore her greying hair in Indian-style braids, thought she had astral projected. "I was watching my daughter fix dinner for her husband. They live in the Midwest." Evelyn's friend and co-worker Maria was a dark-haired beauty in her late twenties who reported that she had fallen sleep. "I don't remember anything."

Calvin returned his attention to Evelyn. "Did you speak with the naked man?"

"Yes, but why were we both naked, Calvin?"

"Maybe you transferred frequencies and couldn't carry any material aspects of this reality into that one."

Evelyn nodded. "He knew I was in deep trance somewhere. I guess he was too. I said, 'This place isn't real, is it?' And he said, 'It's as real as anywhere else. Every reality vibrates at a different rate.' Then he kissed me and just disappeared."

"He was right about realities and vibrational rates. I hadn't planned to cover this until next week, but in light of Evelyn's experience, let me explain a few things." Calvin stood and picked up a piece of chalk from the blackboard. "Your view of reality is based on what you perceive with your five senses. And sometimes with your sixth sense if you learn to be more psychic in this class."

The students laughed.

Calvin continued. "But your view is limited. Right here, right now, we're surrounded by words and music we can't hear. Portable phone calls, radio and television signals, shortwave, CBs, and maybe microwave transmissions are beaming through the room. Just because you can't perceive them with your limited hearing range doesn't mean they aren't there. The same is true of various light waves."

On the blackboard, Calvin rapidly drew a small circle surrounded by several elliptical lines. "I'm not much of an artist, but I can get the idea across. What's this?" The chalk clicked decisively on the board as he finished with a flourish.

"An atom," someone said.

"Right. This is the way you usually see an atom depicted, but it is wa-a-a-a-a-y out of scale. If the nucleus in the center of the atom were the size of a pinpoint, the electron spinning around it would encircle an area larger than this living room. To put it into perspective, the electron is 2,000 times smaller than the nucleus and is orbiting the nucleus at about 600 miles per second. Per second, mind you. The result is an illusion making the electron look the size of this room."

Mary raised her hand and said, "This is basic physics. Are you going to expound on $E = mc$ squared?"

Calvin smiled. "Sure. It was the knowledge that energy equals matter times the speed of light that allowed physicists to explore the subtle aspects of the universe. They found that atoms have a minute proton, neutron nucleus. And the nucleus doesn't remain still. It's moving at 40,000 miles per second. Now, many physicists believe that the nucleus isn't matter at all, but waves. What were once thought to be solid subatomic particles may in reality be waves."

Evelyn asked, "How does this relate to my experience?"

"Everything is made up of atoms: mountains, plants, animals, the chair you're sitting on . . . even your body. If you look up atoms in the encyclopedia it will tell you they are mostly empty space."

Calvin looked from face to face. He had their attention. Focusing on Evelyn, he said, "The atoms in your chair create an illusion of solid material, fabric, padding, springs and a wooden frame. But if the electrons stopped spinning, the chair would simply disappear. The chair is an illusion."

The students looked at each other. Maria said, "Then I'm an illusion. I'm not real."

Calvin laughed. "No, you are reality to all those interacting within this vibrational frequency. But reality doesn't mean quite the same thing when you understand the reality of the atom."

Evelyn shrugged her shoulders, sighed and said, "So another reality could exist right here, occupying the same time and space, but vibrating on a different frequency?"

"Just like different stations on a TV or radio." Calvin replied.

"Then the reality I experienced in hypnosis was as real as this one?" Evelyn gestured, her hands sweeping the room.

"Maybe," Calvin said. "Probably."

"What if I got stuck there?" she asked.

He shook his head. "You probably didn't notice the translucent silver cord attached to your body—in the sunlight, it would be almost invisible. The cord will always draw you back."

"What if it were severed?"

Calvin hesitated. "I don't know."

The phone rang. Calvin seemed glad for the distraction and left the room to answer it.

"You okay, Evelyn?" Maria asked again.

"Evelyn, it's for you," Calvin called from the dining room.

Who knows I'm here? No one. Absolutely no one. She stepped over two of the students lying on the floor.

Calvin smiled, saying, "A man. He wants to talk to the pretty girl with long brown hair who met him in trance. I told him your name is Evelyn."

Shaking her head, she took the receiver. "Hello."

"Evelyn, this is Burward. Do you remember?"

"Of course, but how did . . ."

"I called a few West Coast cities and asked for a listing for Calvin O'Conner. I hit it on the fifth try."

"This is too bizarre to believe." Evelyn forced herself to take a deep breath.

"Can you go back into deep trance on your own?" Burward asked.

"No, not a chance."

"Did O'Conner tape record the session?"

Evelyn glanced into the living room. "Yes, I think so. He usually records everything."

"Then beg him for the tape. Go home and start playing it about midnight your time. I'll meet you at 1 A.M. on the hillside."

"I don't know, Burward. I'd like to, I really would, but . . ."

"Please."

"If I can."

"Better give me your phone number, just in case we don't connect."

Evelyn's heart was racing like a schoolgirl. After hanging up the phone, she related the conversation to the class.

"Can I have the tape, Calvin?"

He shook his head. "Ultra-depth is too tricky, Evelyn. None of us know enough about it."

"Please, Calvin. It's terribly important."

"Can't do it, Evelyn, but I am willing to start hypnotizing you again at midnight so you can keep your 1 A.M. rendezvous. The rest of the class can stick around for the session if they have the stamina. It's 10:30 now."

The members of the class talked among themselves for a few moments. In the end, only Maria agreed to stay.

"All right, I'm going to take a break myself," Calvin said. "I'll see those of you who are leaving next week. Evelyn and Maria, feel free to relax. There are soft drinks in the refrigerator. I'm going to take a nap. Wake me at 11:45 if you still want to make the trip."

When the room was quiet, Evelyn and Maria curled up on the sofa to talk.

"I sense you really like this guy," Maria said.

Evelyn stared out the picture window at the waves breaking on the shore. "There was something special about him."

"Maybe because he was naked." Maria giggled.

"Maybe because I haven't had a date in almost two years, but I don't think so. I've never been so intensely attracted to anyone before."

Maria laid her head on the armrest of the sofa. "You haven't gone out with anyone in two years?"

"I've only had a handful of dates since I was divorced six years ago. Being a loan officer, I meet a lot of men, but none that I've been interested in."

"But at work you always tell me about the latest movies you've seen and . . ."

"I go alone."

"What about your family?"

"My mother and father were killed in an accident when I was six. No brothers or sisters."

After talking a little while longer, Maria's eyes began to flutter and finally close. She began to breathe deeply. Evelyn returned her attention to the slow-rolling waves breaking on the beach and thought about Burward A. Kendall. *Burward. What a name! What a man.*

She looked at her watch. 11:05. Glancing up, she noticed the reel-to-reel tape recorder sitting on the bookshelf. Easing off the sofa, she padded across the room to the recorder. Punching the rewind button, she let it run for a moment, then tapped "stop." Inserting a jack into the machine, she put on the headphones and pushed play. Her voice was saying, "So another reality could exist right here, occupying the same . . ."

It took a few minutes to write Calvin a note, apologizing for borrowing the tape recorder. She concluded the note with, "I need to do this on my own." Propping the note on his chair, she quietly left the beach house with the tape recorder under her arm.

By 11:35 Evelyn was home in her own apartment. After double locking the door and drawing all the curtains, she placed the tape recorder on her desk. Considering the amount of tape on the spool, she concluded that the session had been recorded at slow speed. Listening over the headphones, she marked the place where Calvin began awakening the class from the deep trance. Between the end of his trance induction and the awakening, she spliced the remaining blank tape on the spool. At the end of blank tape she spliced the awakening. *That should give me two or three hours over there before the awakening.*

At 11:55 she brushed her hair and took a good look at herself in the bathroom mirror. *As good as it's going to get.* At midnight, she was lying comfortably beneath a blanket on her sofa, shivering. She put the headphones over her ears, switched on the tape and switched off the light.

Calvin's rhythmic voice soothed her shivering body, and she began to relax. "You're going to go very, very deep. Far, far deeper than you've ever been before. This is an experimental session, so just be open to what happens, flow with your experiences and explore the limits of your potential. Deeper, deeper, deeper, down, down, down."

Focusing upon Calvin's words, her body relaxed until she couldn't feel her arms or legs. Images of her childhood faded in and out—her mother and father laughing—her tears at their grave site. "Deeper, deeper, deeper, down, down, down." Her cantankerous foster parents appeared and disappeared. "Deeper than you've ever been before." She saw a brief flash of her desk at the bank. "Much, much deeper, as you continue to go down, down, down into the deepest possible hypnotic sleep."

"I was afraid you wouldn't come."

She opened her eyes and smiled. "Burward."

He took her in his arms and kissed her tenderly.

"Don't disappear on me again," she said.

He shook his head. "My therapist awakened me. But I'm doing it on my own this time."

The sun was low on the horizon as they walked naked, hand-in-hand down the hill, through the grove of oak trees. Crossing the meadow, they came to the river and sat down on the bank with their feet in the flowing water.

Burward wanted to know all about Evelyn's life. She told him all there was to tell. "Life for me isn't too exciting in Lashera."

"But it's the biggest city on the West Coast."

"I guess I don't take advantage of the opportunities," she said. "Now, it's your turn to tell me about your life."

"I'm in prison. But I have phone privileges, so I tracked you down."

Their eyes met.

"It was a big mix-up over stocks and bonds. I honestly didn't think I was breaking the law but . . ."

"How long, Burward?"

"Ten years in Conseria. It's a prison on the island just off the coast in the Raceen Ocean."

"Why the hypnotic therapy?"

"An experiment in the decriminalization of nonviolent inmates." He laughed.

"Then we couldn't be together, if I were to travel to . . ."

He shook his head. "But we can be together here."

They made love in the twilight on the grass by the river bank. Birds serenaded their union until the light faded and the moon rose.

"That was the most incredible experience I've ever had," he whispered, still breathing heavily.

"Me too."

"I don't want to go back," he said, sitting up, holding her hand.

"Me either." She looked at the shimmering silver cord extending from her body and disappearing into the distance. "What would happen if we were to sever the cords, Burward?"

"I don't know."

"Wouldn't it be worth a try?" She smiled at him.

"We could survive here," he said, looking around. "The place is a garden of fruit trees. I saw a turtle on the river-bank, so there are probably plenty of fish."

"Let's do it before we're pulled back."

"We might die."

"But we might start to live."

Burward stood up, laughed, and walked along the river-bank until he found a large rock. Returning to Evelyn with it in his arms, he said, "Are you sure?"

She looked him confidently in the eye and smiled gently.

"Yes, I'm sure."

"Okay." Burward lifted the rock high over his head and smashed it down on his silver cord. There was a faint sizzling sound and the cord disappeared. "Whew! Wonder what happened to my body back home?"

"It probably disappeared." Evelyn briefly recounted Calvin's discussion of atoms. "My turn."

When both cords were severed the couple embraced. Arms entwined, they stood watching the moon. "Looks like we could be starting a new world," Burward said.

She laughed at the idea. "If so, I can't call you Burward. What's your middle name?"

"Adam."

"Much better," Evelyn said.